BECK
LIFE IN INK 2
ELOUISE EAST

ELOUISE EAST

Publisher: Elouise East

Cover Design: Covers by Jo

Editor: Elouise East

Beta Readers: Emma Brown

CONTENTS

Author note

If you would like to see any potential triggers for this book and any other books I've written, please go to this link on my website: https://elouiseeast.com/triggers

1

BECK

Beck Cavanagh snorted at Dallas's joke, his sides aching from how much they'd all laughed that night. Drink flooded their veins, and they could barely contain themselves, even with the sheer number of people in attendance who stared at them in a mix of disgust and appreciation. They didn't care, though. Their little corner of the world was perfect, even if Beck said so himself. They were all in fine form, even those of them who had recently been added to their tight-knit group, as they chilled out before the Bonser Tattooing event the next day.

His gaze transferred to their surroundings, seeing if he could find anyone remotely interesting beneath the multicoloured strobe lighting to spend a few hours with. He passed over several men, no one jumping out at him. He could do with letting off a little steam, but his skin pebbled as he thought of what it would entail.

Instead, he focused on his friends, new and old.

"How many do you think we'll get done this year? Will we beat last year's?" Dallas asked.

Dallas was a surf dude, through and through. Well, he would've been if he actually surfed. He had the look, but Beck wondered if he would have the balance to stay on a surfboard with how big he was. They all called him a giant because he was six foot six inches of pure muscle and tattoos, but Dallas was...conflicted, from what Beck could guess. Despite being as close as brothers, Dallas liked his privacy, but he spent many nights looking for something in someone. Beck hoped he'd find it soon.

"We pushed it last year," Finn said. "I think we'll end up doing less or break even."

Finn, on the other hand, was more than happy alone. Beck could only describe him as a free spirit, but he'd been with Life in Ink for years and showed no signs of leaving. If he ever did, they'd all be devastated, but they'd support him in whatever he chose to do. Finn was the quietest of them all, but when he spoke, they all listened.

"We have more help this year, though. If you think about it, with Ethan helping Ani with the organisation and Kole helping with the designs, we'll be concentrating more on tattooing on its own. I bet we'll manage more," Joey said.

Joey, who was the owner of Life in Ink, sat across from him, his arm around his boyfriend, Ethan. They hadn't been together for long, but they were, without a doubt to anyone who saw them, made for each other. Beck had always thought he didn't believe in love, but seeing them together had made him reconsider recently. Not enough to go looking for it himself, but to appreciate what Joey and Ethan had.

And with Ethan came his friends, Kole and Christi. Christi and her girlfriend, Di, didn't visit as much as Kole did. Kole was spending more and more time in London as opposed to where he lived in Whitby, and Beck didn't mind it one bit. The man was a genius when it came to art and design, and with Ethan's wily words, he'd persuaded Kole to help them out at the event the next day. If they didn't get more business from Kole's artistic flair than they ever had, he'd eat his motorcycle.

The only person who was missing from their crew was Ani, their manager. They'd all spent the afternoon getting their area ready for the weekend's event, but she'd ended up with a migraine and wanted it gone before the busy following days, so she'd stayed at the hotel and gone to sleep. Beck would've been happy to stay with her to make sure she was okay, but she'd insisted they all head out and have fun because they'd be too exhausted to do so the next day—which was likely to be true.

"What do you think, Beck?" Dallas asked, dragging Beck from his musings.

Beck grabbed his beer, pursing his lips as he considered their situation now compared to last year. "I think Joey has it right. We have extra help. We'll smash it." He put his fist into the centre of the table and the four of them fist-bumped. Kole snorted at his side, and Beck glanced at him, shoving him with his shoulder. "What's got you so amused?"

"Does it really matter how many you get?" Kole asked, but the twinkle in his eyes belied his innocent question.

"You know it. Why not have a goal in mind? It makes hands work quicker." Beck winked at him and drained his beer. "Hey, do you wanna dance?"

Kole stared at the dance floor, his fingertips immediately heading for his mouth, a tell Beck had figured out meant he was uncertain. They had all been told what had happened to Kole a few months prior, and they'd all vowed to make him feel safe again.

"Just you and me against the music. No one else," Beck said into his ear. He pulled back and met his gaze.

Kole nodded once. "Sure."

"We'll be back," Beck told the table and grabbed Kole's hand, dragging him towards the mass of writhing bodies. "We'll stay to the edge. That way, we can hightail it if someone tries something we want to escape."

It wasn't just for Kole's benefit, either. Beck didn't mind his friends touching him, and he often initiated touch himself, but he couldn't stand it when someone stood at his back, danced behind him or touched him without warning. He was fine if someone was in front of him because he could see what they were doing, which was where he put Kole.

"Is this okay?" he asked over the music.

Kole nodded and started moving to the music, a small smile playing on his lips. Beck copied his moves, their hips swaying, their arms rising and lowering, their heads bobbing in time with the beat. A guy moved in behind Kole, grabbing his hips, and Kole jerked forward and spun around to face him. The guy raised his hands and said something Beck didn't catch. Beck kept his hands loosely on Kole's arms as the guy raised his eyebrows and Kole nodded. The guy started dancing in front of Kole, and Kole found the beat again. When Beck stepped back to give him room, Kole's hand gripped the one that was still on his arm and shook his head. Beck stayed where he was, moving in time with Kole, their bodies a bit closer than they usually would be, but if that was what Kole needed to allow a stranger to dance with him, then so be it.

Their little bubble burst when someone squeezed Beck's ass and pushed in against his back. Beck froze, his heart pounding as if he'd run a mile in ten seconds, and his mind went offline. But only for a second, and then he shoved himself away, knocking Kole from in front of him as well, and faced the newcomer.

"What the fuck?" Beck said. "Did it look like I was giving you permission to touch me?"

The stranger grinned and backed off, shaking his head and disappearing into the crowd. Beck's heart continued its sprint, and his gaze studied everyone around him, looking for a threat. A hand rested on his arm, and he jumped a mile, dislodging the hand before he found Kole, frowning at him.

"Are you okay?" he asked, not reaching for him again, and Beck nodded, trying to find the easygoing smile he always had available.

"Yeah, I just wasn't... He made me jump." It was the worst excuse on the planet, but what else could he say? No one knew the truth, and if he had his way, they never would. "Let's get another drink, yeah?"

He headed towards the bar, but he kept an eye on Kole to make sure, first, that he was following, and second, that no one messed with him. Ethan's best friend was good-looking in an "I don't care" fashion. His dark hair was always mussed, reminding Beck of when someone had just taken off a motorcycle helmet. But it was his eyes that got to him. Those deep chestnut-coloured orbs made it seem like he could see everything everyone wasn't saying, and he didn't need that kind of attention at that moment.

"Beer?" he asked Kole when they reached the bar.

"Sure. Do you want me to ask if anyone else wants one?"

Beck shook his head. "I'll get them all one, anyway. If someone doesn't want one, I'm sure Dallas will have it." He grinned, finally finding some semblance of control. He hated it when he lost it like that.

Kole snorted. "I'm sure he will."

While they waited for the bartender to fill their order, Beck asked, "I can't remember what you said earlier. Are you heading straight back to Whitby after the event finishes on Sunday, or are you staying longer?"

Joey and Ethan had been trying to persuade Kole to move down to London for weeks, but Kole was resistant for some reason. Joey was ready to give Kole a job in the shop as soon as he said yes, and Beck could see him fitting in well. He wasn't a tattoo artist—yet—but his designs would make a tremendous impact on them, both as artists and as a business.

"I haven't decided. I'm staying until Monday at least because I don't fancy driving all that way after a long day here, but further than that, I've not decided." He held up his hand. "I know you all want me here, but it's a big decision. I don't have what Ethan has, and it makes it more difficult."

"I can imagine it does with having family up there. You'd miss them."

Kole nodded, his mouth curving gently. "I will."

Beck didn't mention that slip. The present tense of the word instead of the possibility. Maybe he'd already decided, yet he was worried about taking that step. Beck didn't bring it to light, and instead, focused on carrying the tray the bartender had given him for all the drinks.

"Come on. Let's water the rabble." He grinned and followed Kole as he led the way, clearing a path so Beck didn't get the tray knocked from his hands.

"Ah, I wondered where you two had gone," Ethan said when Kole slipped into the booth and Beck followed, placing the tray down. "And now I know."

"You know me. Dancing always makes me thirsty," Kole said, and Beck glanced at him for the excuse. Kole didn't meet his gaze and passed him a drink instead.

"I can't stay much longer, Joey," Ethan said with a yawn. "I won't be any good to anyone tomorrow."

Joey dropped a kiss on his lips. "We'll head back after this one." He transferred his gaze to Beck, his eyes narrowing as he studied him. Beck refused to squirm under the scrutiny and raised his eyebrows.

"Everything okay?" he asked.

Joey leaned forward, resting his arms on the table, and gave Beck his no-nonsense look. "I was going to ask you the same thing."

Beck crossed his arms over his chest and leaned them on the table, too. "I'm fine. Are you ready for tomorrow?"

"Stop changing the subject."

"I didn't realise we were on a subject." Beck gave his trademark grin, but Joey didn't soften, and Beck's front was crumbling. "I'm doing good. I'm looking forward to the event."

Joey stared at him for a long moment and then nodded slowly. "Yeah, me, too," he said, seeming to let his previous worries go. At least for now. He'd circle around to them again at some point. Maybe not that night, but at some point soon, Joey would get him to spill his guts—well, what he thought was Beck's guts. Beck's stomach churned at the thought. All the people around him believed he'd been completely honest with them about his past, but other than telling them he'd been in foster care and some of the awesome stories that had happened along the way, there was a huge part of that time he refused to tell anyone.

No one needed to be burdened with those memories except for him.

They spoke about the event again, none of their minds far from it, and even shared a toast to Elliott, Joey's best friend who dies the previous year, someone who was very close to all their hearts. And then Joey slipped his arm around Ethan and tugged the sleepy man from the booth. Saying goodbye, he watched them until they disappeared and then focused on his beer. He peeled the label off the front and tried breathing through the need to fly out of the bar and straight into a scalding shower.

"Hey, do you want to stay any longer?" Kole asked from beside him.

Beck glanced at him, noticing his lifted chin, and shook his head. Ethan had shared something with the Life in Ink crew about Kole that the man probably wouldn't want known, but it helped them know how he was feeling. Whenever Kole lifted his chin, he was embarrassed about something, and Beck hated seeing that.

"I'm getting tired now," he said, though it was a lie. He doubted he'd sleep anytime soon.

Kole gave a small smile. "Fancy taking a walk back to the hotel with me?"

Beck didn't read it as a come-on at all, but he understood what Kole wasn't saying—he wanted company for the journey somewhere he'd never been before, and after the physical assault he experienced, Beck wasn't surprised.

"Sure." He focused on Dallas. "Yo, Dallas! We're heading back. Make sure you get at least a few hours of sleep. Please." He stared at him, Dallas's eyes bleary and pupil-blown, but the man nodded. Slightly appeased because he knew how much alcohol Dallas could drink and still be coherent, he nodded back and followed Kole towards the exit, looking out for Finn but not seeing him.

The cool night air reminded him he'd left his jacket at the hotel, but he shoved his hands into his pockets and lifted his shoulders to his ears as if that would help warm him. "Fuck, it's cold."

Kole snorted. "Where's your jacket?"

"I left it at the hotel when we ran out earlier."

"Are you part polar bear? Jeez."

Beck chuckled. "I wish." He shivered and sped up when Kole did. "Did you enjoy tonight?"

Kole nodded. "I did." He glanced at him and then forward again. "Thank you for the dance."

"You're welcome. I'm always happy to dance."

"Not always," Kole murmured, acknowledging the event Beck had wanted to ignore.

He didn't reply, not sure what he would say if he opened his mouth with everything being so close to the surface as it was. Kole stepped in front of him just before they went through the front door of the hotel, and Beck stopped, meeting his gaze.

"You don't need to tell me anything, but I wanted to say...if there is something you want to get off your chest, you can talk to me. I'm a good listener. Though you might already have someone, so if you do, you can ignore this. I was just wanting to let you know that I'm...here...if you need it." He inhaled, having evidently run out of air from that monologue.

And despite Beck's stomach churning at the idea of sharing that which he'd never shared with anyone, he found a smile.

"Have you replenished your oxygen levels now?" he teased instead of answering.

Kole rubbed his face and sighed. "Yes, thanks."

Beck shivered again, his teeth setting a record for how loud they could be when they chattered, and he gestured to the door. "Can we get inside now?"

Kole cursed and pushed through the door to the hotel, holding it open for him, and Beck groaned as heat enveloped him, chasing away the frigid January air.

"Not a polar bear, then." Kole snorted, heading for the lifts, and Beck followed, studying the recent addition to their crew in the mirrored doors as they waited. Kole stood straight, his eyes lowered to the floor, but his head kept tilting whenever there was a noise behind them and his throat bobbed.

When the doors finally opened, Kole scooted across the threshold faster than a rabbit being chased by a fox, and Beck stepped in front of him, allowing him to stay behind him if he needed it, and pressed the button to close the doors. Someone yelled for them to hold the lift, but Beck didn't.

Kole chuckled behind him. "That wasn't kind."

"I thought I was being extra kind. We don't need to share." He leaned back against the handrail and crossed his arms over his chest, keeping his attention on the floor instead of the man beside him.

"I still struggle some days," Kole said after a long silence, and Beck peered across at him. Kole stared at the numbers on the display, increasing with each floor they hit. "I hate it," he murmured. "I hate that he's changed who I am." Kole blinked, glanced at Beck and then to the floor. "Sorry." He huffed a small laugh.

The lift dinged, and the doors opened. They were in rooms next to each other, and Beck stopped beside Kole's as he fumbled in his pocket for the key. Beck wanted to say something to acknowledge what he'd said, but he wasn't sure what.

"Thanks for the company," Kole said with a smile when he opened his hotel room door. "I appreciate it." He stepped inside, but before he shut the door, Beck found his voice.

"You're still you. You're just a shaky version of yourself at the moment. You'll find your balance again soon." Beck nodded and turned away, unable to believe the words coming from his mouth.

He clicked open his door and paused when Kole called his name. Glancing down the corridor, Kole's head and shoulder peered around the door frame.

"And you're still you. Whatever happened, you're still you."

Kole disappeared, and Beck entered his room, closing the door softly behind him. And as he sank to the floor and dropped his head into his hands, he considered Kole's words.

Having his childhood ripped away from him had left little time to figure out who he was. He'd learnt to get by, to withstand, to survive.

He had no idea who Beck Cavanagh really was.

2

KOLE

K ole Peterson found it easier to fall asleep than he'd thought it would be, and when his alarm woke him the next morning, he stretched his arms above his head and his feet until cool air touched them before pulling them back into the covers again. He rolled to his side and stared at the light, weakly straining past the edges of the curtains.

That day, he would stand alongside the Life in Ink crew, helping to design tattoos and whatever else Ethan and Ani needed him to do. It wasn't something he'd ever envisaged for himself, but he was excited to stretch his design muscles. It had been a long time since he'd done anything with them—college, to be exact.

His second alarm rang. He'd always been one of those people who needed at least two, sometimes three, alarms to get him moving in the morning. It wouldn't faze Ethan or Christi if someone told them Kole had ten alarms to wake up. The main thing was that he would never be late because, despite having so many alarms, he was always on time or early.

He swung his legs out of the bed and rubbed his hands over his face and through his hair, his fingers tangling in the knots. Exhaling away the leftover sleepiness, he headed for the bathroom and switched the shower on while he used the toilet. Then he jumped right in, moaning at the heat of the water. He let the spray pound down on his shoulders, easing the ache from how he'd slept, and then tilted his head back to wet his hair.

There was something about the feel of the water drenching his strands that loosened his muscles further. Like he was washing something away, becoming new again.

He snorted at his fanciful thoughts and squirted shampoo into his hand. As he massaged it into his hair and scalp, his thoughts drifted back to the previous night and what happened with Beck. When that guy had startled Kole, he'd only found the courage to say yes to dancing with him because Beck was there. When Beck had tried to leave him, Kole couldn't cope, and he'd grabbed for him to stay. But after a few minutes, Beck had frozen and then pushed Kole into the guy and faced off with another one. Despite Kole's panic, he'd seen the flash of fear in Beck's eyes. There was no way he could've left him to fend for himself at that point, even though Kole had been terrified about what was happening.

After that, Beck had been distant but fronting hard. Kole could relate. It was one reason he'd asked Beck about walking back to the hotel. Yes, Kole hadn't wanted to walk back by himself, but he could see Beck was struggling. But despite that, Beck had still protected Kole in the lift. The man was a conundrum. He hadn't believed there were still people around like that. Except for his friends, of course. Though, thinking about it, the Life in Ink crew were becoming his friends, too. He just didn't know them as well, yet.

He finished in the shower, ignoring his hard-on, and dried off. Wrapping the towel around his waist, he strode for the chest of drawers he filled with his belongings when they'd arrived the previous day. He'd already chosen what he was going to wear, so he grabbed the briefs, skinny jeans and T-shirt, and dressed quickly. Then he took the purple shirt from the hanger and slipped it over his shoulders. It was chilly outside, but he wasn't sure if the event would be air-conditioned like it had been the previous day. He'd prefer to wear layers he could take off if he needed to.

Someone pounded at his door, and he checked the clock. Right on time. He shoved his wallet, keys and phone into his pockets, lifted his coat from the hook and opened the door.

"Ready?" Beck said.

"Yep." He followed Beck down the hallway while shrugging on his coat.

"Did you sleep okay?" Beck asked.

"Yes, thanks. I might just have to steal the bed and take it home," Kole joked.

Beck laughed. "This hotel is definitely worth their weight in gold."

The lift deposited them on the ground floor, and they met up with the rest of the crew with hugs and back slaps all around before they left the hotel for the early morning walk to the event, which was being held right around the corner from the hotel.

Ethan dropped into step beside him, hooking his arm through Kole's. "Did you have a good night?"

Kole understood the undercurrent of his question. "I did, and I'm fine. As I said to Beck, I might need to steal the bed. It was damn comfortable."

Ethan chuckled. "They spare no expense when it comes to comfort."

"I can see that. I daren't look at the prices of the rooms. I'm scared I'll have a heart attack."

"Yeah, definitely don't do that. Either of them."

Kole studied him. "You seem unusually chipper for such an early morning."

Ethan hit his arm. "I'm always chipper. I used to get up at an ungodly hour, remember?"

"Just because you had to doesn't mean you were chipper."

"Shut up!" Ethan whined. "It's true, though. I've been spoilt since moving here and not having to get up that early." He rested his head on Kole's arm. "Do you think you'll join me one day?"

Kole snorted, knowing Ethan had been keeping those words in for their entire conversation. "If I leave Whitby, poor Christi will be on her own."

"She's got Di."

"My family is there."

"So is mine."

"I have a job I love."

"You could get a similar job here or you could work with us."

Kole sighed. "You have an answer for everything, don't you?"

"I try." Ethan tightened his hold on his arm. "I just want you happy, Kole," he murmured. "And you don't seem particularly happy right now. I'm worried about my best friend."

Kole rested his cheek against Ethan's head as they walked. "I know you are. I'm okay. I'm figuring things out. But you need to *let* me figure them out. I'm getting there."

Ethan went quiet, but he wouldn't be for long. And he was right. "Okay."

Kole glanced at him, though all he could see was his hair. "What?"

Ethan lifted his head, meeting his gaze. "Okay. I'll back off. Just make sure you come to me if you need *anything* at all. I don't want you to ever think I haven't got your back."

Kole pulled Ethan into a hug, wanting to cry but refraining. "I know."

They pulled back, and Ethan's eyes were wet but resolved. "Don't be a stranger if your decision is Whitby."

"I won't. You'll never be rid of me."

"Good."

"You all ready?" Dallas yelled from his lean by the door to the building where the event was being held.

"We're coming!" Ethan yelled back.

"So is Christmas! And it'll get here quicker if you're not careful!"

Ethan shook his head and lifted his middle finger to Dallas, who just laughed in response. "Come on, before we're accosted by him. I wouldn't put it past him to throw us both over his shoulders and carry us in there."

Kole laughed and followed Ethan to the entrance. He'd been at the venue the previous day, but it still surprised him how big the place was. The cavernous ceilings appeared to reach the sky and a football field could probably fit in the square footage. With how the organisers had laid it out, partitions divided the space evenly between the hundred tattoo companies in attendance, but only enough to show the different spaces, not to stop the flow of visitors. Kole wasn't sure what to expect with the event, though each of them had tried to explain it. But their words had failed to encompass the enormity of the event. As he entered that vast hall, the hustle and bustle of people echoed, creating a cacophony of noise along with music that didn't reach as far as it probably should have.

"Kole!" Ethan called. "Come on!"

Shaking himself, he headed over to their area, a space with four reclinable chairs and trolleys that were filled with tools. Two tables stood in front, one where Ethan and Ani would speak with the clients, and the other for Kole to create the designs. He exhaled at the blank tabletop, steeling himself against the wave of nerves that had him trembling.

"You'll be great," Ethan said in his ear, making him jump.

"I've never done designs for other people before."

"I know. But you're great at it. I know you're worried about letting them down, but you won't." Ethan kept his voice down. "If you decide you don't want to do this, you don't have to."

Kole swallowed. "I want to." And he did.

Ethan squeezed his shoulders. "Okay, then. Get drawing." He threw three pads of plain paper on the table and shoved Kole towards it.

Kole laughed. "Yes, sir."

Grateful for the pep talk, Kole settled down on the stool he'd been given and pulled a pad closer to him. He needed a muse, something to get the ideas percolating. He studied the hall, noticing the designs on the walls, the large banners hanging from the ceiling and the decorative arches. Plenty of ideas, but he needed more. Peering around him, he observed the people, and his gaze snagged on Beck, his head thrown back as laughter bellowed from him, the lines around his eyes and mouth as they deepened, the strength in his body, the wings of the tattoo that peeked around the edges of his tank top. A dark angel.

Feeling the need to draw, Kole grabbed a pencil case from his coat pocket, something he'd stashed there the previous night after worrying he'd forget it that morning, and chose a pencil. The moment the tip touched the paper, he fell into the design. Starting with something small, he sketched angel wings in the corner and steadily continued expanding on the original until he had something he was happy with.

"Woah, I want that!"

The voice startled him, and his pencil ran off the end of the sheet. He snapped his gaze up towards a youngish woman, her eyes on his newly finished design.

"Isn't it a bit big?" the man beside her said.

"No, it's perfect. It's exactly what I was trying to draw myself, but I couldn't get it to look right." She glanced at Kole. "Is it for sale?"

Kole's mouth worked but nothing came out, and Ethan stepped over, leaning down. "Kole, are you willing to sell that one, or is it personal?"

Kole glanced at Ethan, blinked and exhaled, his brain finally coming back online. He cleared his throat. "Yes, that's fine." He handed the paper to Ethan with a smile, his stomach swooping with the idea that someone was going to be carrying his design on their body for a long time.

The woman grinned. "Thank you so much!"

Kole nodded and watched as Ethan led her over to Ani and they finalised the purchase before Ethan took her to Beck. It was both a blessing and a curse that the muse for the design was the one doing the tattoo, but it was the right choice. Beck's flair was extensive and extravagant, and he would do it justice.

Taking a deep breath, he faced his empty drawing pad and let it out slowly. Not even a few seconds later, Ethan drew his attention by bringing another person over to him.

"Kole is one of our designers today. Would you like to explain to him what you're thinking of and see if he can create something you like? Naturally, you don't have to choose his design, but if you like it, we can go from there."

"Yeah, sure," the guy said.

"Fantastic. Let me get you a stool." Ethan grabbed a stool from behind the tables and took it around to the other side for the client. "I'll leave you in Kole's capable hands."

Kole tucked away his reservations and smiled at the guy. "So, what's your name?"

"Andy."

"Nice to meet you, Andy. What are you looking for?"

Andy described what he wanted, and Kole rolled with it. He erased and redrew some things a few times, but eventually, Andy was happy with the result. He took the design over to Ethan and so went the rest of the day. It was exhausting and exhilarating all at once. He took several breaks, especially when his hand cramped, but mostly, he drew to his heart's content. And when there weren't any clients to draw for—whether that was because they'd chosen to ask an artist themselves or because they weren't busy—he drew what he needed to, what his soul pushed to express.

When the announcement came that the event was closing, a ripple of awareness swarmed the venue. While Joey, Beck, Dallas and Finn finished up on their last clients, Ethan and Ani closed up their table, and Kole tidied away his designs. Whether they saw the light of day again was something he'd decide later.

"What was the final figure for today?" Joey asked Ani.

Ani shared a smile with Ethan. "Twenty-nine."

Dallas threw his hands in the air, Joey and Beck hugged, and Finn stood with a grin on his face, the most expressive Kole had ever seen him outside of the shop.

"We're over halfway, baby!" Joey said, lifting Ethan and spinning him around.

"Put me down, you big oaf!" Ethan said, laughing, belying his words by wrapping his legs around his boyfriend's waist.

Kole chuckled at their antics. Their need to break last year's record was cute. He hoped they hit the mark the next day. Kole might need to ice his hand that night if he was to draw for twelve hours the following day. He also needed some sleep. He stood.

"Congrats. I'm glad you're on track. I'm heading back to the hotel." He gestured over his shoulder. "Same time tomorrow?"

Joey held out his hand despite still holding onto Ethan. "You were amazing, man. I appreciate you helping us out so much."

"It's not a problem at all. I've had fun." He smiled. "I'll see you all in the morning."

Kole waved and headed out, torn between wanting to celebrate with them and wanting to crawl into bed and sleep for hours. As soon as the frigid January air hit his lungs, he could breathe a little easier. Why, though, he wasn't sure. It hadn't been stifling when he'd been working, but as soon as they'd stopped, the walls had closed in on him.

He wandered slowly down the street, lit only by streetlights, and the now-regular feeling of someone watching washed over him. He quickened his pace, his pulse pounding in his ears until he started a jog. Only a few steps away from the hotel, a hand grabbed his arm.

"Kole!"

Kole yanked his arm away, held his hands in front of him and backed into the wall.

"Kole?"

He blinked a few times, trying to understand what else the person said, but still only catching his name.

"Kole." Indistinguishable mutterings. "Kole. Beck."

The new piece of information slipped in, and his gaze darted over the face swimming in front of him. The dark hair, the beard, the full lips, the blue eyes staring at him with something Kole couldn't name in them.

"Kole. It's Beck. Breathe for me, okay? Just breathe."

His hearing cleared, and he sank into a crouch as his surroundings came into focus. Nausea swam around in his stomach like a tsunami, his head pounded, and his entire body shook.

"It's okay. I'm here, Kole. I'm here."

Kole glanced up at Beck through watery eyes and launched himself forward. Beck caught him with a grunt but tightened his hold around him.

"I'm so sorry I scared you. I'm so sorry. So sorry," Beck repeated, brushing his hand against his hair, soothing him.

Kole, being the coward that he was, hid his face in Beck's neck, tears streaming down his face. His legs wouldn't be able to hold him until the panic faded, so he didn't try. When would it be over? When would he get his life back? A one-night stand, someone he never thought he'd ever see again, had attacked him, unprovoked, while he was telling his ghost stories on one of his tours. Someone he hadn't thought about once they'd parted ways. Someone who would never be forgotten again.

How could one small thing have such a profound effect on the way he lived his life?

"I've got you. I'm so sorry," Beck continued to say.

Kole heard him whisper something else and other voices, but he couldn't get the energy to rise and run away from whoever it was. Beck had said he'd got him, and for once, Kole was going to hold someone to those words. He didn't plan on moving for a little while, despite how cold he was getting.

"It's okay. Take your time, Kole. I've got you."

If only he could lean on someone for more than a few moments. He needed the respite, but he didn't have a choice. He would not bother Ethan with his burden. He didn't know the artists well enough to ask for help. Christi was busy with Di and their new business venture. Most of his family had told him to get over it by going to therapy. He had no one.

But for these few minutes, he had Beck, and he'd remember the feel of his arms around him, his strength, whenever he needed a reminder that one day, just maybe, he might be able to have that for himself.

3

BECK

Holding a trembling Kole in his arms, Beck called himself every curse word he knew. When someone had been through what Kole had been through, another person didn't just grab them to get their attention. *For fuck's sake, Beck.*

He cradled Kole, muttering his apologies as occasionally people moved around them. The crew had been and gone, Joey physically dragging Ethan away when he'd refused to leave his best friend. Beck wasn't sure if Kole would want Ethan to have seen him that way, but it was too late. Undoubtedly, Ethan would have words for Kole the next day.

But for the moment, Kole was Beck's concern. His body trembled like an autumn leaf hanging by its last stalk, though whether it was from panic or the cold, he wasn't sure.

"Kole, let's get inside. It's getting colder. I need to get you warm."

Kole didn't respond vocally, but he tightened his grip on Beck's coat. Beck's shins were freezing from kneeling on the cold ground, and he manoeuvred to get his feet beneath him while still holding onto Kole with the same strength he had before. He didn't want him to think he was letting him go.

"That's it. I've got you," he said as Kole responded to the move and rose with him. He guided them towards the hotel, and the doorman opened the door for them with a sympathetic expression. Kole kept his face buried but loosened his hold once they were inside.

Wasting no time, he aimed for the lifts, reaching to call for it before putting the hand back on Kole's head. Their reflection showed how small Kole seemed to want to be, and the pain ravaging his own face. Barely keeping his memories under control, he focused on Kole. On how he felt in his arms. On holding him tight enough to make Kole feel safe. On apologising for scaring him.

When the lift finally arrived, he bundled them both into the small space and counted the seconds until it deposited them out. He guided Kole down the hallway to his room.

"Kole, do you have your key?" he asked gently.

Kole stiffened but then nodded. His grip loosened on Beck's T-shirt, his hand smoothing down his front until it left his body to reach into his pocket. Pulling out a keycard, he trembled as he held it out. Beck took it and opened the door, hesitating on the threshold when Kole seemed reluctant to let him go.

"Can you..." Kole sniffed and pulled away, not finishing his sentence. "Thank you. I..."

"You don't need to say thanks. Not for this." It was also one of the last things anyone needed to apologise for. "Do you need anything?"

Kole shook his head, but he visibly shook as he wrapped his arms around his waist. Beck wanted to enfold him in his arms again, but he didn't want to overstep his boundaries. Maybe they were past that, but he wouldn't do anything without Kole's express permission.

"I'm only next door, and you have my number if you need anything at all. Okay?"

Kole nodded again, and though Beck wasn't sure leaving Kole alone was the best option, he stepped back. Before he left, he said, "I'm going to come back in a bit with some food. Make sure you answer your door. I would hate to break it down."

It brought a slight curve to Kole's lips, which eased Beck's conscience a little. "Okay."

It wasn't the confident acquiescence the man would usually give, but it was something.

"See you in a bit," Beck confirmed.

He left the room, closing the door tightly behind him, and stared at it for a few seconds before heading to his room down the hall. It was identical to Kole's except the opposite way around, the beds being against the same wall. He wasn't completely confident, but he believed he would hear Kole shout if he needed him.

Stripping off his T-shirt, he grabbed his phone and texted Joey with an update about Ethan's best friend.

BECK: *Kole is in his room now. I'm going to order us some food and make sure he eats before he gets some sleep. I'll keep an ear out as much as I can tonight.*

JOEY: *Thanks. That's helped Ethan to relax. We knew it was bad, but we didn't know how bad he could get. I thought therapy was helping.*

Joey must've been waiting for an update to have answered straight away, but Beck pursed his lips at his words. Therapy wasn't something that helped or didn't. Sometimes, it helped that week. Sometimes, it didn't help at all. Sometimes, it felt like jumping forward three steps before going back ten. It was a fluid experience, and one everyone felt differently about.

Beck shook himself, not wanting to take himself back to the times he spent in a therapist's office, hoping they had a magic cure.

They didn't.

BECK: *It is helping, but he'll have relapses, the same as anyone. Give him time. I'll let you know if there are any problems.*

JOEY: *Thanks. Unless we hear from you, we'll see you both in the morning.*

Beck didn't respond. Instead, he grabbed the takeaway menus from the drawer and flicked through them, deciding on Chinese. He wasn't sure what Kole liked, so he ordered several dishes, knowing whatever they left, they could take home the following day. The rooms, thankfully, had small fridges. The takeaway place said they'd deliver it to the reception desk, so he rang down and asked them to let him know when it arrived. Then he took a shower and dressed in joggers and a fresh T-shirt.

Settling onto the bed, he flicked through the films and shows available on the TV, but nothing held his interest enough to watch it. He turned it off again and threw the remote onto the bottom of the bed. Just as he was about to go out of his mind, his room phone rang. When they said their food was there, he sprang up from the bed, slid on his trainers and left his room. He thanked the receptionist and carried the food back up. Maybe he'd gone a little overboard, but he didn't care.

Taking a deep breath, he knocked on Kole's door, exhaling in a rush when Kole yelled for him to hang on. At least the man was true to his word, and from those few words, Beck relaxed at the calmer tone he had.

Kole opened the door, wearing similar clothes to Beck but with droplets of water soaking into the material, and waved him in. "Sorry, I was just finishing in the shower."

Beck ignored the wet material as much as he could. "No problem." He held up the food bags. "Dinner awaits."

Kole grinned and stepped back from the door, gesturing for Beck to follow. "I'm surprisingly hungry."

"Stress can do that to a person," Beck replied and then felt shitty for bringing up the elephant in the room. "I got Chinese, but I wasn't sure what you'd like, so I ordered a load of stuff. Don't worry, though. Whatever doesn't get eaten, we'll take home tomorrow."

"You didn't have to go to any trouble."

Beck chuckled. "The only trouble was picking up the phone and ordering my favourite food." He placed the bag on the small circular table in the corner of the room by the window. "Do you have a favourite?" he asked as he pulled the plastic containers from the bags.

"Not really. Though I suppose I tend to choose noodle options over rice."

Beck grinned. "Well, it just so happens..." He pointed to the containers in order. "We have chicken chow mein, vegetable lo mein and Singapore noodles. Do any of those sound good?"

"I wouldn't say no to vegetable lo mein."

Beck handed it over. "Knock yourself out."

Kole took it and settled into a chair at the table, tucking one leg beneath him as he sat. Beck handed him a bottle of water from the fridge and sat opposite him before freezing and clearing his throat.

"Um, is it okay if I stay to eat? I can go back to my room?" he said.

Kole smiled, his cheeks bulging, before he covered his mouth with his hand. "It's fine," he mumbled.

Beck relaxed and dug into his beef in black bean sauce. Silence descended, but it wasn't fraught with tension like he assumed it would be between them. After all, they didn't know each other that well. If he'd been the type of person to pry, he would've asked questions Kole probably wouldn't want to answer, but Beck understood the need to keep quiet. To let things lie. To figure it out on his own.

"Is tomorrow going to be the same as today?" Kole broke the silence after taking a sip of water.

Beck nodded, chewing and swallowing his mouthful before answering. "Yep. Everything will happen the same. There might be a few more people than today because some people work Saturdays, but some might be repeat people who bought a weekend ticket."

"Is there a limit to how many people can attend?"

"Yeah, but I think it's a fairly high number due to the size of the place. And people don't always stay all day, so there will be some leaving and some entering at different times. I don't know the figures personally, but that's just what I've seen over the years."

"How long have you been doing this event?" Kole forked more noodles into his mouth, chewing slowly.

Beck blew out a breath and propped his chin on his fist, his elbow on the table while he figured it out. "Six years? Or is it seven years? Six or seven." He shrugged. "Not to toot our own horn, to borrow Finn's phrase, but we're one of the best in the country, if not further afield, so having us there makes the event bigger."

"You all deserve the praise you receive. It's hard-earned and right. You all work damn hard, from what I've seen. And I'm not just talking about this event. I've rarely seen the shop empty when I've visited."

Warmth flowed through him at Kole's words, and he ducked his head, focusing on his food. "We have worked extremely hard to get where we are, but if it wasn't for Joey..."

Kole smiled. "He seems the type to befriend someone and never let them go."

Beck laughed, covering his mouth when his food threatened to fly across the table. Kole chuckled and handed him a napkin, which he held to his mouth.

"Sorry," Kole said, his cheeks flushing.

He cleared his throat and waved his hand. "It's okay. You were right on the nose with that description." He wiped his hands on the napkin, sitting back in his chair. "People flock to Joey. There's something about him that's so..." He shook his head. "I can't describe it, but he's so good with people, and they remember that. It forges a bond, and when they return, it deepens. And so on. People can't help it because he's Joey." He sighed. "As for us, we kind of fell into it. Helped out here and there and then never left. Though I fully expect Finn to go his own way at some point."

"Why's that?"

"He's more of a loner, really. He puts up with us, but he's happy to stay behind the scenes. He'd be ecstatic if we told him he could hide out in his room all day and night and we'd just send people in to him." He chuckled. "He prefers his own company most of the time, though he makes allowances for us now."

"I can see why. You are all such good people."

Beck preened a little at the praise but ignored it and took another mouthful. They descended into silence again until they finished their food. With plenty left, Beck stacked the containers back into the bags and stood.

"I'll leave you in peace now." He picked up the bags and headed for the door, pausing with his hand on the handle. He tilted his head to the side but didn't look at Kole. "If you need anything at all, please let me know. I'm not...new to this...these feelings, though I don't advertise it. *Please* let me help if you need it."

Kole remained silent for a long moment, and Beck opened the door, believing he wasn't going to respond. As he pulled the door closed, Kole said, "I promise I will tell you if I need anything."

The relief that filled him made him lightheaded, and he leaned against the wall for a second before heading back to his room. He couldn't help but remember Elliott, Joey's best friend. The man had been in pain, and no one had seen it because he'd hid it. And the result had been the man taking his own life. After the police had implied why, Beck had wanted to help Joey with his pain, but his own had come back in full force, and he'd spent several days talking with his therapist before he could face anyone. He could've been where Elliott had been. It could've been him who'd decided he couldn't take it anymore. One more step in that direction, and he would've never met the Life in Ink crew.

He shook his head as he went through his nighttime routine and climbed into bed. It was so hard to understand that all it took was a step in the wrong or right direction and two people went on completely different paths, even in the same originating situation.

Sliding his hand behind his head, he stared up at the dark ceiling, hoping Kole would listen to him and call him if he needed help. Maybe if they had seen that Elliott needed that opportunity, he would've still been there, but no point in thinking what-ifs. It would drive a man crazy.

Several hours later, he was back at his station at the event, ready to ignore a cramping hand when the tattooing became too much for it. He studied his friends and grinned at Ethan's exuberant hand, gesturing as he spoke with Kole. The latter looked ready and willing to get to work, his hand fiddling with the pencil on his table while he spoke with Ethan. He laughed, throwing his head back, and Beck followed the long line of his neck, lingering on the man's lips before jerking his gaze away.

Fucking hell, Beck. Get a grip.

Beck closed his eyes and crossed his arms over his chest, taking a few deep breaths to get rid of the images wanting to encroach on his mind.

"You okay, man?" Dallas asked, clapping his hand on Beck's shoulder and making him jump.

He snapped open his eyes and nodded. "Yep, all good. I love being here, but I'm knackered already." He chuckled, trying to cover for his inappropriate thoughts.

"Yeah, I get that. We're going to break the record, though, man. I can feel it in my bones." Dallas's voice took on a pirate-esque tone, and Beck had to laugh.

"You're a dork."

"I wholeheartedly accept that description."

"Calling all tattoo artists. Please be advised, the doors will be opening in five minutes," the announcer said.

Dallas called everyone over and held out his fisted hand. "Let's do this!"

Everyone rested their hands against Dallas's and echoed his sentiment and dispersed to their relevant positions. Ethan and Ani manned the front desk, so to speak. Kole settled at his table with paper and a pencil. And the tattoo artists stood beside their chairs and equipment. Each of them—even Finn—vibrated with excitement. As Joey had mentioned before, they didn't need the exposure the event gave them, but it never hurt to keep their company in people's minds. After all, their rise to fame thanks to some celebrities could easily come crumbling down around their ears, just as much as a celebrity's fame could. Nothing was set in stone, so they needed to ride the wave as far and as fast as they could, making sure their foundation was secure in case something happened.

Being able to travel to reach customers was a bonus, and something Beck enjoyed. Visiting new places and old kept things interesting, but he especially liked Paris. Annabelle was one of their Paris customers, and though they had others living there, she was his favourite. She was so carefree and easygoing that he often wished he could be her. Seemingly not having a care in the world. He was sure she did, but she could cope or ignore them in favour of living her life. Beck could only hope to get to that place eventually.

As the day wore on, his gaze found Kole more and more often, so he saw when the guy had done enough. He caught Ethan's attention and gestured to Kole. Ethan glanced at Kole and then back at Beck before nodding and mouthing, "Thank you." Ethan headed over to the man, and they disappeared, leaving Beck to go back to cleaning his equipment in the brief break he had. He knew the exact moment they came back, too.

Near the end, several reporters turned up, wanting to cover the last moments of the event, and one came over to Beck.

"How has it been for you?" the reporter, Jack, asked.

Beck grinned at the camera. "It's been an amazing experience, as always. Customers have been fantastic, the atmosphere unmeasurable, and I can't wait to do it again next year."

After a few more questions, Jack moved on, and Beck focused on his last customer.

"What's the final score, Ani?" Joey asked when the event had closed and they packed away.

"Do you want to tell them, Ethan?" Ani raised her eyebrows.

"No, you do it."

"I really think you should," Ani said, nudging Ethan's shoulder.

"But you've done this before. It should—"

"I don't care who tells us, but please tell us!" Dallas said, throwing his hands in the air.

Ani and Ethan laughed, and Beck realised they'd done it on purpose.

"Sixty-one," they said in unison.

Beck, Joey and Dallas roared at the ceiling, waving their hands in the air. Finn just grinned. They'd done it. They'd fucking beat their record. Beck bounded over to Kole and tugged him into a hug. Kole laughed in his ear and returned the gesture.

"Congrats."

"Thanks." Beck pulled back and stared at him. Then, when he should've pulled back, he continued staring, mesmerised by the different shades of brown flecks in his eyes. But then he came to his senses and stepped back, gaze on the floor.

He couldn't have Kole. It wasn't fair to the man to deal with Beck's issues and everything he was dealing with himself. And, for once, he hated the idea of pretending to be something he wasn't. He didn't want to do that with Kole, and he would have to if he went that route.

No, he was better alone.

4

KOLE

K ole rolled his eyes and shook his head. "I'll be back again before you know it."

Ethan pouted, something he'd only started doing when he figured out Joey had caved almost every time. "But that's still too long. I need my best friend."

Kole chuckled and dragged Ethan into a hug. "And I need you, but we'll still be best friends like we have since you moved here." He clapped his shoulder and opened his car door, the sounds of Monday morning traffic ringing in his ears. London traffic was awful at the quiet times, but during busy times, it was a nightmare. Unfortunately, Kole had to get back, so he had to brave the miserable and inevitable traffic jams.

"Think about it, though, yeah?" Ethan said, his forehead creasing as he crossed his arms over his chest.

Kole smiled at him, even though his stomach swirled at the idea. "I will. I promise."

And he would. He just wasn't sure what his answer would be. It was a big thing, moving clear across the country. He'd been thinking about it for weeks. Ever since Ethan had moved down there with Joey.

He climbed into the car, waved and pulled out of the parking space. Heading down the alley beside the shop had been a hyperventilating experience the first time he'd done it because it was so narrow, but he was getting used to it. He paused at the entrance, looked both ways and pulled out onto the road. It took him less than five minutes to hit traffic, and while he paused, he fiddled with the radio. He hadn't bothered upgrading his system when new ones came out because he was happy flicking between radio stations, depending on what or who was on. It sometimes got tedious when they all had adverts on at the same time, but he managed.

As the miles between London and Whitby went by, he thought about that weekend. Designing those tattoos and then seeing them come to life on someone's body was an amazing experience. But then thinking about that led him to what happened on Saturday night.

He couldn't believe he'd lost it, but he was both grateful and annoyed that Beck had been the one to see it. Losing it because he'd thought someone was following him was not right. He wasn't right, and the man Kole could admit only to himself he had a crush on was one of the last people he'd wanted to see it. Despite that, Beck had been a rock. Kole wanted to do something for him, but he didn't know what. He'd have to think about it and maybe speak to Ethan to get some insights into the man. Obviously, that would only be for repaying him, not for anything else. He didn't want to gather intel about him so he could slyly get to know him better. Of course he didn't.

He couldn't stop the grin from spreading across his face as he drove into Whitby. The scent of the ocean, the distinctive squawk of the seagulls and the view from the top of the cliffs sank right into his soul, and the tension he hadn't realised he'd been holding leached away. Winding through the well-known streets, he headed for his parents' house. However much he wanted to sleep after the long journey, he needed to get the visit over and done with; otherwise, his aunt would start banging his door down when he didn't want her to. It was because she cared, especially after what happened, but he was done being a victim that everyone had to be careful around. He was grateful most of his family didn't care.

As he parked in their driveway, he wondered whether he could stop people from seeing him like that if he couldn't see it in himself. Maybe he had to change his own thoughts before other people did. He sighed as he climbed out of the car. More therapy was in his future.

He knocked but unlocked the front door with his key. "I'm back!" he called, locking the door again behind him.

"Kole! I wasn't expecting you back until a little later," his mother said, drying the dishes.

"I have a tour tonight, remember? I wanted to get back in time to rest before then."

His mother's mouth pursed. She hated him doing the job, and he couldn't understand why. It was nothing to do with what happened to him, which could've happened to him even if he'd been working in a supermarket or an office. The location was unlikely to have changed the outcome.

"Are you able to stay for dinner?" she asked, heading into the living room. "Your dad is cooking chicken curry."

Kole shook his head. "I don't have time. I just wanted to pop in so you could see that I survived my foray into London and back."

"How did it go?" his dad said, entering the room and ignoring Kole's outstretched hand.

"Jordan! The least you can do is say hello first," his mum chastised, though she didn't mean it. Appearances and all.

His dad looked at him and said, "Hello, Kole," all while rolling his eyes behind his wife's back. Kole's mouth twitched, but he held back his laughter, knowing how his mother would react if she saw. His dad was less strict than his mother, but he had his funny moments.

"It went well, thanks. I designed a few tattoos for people. It was amazing watching it go from that design to an actual colourful piece of art on someone's skin."

"It's a waste of money, if you ask me."

"Emmeline," Jordan said. "Just because you don't like tattoos doesn't mean other people don't. And someone now has Kole's artwork on their body."

Kole's chest expanded after deflating a bit with his mother's words. No, not everyone liked tattoos, but that was a personal choice, the same as anything. His mother huffed and headed out of the kitchen. She had opinions and she wasn't scared of telling anyone who asked what they were. His dad, on the other hand, was more easygoing and laidback, finding the humour in some situations. He couldn't help but want to be more like his father rather than his mother. Although saying that, he wanted to be more like Auntie Ava. She was even more lighthearted than his dad, and she meant the world to Kole. He hoped he'd be able to visit with her that week.

Kole and Jordan spoke about the weekend for a while longer before Kole said he had to go. He went to find his mother.

"Look after yourself, okay?" she said. And though there wasn't a lot of emotion behind it, he knew she meant it.

"I will."

It took him several more minutes to extricate himself from the house, but then he was on his way home. When he finally closed his front door behind him, he sighed, barely keeping his knees from dropping him to the floor. He needed a shower to wake him up; otherwise, he wouldn't make it through the tour that night.

A few hours later, he pulled on his black jeans, black shirt and black jumper—why not go the whole way into looking dark and mysterious—and shook out his cape. Checking the time, he grabbed a sandwich to eat before sitting at his table and laying out the face paint he used. It was usually a toss-up between a skeleton or vampire, or half of each, but he wanted to change it up a bit. Maybe a werewolf? Or actually go the whole ghostly way and become the ghost he often depicted. In the end, he chose his usual skeleton, and quickly applied the face paint he'd done hundreds of times before.

Once he was ready, he locked up and headed down the street. His house was on the opposite side of the harbour from where he started his tour, but the walk was never horrible, even in wet and windy weather. He never drove, no matter what, because, if the weather was that bad, they would cancel the tours.

Waving to his neighbour, he crossed the bridge, shivering a little at the biting breeze coming from the water, and began the winding incline up to the Whalebone Arch. It was one of the tourist attractions, and even though Kole had grown up with it being part of the landscape, it was an impressive sight. Once he stood beneath it, he took a photo and sent it to Ethan.

KOLE: *Do I look like the whale ate me before he died?*

Not waiting for a reply, he brought up the bookings for the tour, glad to see it was full once again. He would've loved to make this his business, working all hours of the night with his gift of storytelling, but it was a harsh business to get started in, and he wasn't sure how his employers would react if he started an opposing business venture, which might take money away from them. It shouldn't be something he considered, but he couldn't help but want a peaceful life.

"Good evening!" he said to a couple who stopped beside him. "Are you here for the ghost tour?"

"We are," one said.

"Fantastic. Can I take your name, please?"

He marked them off and asked where they were visiting from, and continued to do the same for those who joined. Checking his watch, he said, "We're just waiting for two more people, and then we'll start." He chatted with some of them, and then the stragglers arrived.

Kole froze, staring at the one person he didn't want to see. Ever again. He held up his hand. "No, Andrew."

"Please, Kole. Let me explain."

Kole swallowed, his knees trembling. "No. If you've booked onto the tour, go back and request a transfer or a refund. You will not be on this one."

Andrew's face fell, but he stepped away. Kole smiled at the rest of the visitors. "I apologise for that. So, welcome to the Ravenwood Whitby Ghost Tour. I'm your host, Kole, and I promise you stories, scares and sass for the next hour and a half. Before we set off, do you have any questions?" No one said anything—which was the usual response—so he set off on his first pirate story as they made their way down the path. He tried to ignore that Andrew had been there, but he kept checking over his shoulder in case he followed them. He was more reluctant to go into the shadowy alleys and nooks of the town, knowing he was nearby, but he wouldn't let down his visitors. Plus, he had an alarm in his pocket, one he had taken to carrying since the incident.

Bracing himself, Kole said the words to get the pirate to jump out at them, and screams rent through the air, followed by laughter. He grinned. "I thought you might like that one. We'll walk a little further, and then I'll regale you with the second of my stories."

Gavin, the ghost pirate actor, dropped into place beside him. "Are you okay? I saw who turned up."

Kole exhaled. "Shaky, but he seems to have stayed away. I don't know why he booked onto the tour when he knows he's not supposed to be near me."

"He probably knows you won't call the police on him." Gavin gave him the same side-eye he would've got from Ethan had he been there.

Kole sighed. "It's a waste of time. Mine, the police, everything. They won't do anything about it other than note down that he was here."

"But what if you don't report all these minor incidents, and something happens, Kole? The police will think it was a one-and-done rather than a build-up."

"You've been watching too many crime shows." Kole elbowed him.

"Maybe. But I'm also not wrong."

"Fine. But I'm not calling them tonight. I'll tell them tomorrow."

Gavin blew out a breath and shook his head. "I don't agree, but it's your choice. I'm sticking around tonight, though."

Kole wouldn't admit how much he'd hoped Gavin would say that. There wasn't much anyone could do if something happened, but knowing there was someone on his side helped settle his nerves.

He continued through the streets, scaring them with his stories of headless horses and ghostly apparitions, and sending their blood pressure through the roof when people jumped out at them, and by the end of the night, finishing at his favourite spot—the top of the 199 steps—he grinned.

"Thank you so much for your company this evening. I hope you join me again soon. And please remember to leave a review!"

He turned to face the view, the lights from buildings flickering on and off throughout the town, up the cliffs and down to the harbour. The sounds from the arcades and pubs spilt into the night and rose to him on the breeze. It was chillier up there, but he didn't care. It helped clear his head.

"Kole."

Kole screeched and stepped back, holding out his hand. "Andrew, you can't be here. You know this."

"I just want to explain."

He glanced around, trying to see where everyone had gone. "The police will be upset if you're here, Andrew. You don't want that."

"The police are idiots!" Andrew yelled, throwing his hands in the air.

Kole's heart raced, but his shoulders loosened when Gavin came running towards them. His colleague stepped between them.

"Leave now. The police are on their way."

Andrew cradled his head and growled. "I just want to explain!"

"Then explain to the police, and they will let Kole know," Gavin said.

Andrew took a step forward, and Gavin stepped back into Kole, who gripped the back of his costume. He wasn't sure what Andrew was going to do, but thankfully, after sending a frenzied look at Kole, Andrew turned around and raced down the steps. Kole's knees stopped holding him up, and he sank to the floor.

"Holy shit," he muttered. "I'm not sure I can take this any longer."

Gavin crouched beside him. "What do you mean?"

His eyes darted around as the decision settled inside him. "I'm moving to London," he said, meeting Gavin's gaze.

"I didn't know you were moving."

"Split-second decision. I can't stay here, Gavin. Not after this. He'll just haunt my footsteps as well as my dreams. I can't do it."

He had never been close friends with Gavin, but they all knew what had happened to him, and they had been asked to keep their eyes open. It was great for people to have his back, but his nerves couldn't take any longer. There was no guarantee Andrew wouldn't follow him to London, but he had to take the chance.

Now he just had to break the news to his family.

While they waited for the police to arrive, Kole checked his phone, having forgotten he'd messaged Ethan until he saw his reply.

ETHAN: *Yes, actually. That's pretty scary. Let me know when you're done.*

KOLE: *I'm done, but Andrew was here. He didn't do anything, and Gavin stayed with me. We're waiting to file a police report, and then I'll be going home. Don't worry. I'm fine. I promise. But you're getting your wish.*

ETHAN: *What? That asshole! I'm going to come up there and show him what I could fit into a place where the sun doesn't shine! I'm going to call you later, so tell me when you get home. Don't walk home by yourself. Please. And what wish are you on about?*

KOLE: *You better start looking for a place I can afford down there. It'll take me a while to pack up and convince Mum I'm not making a rash decision.*

ETHAN: *SERIOUSLY? Fuck yeah! I'll get Joey on it right away. We'll find you some place in no time.*

Kole didn't reply straight away because the police arrived, and as he thought, they couldn't do anything about it, but they would add it to the folder about the case. Gavin walked him home, and Peter, the owner of the tour company, called to check on him.

As he stood in his living room, he looked around. It wouldn't take that long to pack up if he was being truthful. But was he making the right choice? Images of Ethan and Joey swam into his mind, followed by the Life in Ink crew, followed by the memories of how Beck held him when he'd lost control. Kole's heart skipped a beat. Although he doubted Beck wanted any kind of relationship with him, that Kole liked the idea of trying was a step in the right direction.

After calling Ethan to reassure him, Kole went to bed. Despite knowing that he'd get embarrassed when he next saw him, he couldn't stop thinking about Beck and how he'd looked at him as they'd hugged at the event. He'd been sure Beck was going to kiss him, and his stomach had swooped and swirled, readying for it, but then he'd pulled back.

Did Kole have the confidence to make a move on Beck when he moved to London?

5

BECK

B eck had tried to drown the "what-ifs" from his head by searching for someone to share his bed, but whenever he found someone, it was never their eyes that gazed back at him. And each time, he found an excuse to end the night early. His frustration built, but it didn't matter how many times he told his reflection that he couldn't have Kole, his brain—and his dick—didn't listen. Luckily, it hadn't bled into his work, and because of that, he found himself working longer hours in the two months since the Bonser event.

The following morning, he had to stay at the shop as it was his turn. He'd not long been back from a trip to Amsterdam to tattoo Sem van der Berg, a top male model, while he was home. The Netherlands' capital was a beautiful place, but Beck loved his home city much more, despite London having the reputation of being dirty, packed like sardines and never sleeping.

He stared at his TV screen as the images flashed across it, words spoken that never registered with him. What he wanted was to sleep, but that was difficult when his own screams woke him repeatedly through the darkened hours. His body was sluggish, and he laid down, shoving a cushion beneath his head and tucking his feet under another. Blinking several times to remove the gritty feeling, he relaxed as much as possible, hoping sleep would come.

Beck ran through the forest, laughing as his foster brother and sisters chased him. He jumped over a log, rounded a tree and crashed into something—someone. Falling to his ass, Beck growled up at Drake.

"Drake! Watch where you're going!"

He clambered to his feet and brushed his trousers off, groaning when Allan, Rebecca and Sarah caught up. Beck threw his hands in the air.

"That's not fair!"

Drake stepped closer, gripping his shoulder in a tight hand. "I'll make it up to you tonight."

Beck shivered at the promise in the other boy's eyes. Drake was two years older than his eleven years, and he didn't like him one bit. He often pretended to be nice and kind and helpful, but when their foster parents weren't looking, he could be mean and hurtful—with his words and his hands. Beck had learnt many things during his years in the foster system, and being beholden to someone was never good.

"Don't bother," Beck said, shrugging him off. He turned to the others, pointing at Sarah. "Your turn."

Sarah shouted and pumped her hands in the air and set off through the trees. Beck, Allan and Rebecca counted to ten. Allan and Rebecca set after her first, Beck giving them a headstart because they were younger than he was. But before he could join them in the hunt, Drake shoved him against a tree face first, covering his back with his body.

"You know something, Beck? You should be a little kinder to the person who shares a room with you."

Drake pushed against him, shoving Beck's groin against the tree and causing him to whimper as pain streaked through him.

"Let me go, Drake!"

He tried to push away, but Drake forced him back again.

"Be kind, Beck. You never know what you'll end up getting."

Drake disappeared, and Beck pushed off the tree, brushing himself down again. He glared at Drake's retreating back and sighed. Maybe he'd go to bed early so he was asleep by the time Drake came into the bedroom. Maybe then he'd leave him alone.

Laughter reached his ears, and he shook his head, sprinting off in the direction of the foster siblings he actually liked.

Beck startled awake, but it only took seconds for him to reorient himself. Waking up on the sofa was a regular occurrence, as was the sweat coating his skin. He breathed deeply before pushing to sit upright. His head spun a little, but he closed his eyes and waited until it passed. Once it had, he headed for the kitchen; coffee was calling his name. While he waited for the kettle, he stared out of the window into the early morning light, watching the commuters drive past his flat.

It wasn't a luxurious place to live, but it was his, and he couldn't be happier with it. His little house was between an estate agent's and another house and had two floors. The first floor had a living room, kitchen and bedroom, and the top floor had two small bedrooms. He rarely used the top floor, except for storage, but it was handy if anyone needed to stay over. Not that anyone did.

The noise from the road wasn't as loud as he'd found it to be in other locations, so that was a bonus, but it sometimes got worse whenever there was an event going on at the bar or club down the road. But as he didn't sleep much, it wasn't a huge issue. Sometimes, he even went to join them.

The kettle clicked off, and he poured the hot water into the mug, the scent of coffee rising into the air. Despite being extremely hot, he wrapped his hands around it and stared out of the window some more. He had plenty of time before he had to be at work, but he would be there far too early, anyway. What else did he have to do? Between pining after Kole and nightmares about his past, he didn't have much taking up his time. Tattooing was the best release he ever had.

Once he finished that coffee, he made another and headed for the shower, finally washing off the nightmare he'd experienced. He didn't feel much about them anymore; they were just...there. If he didn't dwell on them, he was fine. But sometimes, nausea and headaches accompanied them. By the time he was dressed, that coffee was making its way through his body. He made one more for the road, which should give him enough energy to keep him awake for several hours, especially with more caffeine throughout the day. No one would be the wiser.

The radio kept him company on the thirty-minute drive to Life in Ink, and despite getting caught at every possible traffic light he could, he still made good time. He unlocked the door, switched off the alarm and locked the door behind him. He still had over an hour before he needed to open the doors to the public, so he dragged his ass up the stairs to his studio, flicking lights on as he went.

Immediately, he turned on some music, nodding his head when Bon Jovi started playing. No one could ever go wrong with Bon Jovi. Going through his usual routine, he set his studio up, pausing only when he received a message from Joey through the group chat.

JOEY: *We have some amazing news!*

He waited, but nothing else came through, so he typed:

BECK: *You're pregnant! Congrats!*
JOEY: *Close, but not quite.*

He knew sarcasm when he read it. He waited again, but still nothing. Sighing, he sent another guess.

BECK: You're emigrating to Australia?

JOEY: A little bit closer.

BECK: You're eloping?

JOEY: Your guesses suck. Anyone else?

DALLAS: You're pregnant?

DALLAS: Shit, Beck already did that one.

DALLAS: You're marrying a prince?

JOEY: I've found my prince, Dallas. Don't need another.

BECK: You're closing up shop.

JOEY: What a traitorous thought! No way!

DALLAS: You've found someone to pay off your huge gambling debt from our visit to Vegas three years ago?

JOEY: I didn't have a debt! Asshole!

JOEY: If anyone did, it was you.

DALLAS: Get real. I won plenty.

BECK: Ethan has decided to dump your ass because he realised I'm a much better catch?

JOEY: In your dreams.

ETHAN: I didn't know you cared so much, Beck.

BECK: You're a prince, so Joey says. I think I deserve a prince.

ETHAN: You truly do, and you'll find one.

FINN: You've finally persuaded Kole to come and work with us?

The conversation stalled for a moment, no responses at all, and then Joey started typing.

JOEY: How the fuck...?

JOEY: Yes. Kole is coming to work for us.

Beck's breath caught in his throat as he stared at the words, questions tumbling through his head in no particular order. When? Why? How? Where? When? He licked his lips, needing to ask the question, but not wanting to appear too keen. Luckily, though, Dallas beat him to it.

DALLAS: *Yes! When is he starting?*

The doorbell of the shop rang, and Beck glanced at the time, cursing when he realised it was time to open up. He shoved the phone into his pocket, even though he needed to know the answer like he needed to breathe. The doorbell sounded again, and he jogged down the stairs and to the door.

"Hold up!" he called, unlocking the door and flipping the sign to "open." "Sorry about that. I was…"

He trailed off when he was met with a familiar face, and suddenly, he didn't need to know the answer. He was staring at it—him.

"Hey. Joey said it was okay to drop in today. To see how things worked. Is that…okay?" Kole asked, still standing on the threshold.

Beck blinked. "Yes, of course!" He stepped back. "Come on in. I've only just been told the good news, but I wasn't told when you were starting." He closed the door and focused on opening the blinds. Inhaling, he faced the man who had made him want to fall asleep because he saw him in his dreams—when his brain let go of the nightmares, that was.

Kole winced. "Sorry about that. I hadn't realised they were keeping it a secret."

Beck waved him away, even as his stomach flooded with butterflies at being so close to the guy again. "It's all good. It was a good surprise, that's all." He rounded the desk to see the calendar. Nothing said anything about where Kole would be working from. "I'm not sure where you're going to be, but I'm sure you could use Dallas's studio today. He's on his travels today."

Kole shook his head. "I'm good just sitting in one of these chairs and doing my thing. I doubt I'll have many people wanting me to do something for them."

Beck smiled. "You will. As soon as word spreads that you're working for us, that you were the one at the Bonser event, people will start flocking. I know it."

Kole licked his lips and lifted his chin, though Beck could see the uncertainty in him. "I don't know about that, but thank you for saying it."

"Do you want a tour, or have they done that already? Wait. Where are you staying?"

"Joey found me a small flat not too far away. It works for now, but maybe I'll find something else, eventually. I don't think it's my forever home."

Beck nodded. "I can understand that. There are so many places, good and bad, in London that it may take a little while for you to find something you like."

"Same everywhere then." Kole grinned and put his bag on the counter. "I'll just sit here and wait until Joey or Ethan are around."

Beck didn't want him to feel unwelcome or unsure, so he settled on giving him a task. "How about you draw some designs for us to put on the wall? Like these." He moved to the designs covering the walls. "Each of us has designs on there that people can choose from or they can request something from the designer of their choice. Or bring something in themselves. Either way, if you get some drawings done, something with your flair on it, we can put them up and see what happens. I bet you'll get more work than you think you will."

He could see Kole wasn't convinced, but he nodded. "I'll start scribbling." Settling into a chair in the waiting room, Kole pulled his things from his bag, laying them on his lap. He opened a regular artist's pad, chose a pencil and tapped it against his lip as he stared at the blank page. Beck knew all this because he watched. He couldn't help himself. He took in the way he held his pencil. The way he scraped his teeth across his lower lip while his hand brushed across the page. The way he tilted his head when he paused to study what he'd already created.

Beck only stopped when the bell rang to signal someone had opened the door. Blinking and shaking his head, he focused on the newcomer, and stood, smiling.

"Leyton! How're things? Not seen you in a while."

Leyton was a huge mofo, originally from Nigeria, and he had a huge array of tattoos over his entire body. There wasn't much space left for big designs, but smaller intricate ones would work in the spaces left. Beck had thought the man had been messing with him when he told him he was a preschool manager, but once he'd seen him in action at an event they'd been invited to at the preschool itself, Beck had known it was a role Leyton had been born for. The man had settled onto a chair, rested his arms on a table on each side, and let the children colour his tattoos. He'd sat there for hours. *Hours*. And the kids loved it. It was why he always had only outlines done on his arms and legs. The rest of him was a waterfall of colour.

"I'm a busy man, Beck. Especially now I have a baby to look after." Leyton grinned.

Beck gaped. "Seriously? When did that happen?" He rounded the counter.

"We'd been thinking about it for a while but decided to go for it. We hadn't told anyone because we didn't want the hell of having to explain if or when it happened. But now little Maria is in our arms, we're telling the world."

Beck shook his hand, wishing he could get the courage to hug him, but he reserved that for close friends only. His body didn't like it when he touched strangers for too long—it was maybe the reason his one-night stands didn't stay for a second night.

"Congratulations! I'm so happy for you."

"Thanks," Leyton said. "So, are we still on for today's session?"

Beck returned to the other side of the counter and checked the diary. "Yes, definitely. Joey should be here in a few minutes, but if he isn't, I'll yell for him." He winked, and Leyton laughed. "While we're waiting, though, I want to introduce you to our newest team member. Kole?"

Kole blinked, seemingly coming out of a trance-like state. "Sorry, what?"

Beck chuckled. "This is Kole's first official day, but he joined us at the Bonser event a couple of months ago, and he was very popular. We're expecting great things from him."

Kole licked his lips again, distracting Beck, but then stood and held out his hand. "Nice to meet you."

"You, too. You won't go wrong with this crowd. What styles do you do?"

"Um, I don't really know if there's a specific word for it, but I like tribal design and mandalas, so I try to combine the two to make something unique."

Leyton whistled and nodded. "I like the sound of that. Do you have any you've already created?"

Kole seemed like he held his breath as he handed over the pad he'd been working on. Leyton flicked through the pages, making Beck wish he'd stepped closer to see them, but he didn't interrupt.

"I love these," Leyton said. "Do you think they'd still work in a small design?" he asked Kole.

Kole's mouth worked but nothing came out straight away. "I'm not a tattoo artist, so I don't really know..." He looked at Beck, who rounded the counter again and looked at the design, marvelling once more at Kole's talent.

"Which one?" he asked Leyton. When he pointed it out, Beck scrutinised it a bit more and nodded. "Yes, that could easily be reduced in size. It might work better if there was one less row inside the circle, but it wouldn't be impossible to do. You know us. We're always up for a challenge."

"We wouldn't be who we were if we weren't," Joey added as he entered the room from the stairs. "Leyton, my man." He hugged him. "How's Eamon?"

"Great, thanks. Do you think we could have a change of design for today? I love this."

He held up Kole's design, and Beck watched Kole's cheeks darken, but his eyes sparkled as Joey and Leyton discussed his design. That was what it was all about. The rush they felt when their designs or work were appreciated. The pleasure when theirs were chosen to be forever inked onto someone's body. The satisfaction when everything went right.

As Joey asked Kole if he could take the page from the pad and Kole nodded, Beck couldn't stop a smile from spreading across his face. And when Joey and Leyton climbed the stairs, he stared at Kole.

"I'm not usually someone who would say I told you so, but..."

He grinned at Kole when he threw a pencil in Beck's direction, but then dropped into the seat again and retrieved a new one—and a new page. Beck had paperwork to get on with until his client turned up in an hour, but he stealthily watched Kole as he drew line after line and wished he would draw on Beck's body instead of paper. The feel of a pen dragging across his bare skin while Kole leaned over him. The images had Beck restraining a groan and adjusting himself in his jeans.

He had to remind himself that Kole was off limits. If only because Beck wasn't a relationship type of guy. If he had been, he would drag Kole to him and keep him, but he wasn't. And it wasn't fair to Kole to give him hope for that.

It didn't stop him from wanting him, though.

But then the memories came back, followed by nausea, trembling and a headache.

When would Drake leave him alone?

6

KOLE

When Beck finally disappeared from the front desk, Kole took a breath. He'd felt the man staring at him as he drew, and electricity sizzled in his veins as he tried to ignore him. It hadn't worked. He'd been aware of every rustle, every move he made. Kole's hand had trembled as he concentrated half his brain on drawing something remotely usable.

He stared down at the paper and froze. The image he'd drawn was something different from his usual sketches. It still had the tribal mandala effect, but to one side, a man's face appeared in profile. The mandala was where the man's brain would have been, and the tribal designs were integrated into the hair. He knew who it was and that it would never see the light of day, but seeing the conundrum that was Beck on paper in that form was disconcerting.

Turning to a new page, he tapped his pencil in the centre, seeing where his brain was going to take him next. As he settled, the door chimed, and Ani entered, her expression brightening when she saw Kole.

"Kole! I'm so glad you're here. Have they helped you to settle in?" she asked, rounding the desk and putting her stuff away.

"They've been great. They weren't sure what had been decided on where my base would be, but I'm happy sitting here."

"Oh, no, no, no. That won't do. Not that I don't want to see your face all day every day, but you do have a space to do what you wish. You'll need to get away from the hustle and bustle of the front here; otherwise, you won't be able to concentrate. Follow me."

She waved at him, and he stood, gathering his things, but the door chimed again, garnering Ani's attention.

"Denny! It's good to see you," she said, rounding the desk to greet him. "You ready for more?"

"Always."

"Beck's upstairs. You know the way."

Denny nodded, but Kole was ashamed to admit he was a little starstruck. Standing barely five feet from him was a member of The Ports, a band he religiously followed. Yes, he was a boy band fan.

"Oh, Denny, have you met Kole yet? He's our newest addition."

Denny smiled at him, and Kole's stomach swirled. How many times had he looked at that smile and wished someone focused something similar on him?

"Nice to meet you, Kole. You've joined a great family." They shook hands.

Kole finally found his voice. "Nice to meet you, too."

Denny let go and headed for the stairs. "I'll see you in a bit."

When Denny disappeared, Kole swallowed. "Holy shit. I gotta get used to this."

Ani laughed and followed in the celebrity's wake. "You will. Soon, it'll be old hat to you, especially when it comes to princes and their friends, like Donovan and Christian."

"Who are they?"

"Donovan is Beck's friend, and Christian...that's Prince Christian." Ani grinned.

Kole gaped and gulped. "Okay, fingers crossed." He was sure he'd dropped into an alternate world.

Ani showed him to a room set up exactly like all the others, with tattoo equipment and chairs.

"I don't need all this," he said.

Ani waved him away. "You don't need to. It's here for if we have a visiting artist, which we rarely do. Besides, we have two more rooms like it."

Kole studied the space and could see the potential. Even the equipment didn't faze him like it might've before. The idea of being able to ink someone was not as scary as the first time.

"Thanks. It's perfect."

"Don't feel like you have to stay up here secluded. You're welcome to join us downstairs whenever you want, but we wanted you to have your own space if you wanted it."

Kole's throat closed, making it difficult to swallow. "Thanks."

"I'll leave you to sort yourself, but come down in a bit. Once the scariness and overwhelm has eased." She squeezed his hand and left.

And then it was Kole, standing in the centre of a room that had been given to him without any questions asked. Had he made the right choice? He wandered over to the window, putting his bags on the desk, and looked out. The cars roaring past were muted by the windowpane, but the view was nice. He could see himself being happy there. If only he could find someone to share his life with.

Beck's face flashed through his mind, and he didn't push it away. It was futile, but he couldn't deny his attraction. He wanted to see whether Beck was willing to give them a try, but he needed to build up the courage first. He would, but he didn't know when. He didn't want Beck to think he'd moved to London for him because it wasn't true. He'd moved for himself. Beck was an extra he hadn't expected. But he was determined to move past his anxiety. What Andrew had done to him wasn't nice, but he needed to live his own life now.

Okay, he had work to do on getting over the feeling of being watched, but he could do it. He'd already decided to find a new therapist to talk it over with. One step at a time, he was doing. And so far, it was working.

Settling at the table, he got to work, wanting to crank out some ideas for Life in Ink to prove hiring him wasn't a mistake.

When a knock came, he lifted his head, groaning at the crick in his neck. "Yeah?"

The door opened, and Ethan popped his head in, grinning. "How're you doing?" he asked, coming further into the room.

Kole stood, dragging his best friend into a hug. "I'm good. How are you?"

"Awesome! I'm so glad you're here." He wandered over to Kole's desk. "Wow. You've been busy." He flicked through the strewn pages. "These are amazing."

Kole flushed at the compliment. "They're okay. Some need some tweaking, but they're not bad."

"Let's take these to Ani. We can put them up on the wall now, and people can start looking through them."

"Oh, I don't think they're ready for that yet."

"They are. Trust me."

Knowing he wouldn't dissuade him, Kole shrugged, and Ethan grabbed a few and gestured for Kole to follow him.

"I know you're scared, but these *are* great, Kole. I wouldn't tell you they were if they weren't. I respect you too much for that."

Kole didn't reply, knowing it was true. Best friends didn't coddle each other. It didn't mean he wasn't scared. But, if he'd managed it at the Bonser event, he could do it here.

"Where shall we put these, Ani?" Ethan asked when they entered reception.

Ani flicked through them, a smile creeping across her face. "These are great, Kole. Let's put two here, and then these three over with the others."

She bustled around, clipping the pages into the frames already set up on the wall. Seeing his designs next to the others was a mind-exploding image.

"Now, anyone who comes in can either buy this design, or request something similar, and you can work with them to design it how they want it."

Kole exhaled. "This is..." He shook his head, unable to explain.

Ethan slid an arm around his shoulder. "I know, but how cool is this, eh?"

Kole chuckled, and finally, some of the weight on his shoulders lifted. "It is cool, yes."

He studied his work amongst the other artists—Joey, Beck, Dallas and Finn—and almost couldn't believe where he was. He'd dreamt of being an artist for years but decided it wasn't for him when his work was heavily criticised throughout school. He wasn't cut out for the cutthroat business that it was. But here, he felt like his work mattered. That he had something to say in his designs. That others wanted to listen to. It was a little overwhelming.

"How are you finding the apartment?" Ethan asked, dropping into a chair and crossing his legs. His phone was already in his hand, something he was rarely without lately. But keeping track of Life in Ink's schedule was a full-time job in itself.

Kole settled beside him, linking his fingers on his lap. "I like it. How you managed to find something that had even the briefest of views of the river was incredible."

Ethan grinned. "Joey has connections, that's for sure. I'm glad you like it. I want you to be happy here."

"You just don't want me to go back home and leave you to fend for yourself amongst this lot," Kole joked, waving his hand to the ceiling.

"I'm not denying that, but I'm also adding that I love having my best friend around." He leant forward. "Are you up for a night out tonight? Just dinner and a few drinks to welcome you?"

He hesitated, but he wanted to spend time with everyone instead of hiding away at home, so he nodded. "Sure. Where are we going?" He snorted. "Not that I would have one clue if you told me."

"Actually, we're heading to that restaurant we went to when you came last time. Not the Bonser event, I mean."

"Oh, that Indian place?" Ethan nodded. "The food was nice there."

"We have a reservation for seven o'clock. Is that enough time?"

Kole nodded. "That'll be... Hold on a minute. How do you have a reservation already if you were only just asking me?"

Ethan smirked. "I already booked it. I would've forcibly dragged you there if you'd said no."

"Good to know."

"You're welcome to head out now if you want a breather before tonight," Ani said. "If anyone comes in asking about your designs, we can book them in for tomorrow."

Kole inhaled and smiled. "No, I think I'm good. I love being here."

And he did. Even when, in the next breath, a small group of twenty-somethings entered, making a lot of noise about each getting a tattoo and taking forever to choose, and turned the place into a loud group meeting. Their excitement and interest were palpable. Kole disappeared behind the desk so he was out of the way, but he stayed to listen to their conversation, taking titbits of information about what they liked and didn't like to use in his future designs. Everyone was different, but if he could get ideas about what people liked, it would give him some reference to go with.

When the group finally decided, Ani and Ethan worked at fitting them in for appointments. Beck was almost finished with Denny, and Joey was nearly done with Leyton. Dallas was due at any time. So that meant each tattoo artist had three people to ink. Luckily, all the designs were fairly small and easy, from what Kole could see.

"Do you want to watch?" Ani asked Kole, but he shook his head.

"I saw some at the Bonser event. I know how it works, thanks. I marvel at how different people are. One liked one design, but another hated it, and so on. It's weirdly wonderful."

Ani grinned and clasped his shoulder. "That should probably be our slogan. Weirdly Wonderful in every way."

"Are you channelling Mary Poppins, Ani?" Joey asked as he descended the stairs, Leyton following behind.

Ani chuckled. "If only. Life might be a little easier if I was."

Kole watched the workings of getting clients into rooms and everything else involved and then retreated to his room to work on some more designs. That time, he wanted to try something colourful. Beck's angel wings came to mind as he drew, and he incorporated some similar lines and textures. Before he started the colours, he added some shading, but before he could continue, someone knocked.

"Come in."

Beck entered with a smile. "How're things going? Ani said you'd been cooped up in here for hours."

Kole checked the clock. "God! I have. No wonder my back aches. I got distracted."

"Can I look?" Beck asked.

He didn't think the design would get him into trouble, if Beck even noticed the similarities to his wings, but it still made his stomach churn. "Sure."

Beck moved closer, resting one hand on the back of Kole's chair, and the other beside his paper. At first, he said nothing, and Kole began to worry, but then he shook his head. "Exquisite. I see you kept it within a circular design. If you wanted to change it up a bit, you could extend the wings a little from either side, as if they were emerging from the design itself."

Kole studied it and saw what Beck meant. He picked up his pencil and sketched a few light pencil marks to get an idea of what it would look like.

"I like it. I'll add that tomorrow with some colour, too."

"I keep meaning to add a little colour to my wings, but I never get around to it."

Kole spun the chair around, dislodging Beck's hand. "Why not?"

Beck shrugged. "It's one of those things I keep telling myself to do, but then life happens. One day, I'll get one of the others to do it."

The idea of getting his hands on Beck's skin and colouring his designs made Kole want to train to be a tattooist straight away, but he wasn't sure if it was his calling or not. It was something to consider later on, after he'd found his feet doing the job he'd already been given.

"Are you ready to break the joint?" Beck asked with a wink.

"I need my bag, but yeah."

He reached across and grabbed it, throwing it over his head to cross his body, and followed Beck from the room. They met with Dallas as he exited his studio.

"Hey! Are you figuring shit out?" he asked Kole.

"Getting there."

He loved how interested they all were. They weren't asking questions just for the sake of it, they wanted to know the answers to them, too. When the clock ticked over to six-thirty, their group cheered, and Ani flipped the sign over to closed.

"Go on, you bunch of twits. Get moving. I'll lock up," Ani said, laughing.

"I'll keep you company," Kole said, not wanting to leave her alone. It wasn't because he thought she couldn't look after herself, it was because he would've done it to anyone to ensure they weren't left alone.

"Me, too," Beck said. "Three is better than one. Or two."

Ani shook her head. "You didn't have to, but I won't argue."

She set the alarm and locked the doors, giving the place a quick once over before seemingly being satisfied. Then they all headed towards the Indian restaurant, which, if Kole wasn't mistaken, was only a ten-minute walk away. Their conversation was light and easy, and it felt like he'd known them for years rather than months. What was it about these people that made him feel...safe?

As soon as he thought that, he had visions of them being hurt, and goosebumps rose across his skin. The same feeling he got when it seemed like someone was watching him. He glanced over his shoulder, checking behind them, but couldn't see anyone of significance. He tried to shake it off—after all, it was all in his head—but it was hard. It was only when Beck rested his palm on Kole's nape that he was able to breathe properly.

When they reached the restaurant, Beck paused, leaning down. "Are you sure you're up for this? I can take you home."

Kole wanted to take the excuse and hide away in his new apartment, but he couldn't. He needed to start fresh, even if old memories and thoughts were trying to keep him down. Determined not to let them win, he shook his head. "I'm good." He licked his lips, deciding to take a huge leap of faith. "But promise me one thing?"

Beck tilted his head and nodded. "What?"

"The next time we get together, it'll be you, me, a bottle of tequila and a bed?"

Beck's breath caught, but then he smiled, the tip of his tongue caught between his teeth. "I can promise that." He leaned down, brushing his lips across Kole's briefly before stepping back. "Time for food. Rain check?"

Kole nodded. "Not too long, though, yeah?"

"Wouldn't dream of it."

Exhaling quietly, Kole walked in behind Beck, proud of himself. He'd made the first move on other people before, but since Andrew had shaken his confidence, he hadn't wanted to try. But Beck had wormed his way into his brain, and he couldn't leave well enough alone. Despite being scared to death that he'd ruin things, he needed some relief, and what better way than to spend a night with the man who kept haunting his dreams?

"Oh, and Kole?" Beck said, stopping a few metres from their table, where everyone else waited for them.

"Yes?"

"Let's make it a day we haven't got to work the next day. I plan to take my time with you."

Beck winked and settled beside Ani at the table, immediately jumping into the conversation and making everyone laugh. Kole, however, had lusty images running rampant in his head and couldn't get his legs to work.

How the hell was he going to survive whatever Beck had planned for them?

7

BECK

Working alongside Kole was pure torture. Sometimes, Beck wouldn't see much of him because one of them would be locked away in their room working. And other times, Kole would sit in reception to draw and chat with Ethan and Ani. And when he did that, Beck saw him every time he had a new client.

Their agreement to spend time in bed hadn't happened because Beck had been called away to tattoo some people the day after Kole had started working there, so he'd been away for two days, and since, they'd not mentioned anything to each other. Beck wanted to take what Kole said as golden and make a date, but what if he'd changed his mind and was happy to think Beck had, too? He didn't want to make things awkward for them at work.

As time drew closer to the weekend, he decided to take a chance. He found Kole in reception, with his elbow on the back of the chair and staring out of the window at the dismal weather. Glancing around, no one else was there, so he settled gently beside him.

Kole still jumped, but he smiled when he saw him, his shoulders lowering from around his ears. "Hey."

Beck smiled. "Hey to you, too. How are you doing?"

"I'm getting inspiration from the rain. Have you got a client?"

"Not yet," Beck said, mirroring Kole's position and crossing his leg over his knee to get that little bit closer to him. "I wanted to ask... Are you still up for a night?"

He watched Kole's face carefully, wanting to see every nuance that crossed it, to ensure he didn't misjudge the situation. His expressive eyes told a story of pain and hurt but also joy and humour. The echoes of the lines around his mouth and eyes told of laughter and grief. Beck wanted to stop the hurt and pain from touching him, but it wasn't possible. Experience had taught him that.

Kole's pale skin flushed, and he nodded. "I'd like that a lot."

"Are you free on Saturday? I don't have to work on Sunday," he explained, the meaning behind his words clear from his statement the other day.

Kole's flush darkened, and Beck wanted to feel that heat against his skin. So, he reached forward, giving enough time for Kole to pull away if he wanted to, and when his palm cupped his cheek and the heat warmed his skin, Kole's eyes drifted closed, and he leaned further in.

"I'm free," he whispered, opening his eyes again. His hazel eyes had darkened to a conker colour, and Beck wanted to kiss him. He even leaned in before coming to his senses when voices sounded.

"I'll pick you up? Seven o'clock?"

Kole nodded, eyelids heavy and needy, and Beck almost changed his mind because feasting on those lips would make everything better, in his opinion. But he would have to wait two more days. He brushed his thumb over the mounds and slid his fingertips across his cheek until he no longer touched him. If he wasn't mistaken, though, a whimper came from Kole when he let go. That was something to explore later.

The doorbell chimed, and Beck glanced up, his next client nodding at him. "Hey, Toby. How are you, man?" He stood and shook hands with the man. "Toby, this is Kole, the newest addition to the Life in Ink family. Kole, this is the gentlest giant to ever have walked in here."

Kole stood and held out his hand to shake. Toby engulfed his tiny hand, but Beck knew Toby didn't have a hurtful bone in his body.

"The gentlest giant? What about Dallas?" Kole said. "Nice to meet you."

"You, too. What do you do for these misfits?"

Oh, how that word fit them so well. Beck grinned and waited for Kole's answer. He was still a little shy about his work, but he was better than he had been on day one.

"I'm an artist." Beck beamed at the use of the word Kole had declined several times at the beginning. "I create designs for Beck and everyone else to use if they wish."

"Which are yours?"

Beck held up his hand. "Ah, ah, ah. You know the rules, Toby. You've been here enough. You have to guess."

Toby sighed dramatically and then stepped closer to the wall. He studied it while Beck studied Kole. He dragged his teeth over his bottom lip, and Beck wanted to pull it free and soothe the battered skin with his mouth.

"This one," Toby said.

Kole grinned. "Yes."

They talked about his designs a little before Ani came back into reception. "I thought I heard voices." She hugged Toby. "How are you?"

"Good, thanks."

"I see you've met Kole."

Toby nodded. "He was just showing me his work. Can I grab what I want?"

Ani waved her hand. "Sure. You know what to do."

As Beck and Kole watched on, Toby took two of Kole's designs and put them on the counter. He could see Kole wanted to protest, but it was only because he didn't think his work was good enough or he felt Toby was doing it to be kind. When Kole stepped forward, Beck slid a hand up his arm and stopped him. It was the first time Kole hadn't flinched at an unexpected touch.

Kole glanced at him, and Beck shook his head. Kole sighed and stepped back, turning to look out of the window again. He'd get used to it because his work was amazing. They just needed Kole to believe it, and that would come with time.

"Thank you for these, Kole. I can book in at least two more sessions now."

Kole smiled at him. "I'm glad you like them."

Beck decided to give Kole a breather. "Come on then, Toby. Time waits for no one."

"Ain't that the truth."

He headed for the stairs, barely stopping himself from checking on Kole again. When they entered his studio space, Beck closed the door.

"He's got talent, that one has," Toby said.

Beck grinned. "He does."

Toby settled into the chair, pulling his trouser leg up so Beck could continue the tattoo on his shin. It was a painful area, but one many people liked to tattoo as it looked good.

"We should get this finished today unless the pain gets too much. Remember to tell me if it does."

"Will do."

Beck put on his music, and Toby pulled out his phone to read. Settling on his stool at Toby's feet, Beck dropped into what he called his tattooing brain. He lost himself to the rhythm of the machine, the sound, the scent, almost able to taste the ink in the air. Nothing was better than that.

Toby had to stop several times, the pain becoming too much, and when his two hours were up, only a small amount remained. Toby sighed. "I wanted it done today."

"I don't have any clients until four o'clock today. Do you want a break, and then we have a go at finishing it?"

Toby raised his eyebrows. "Are you sure?"

Beck nodded. "I know what's it like when you just want it over and done with. It shouldn't take more than half an hour to finish up. Give yourself a breather though. Get something to eat and drink from the café down the street and then come back. I'll get Ani to put you in the diary."

"Thanks, Beck."

He cleaned and covered the tattoo with a temporary covering and led Toby downstairs. "See you in a bit," he said to Toby.

"Do you want me to bring anything back?"

Beck shook his head. "No, I'm good, thanks."

"Ani?" Toby asked.

"I'll take a blueberry muffin if they have one, please."

Toby smiled like she'd given him the sun, and he nodded and left. Ani glanced at him. "Did you not get finished?"

Beck shook his head. "It's the most painful section right now, and it was a bit much for him. Should only take half an hour once he comes back. Anyone else booked in since I was up there?"

"No. You're slammed from four o'clock, though."

Beck leaned over to view the calendar. "Wow. I only had two booked in when I looked earlier."

"We've had a good morning."

Beck grinned. "I can see that."

He headed back to his studio to clean up and then grabbed a sandwich before settling on his stool with his phone. He didn't often do the doom scroll through the various social media platforms because that sucked hours of his time before he realised it, but with only a few minutes until Toby returned, he knew he would have an excuse to turn it off.

The first brought up a picture of Denny. They'd become friends with the guitar player for The Ports when Joey had been going through the issues after his best friend's death. Elliott had been a vital part to their lives, and he was sorely missed. It had turned out that Denny and Elliott had been together, and when Denny had told them, they'd done what they always did and brought him into their fold. This picture was like many others out there. A group one with his bandmates, but Beck could see he wasn't happy. It was in his eyes. He'd had many problems with the management for the band, and if it had been Beck, he would've quit already.

Scrolling further down found a few pictures of acquaintances, some from the tattoo shop that Ani put on to show what they'd created that week, and several about local events happening. But what caught his attention was a photograph of Joey and Ethan. They looked loved up in the restaurant they'd been to the other week. It wasn't them that had him focused on it. It was the background, where Beck and Kole sat, leaning into each other, Kole's mouth at Beck's ear as he whispered something. They looked very much like a couple.

He saved the photo to his phone and closed it. Could he try a relationship with Kole? Would it work? He sighed and shook his head. The lies he would have to tell weren't the foundations of a good relationship, and that in itself made the decision. As much as he liked Kole, he didn't think he could do more than have sex with him. It would ruin them both.

The bell rang, and he shoved his phone into his pocket and raced down the stairs, shouting, "Coming!"

The rest of the afternoon passed in a blur of tattoos, ink and designs, and he loved every minute. He didn't get to see Kole again before he left for the evening. The following day, he would be travelling, so he said he'd see everyone on Monday. He wasn't looking forward to his appointment, though he loved the Cornwall coast. His client was a complete and utter bitch—and that was him being polite—and she complained about everything.

It was more hassle than it was worth, but she brought in too many new clients to them for Joey to cancel her completely.

However, he wouldn't be there long, and he planned to visit the beach while he was. Might as well make the most of the time he had. It didn't matter that it was still freezing cold, the sound and scent of the beach was enough to relax most muscles in his body. He wasn't a fan of going into the water but listening and watching it was enough.

Having already eaten at the shop, he didn't bother to go into the kitchen other than to stick his head in the door to make sure the place wasn't burning down. Then, he headed into the living room, still too wired to sleep. Flicking the TV on, he dropped onto the sofa and scrolled the channels. It would probably take him far too long to choose something, and he'd be on his way to sleep before there was any point of pressing play, but it kept his mind busy.

He finally settled on an animal programme and stretched out, resting his head on one cushion and his feet under another. His eyes were heavy as he watched, his blinks lasting longer until all he could see was Kole's face on the back of his eyelids. He focused on the little quirks he'd seen—the small upwards curve to the corner of his lips when he was placating someone, or the small chicken pox scar on his chin. His mind focused slightly lower, remembering every detail he could. The way he walked. The way he occasionally broke out a genuine smile that almost reached his eyes. The way he spoke. His hand gestures. His scent. The way he treated others. So many things about him were sexy, and most had nothing to do with his body.

Having thought that, his mind veered in a different direction. Beck had held him against him, knew what he felt like, and he liked what he'd seen. He slid his hands to his jeans, unfastening the button and zip before slipping his hand inside and cupping his cock. When he was on his own, he could let his thoughts go wild. He could be true to himself.

Instead of taking control of Kole, he would hand that control over, knowing Kole would never hurt him. Knowing he would respect his wishes and not take what wasn't his to give. Beck would happily kneel for him, staring up at him, waiting for his next order. And as Kole fed him his cock, making him choke on it, Beck's climax would barrel down on him, unexpected pleasure coursing through him. And instead of being upset, Kole would cup his cheeks and smile, saying he was proud of him. At that point, Kole would take him to the bed, turn him onto his hands and knees and slam home, making Beck feel every inch.

Beck pressed his head back into the cushion and came in his clothes, the pleasure too extreme to be denied. His chest heaved as he tried to breathe enough air, and his body felt so heavy, but also light, as if he'd reached a milestone or something.

Opening his eyes, he turned the TV off and pushed himself off the sofa. The warm water of the shower spray was welcome, but it reminded him of how it was in foster care. Depending on the people he stayed with depended if they had hot water to shower in or not. It wasn't always available for one of two reasons. One because the foster parents didn't want the bills to be too high, or two because they couldn't afford to heat the water. After all, heating the water cost money just like feeding kids did, and occasionally he hadn't got that either.

He luxuriated in the warmth, knowing he would never have to go through that again, but eventually, he got sleepy again. Shutting off the water, he dusted a towel over himself and climbed into bed. Shoving a hand beneath his head, he stared at the dark ceiling.

He wasn't that child anymore. He had food to eat, water to drink, hot water to shower in, a bed to sleep in—another thing that wasn't a given in a foster home—and a roof over his head that no one could take away from him. Well, they could, but he could easily find somewhere else.

He huffed at his thoughts and flipped over to thinking about Kole again. His fantasies were one thing, but he wouldn't be able to offer Kole his submission. He had been through too much to hand it over without a care in the world. He would continue to pretend to be a dominant person as it was how he'd survived the years after... Stopping on that path, he refocused again. What could he do with Kole to make their night almost perfect? Should he order them dinner? He'd have to do something because if he planned to take his time with him, they'd need sustenance. Could he tire Kole out? He seemed like the type of guy who would tire easily, mainly when Beck held him on the edge long enough. He was looking forward to seeing if he could do that.

Heaving a sigh, he watched the lights dance across the ceiling whenever a vehicle passed by. As worn out as he had been after his orgasm, he was wide awake again. Would he ever be able to sleep a full night? Probably not because his nightmares still echoed around his brain, ready to appear when he least expected it to.

Reaching for his phone, he put on some soft music to dull the thoughts and closed his eyes and mouth to reduce the sensory input, leaving him with just the music, the scents and the feel of the bedcovers, something that helped to tether him to the present instead of letting him fall back into the past.

As he lost himself in those remaining senses, his mind traitorously whispered, "*But what if Kole is different?*"

8

KOLE

Kole was a jittery mess all day on Saturday. So much so that he locked himself away in his studio—he still couldn't believe he had one—and daydreamed about how things might go. He refused to let his thoughts wander into "bad" territory because he didn't want his fears to take hold and stop him from enjoying what Beck was offering. He wasn't stupid. Beck wouldn't want a relationship with him, but while he was offering satisfaction, who was Kole to say no?

Ethan asked him several times if he was okay when he'd checked on him, and all he could say was yes. He wasn't going to say anything about their "date" because it wasn't a date. It was a mutually beneficial agreement.

And Kole couldn't fucking wait.

He had an itch that needed scratching and Beck was the one to do it.

By the time he finished work, his hands shook, and he could barely hold his pen. He said goodbye to whoever he saw on his way out but didn't actively seek anyone out. He wouldn't have been able to start a decent conversation even if he had.

Home was a small one-bedroomed flat that he would probably never decorate. It still had the white walls and ceilings, the wood effect countertops, cupboards and flooring and a plain white bathroom suite, but it worked for him. He didn't need anything fancy. Having no clue where his future would take him, he'd finally decided, upon taking the chance to move to London, that he would take things as they came and not worry unduly about things he might not be able to change. It was making life easier for him—at least at the moment.

Checking his phone, he saw he had a little over two hours before Beck would be there to pick him up. Kole froze, his hand staying mid-air as he reached for a mug, and the air caught in his lungs. He hadn't even asked why Beck was picking him up. He'd expected them to just spend the night with each other. Were they going somewhere? Or was Beck just picking him up to take him to his house?

Kole's hand resumed its movements, bringing down his favourite mug. Trying not to think about what that evening might entail was hard, but he blanked his mind as much as he could, watching the colours of the tea mix with the water, changing it until he was happy with it, and then he added a splash of milk. Stirring his brew, he lifted it to his lips and blew across the top, sending steam into his face. He inhaled and closed his eyes for a brief moment and then headed for the sofa. Time. He just needed a few minutes to get his head levelled, and then he could get himself ready.

Letting his mind drift as he finished his tea, he finally relaxed enough for his muscles to tell him exactly how tense he had been. The last dregs of tea slid down his throat, and he stood, deciding on a semi-long soak in the bath. He had time. Putting the mug in the kitchen to clean up later, he headed down the hallway, pausing when a knock sounded. Frowning, he backtracked and looked through the peephole. Eyes widening, he stared at the Beck-shaped person on the other side of the door.

Inhaling, he opened the door. Beck had his hands braced on either side of the door, his head lowered, but his eyes on Kole as soon as the door revealed him. Kole's breath caught.

"I'm sorry," Beck said. His nostrils flared as he inhaled audibly. "I couldn't wait any longer."

He stepped forward, slamming into Kole with the force of a tornado, his arms sliding around him the only thing keeping Kole from falling to the floor. But Kole didn't care because Beck's mouth was on his, and it was heaven. His eyelids fluttered closed, and he opened for Beck's questing tongue. The taste hit him like a drug, a hint of mint as if he'd chewed one before he arrived, a tang of tomato, possibly from his dinner, and everything that was Beck. Then, when Beck groaned into his mouth, Kole forgot everything but holding on as Beck ravished him. His fingers gripped the back of Beck's shirt, and he just felt.

Distantly, there was a thud, and then they were moving. Kole stumbled, but Beck kept him upright and then went further by grabbing the backs of his thighs and lifting him. Kole yelped into Beck's mouth and wrapped his legs around his waist automatically, his arms tightening around his back and neck. And then they were kissing again, Beck carrying him forward.

"Ah!" Kole shouted when his stomach dropped as he fell backwards. Luckily, he bounced on the sofa cushions and was covered by a warm body seconds later.

"Fuck, Kole. You're addictive," Beck groaned before joining their lips again.

Blood rushed to Kole's cock, and he thrust upwards, grinding against Beck and feeling the answering hardness press back against him. No doubt crept in, no shiver of unease, and no lifting of the hairs on his arms—well, unless he counted the good lifting of the hairs. Because what Beck was doing with his mouth and hands was pure physical goodness.

Kole grabbed Beck's T-shirt, finding the hem and pushing it up until Beck had no choice but to pull back so he could take it over his head. His fingertips tingled where they touched naked skin, and Beck's breath hitched, his eyelids drifting closed before snapping open to pierce Kole with the bright blue orbs. Kole's gaze took in the dark accents of his hair, eyebrows and beard over his tanned skin and the lines at the edges of his eyes but also the lines creasing his forehead. He was a conundrum, and one Kole wanted to figure out. He seemed to have so much laughter in his life, but when they were alone, that laughter was muted, and his seriousness—pain, even—became clearer. He wanted to help whatever worried him. Take away his pain.

Kole blinked rapidly, exhaling. "Fuck me, Beck," he whispered, needing to divert his thoughts. He couldn't be thinking of more because they were just a friends-with-benefits thing. Nothing more.

Beck unbuttoned the first few of Kole's shirt and then dragged it over his head before fusing their lips and swallowing Kole's hiss of delight as their chests touched. Their hips kept moving, bringing Kole closer and closer to the edge, but he pushed it away, not wanting to come until Beck was inside him. His hands went to Beck's jeans, unfastening them and pushing them down before using his feet to finish the job and kick them to the floor. Beck followed suit with Kole's trousers, briefly lifting off him to yank them off his feet and somewhere behind him. Then he covered Kole's body again, and Kole sighed.

"So warm," Beck muttered, his face nestled into Kole's neck while his tongue tasted his skin.

Kole hummed as he dropped his head to the side, giving Beck more space, all the while grinding against him and sending his arousal skyrocketing. They should slow down, but his mind was too far gone to object. He needed Beck like the blood that ran through his body—and focused in his cock—and he wanted more.

"More," he said, moving his legs to the side and wrapping them around his tempting lover. "Give me more," he murmured, his hands sliding down Beck's back to his ass. Squeezing the tight muscles, he ground up again.

"Jesus, Kole." Beck lifted his head, bracing his hands by his head. "I need my jeans." He scrambled off, ignoring Kole's complaints, so Kole pressed the palm of his hand against his dick, groaning as electricity sparked through him. Beck paused, glancing over his shoulder, eyes darkening as they focused on Kole's movements. "Fuck."

Beck rummaged in his pockets until he returned with two packets. Kole breathed easier, glad one of them was thinking straight. It certainly wasn't him. Beck knelt between his legs once more, and Kole scraped his teeth over his lower lip, knowing what he wanted to say, but it wasn't his place. Beck was the more dominant of the two of them, and he didn't want to ruin what was happening by giving orders—even though he wanted to.

"Let's get these off, shall we?" Beck hooked his fingers in the waistband of Kole's briefs and paused, and Kole realised it hadn't been a rhetorical question.

"Definitely. As long as yours go, too."

Beck grinned. "Wouldn't want anything less."

Stripping off Kole's and then his own, Beck crawled back up Kole's body, kissing skin as he went.

"Inside me, Beck. Please."

"Your wish is my command."

He spent several long minutes stretching Kole's hole while their tongues duelled and retreated repeatedly.

"Now!" Kole ordered, unable to keep his words inside any longer. "Do as you're fucking told, Beck."

Beck exhaled into his mouth, his muscles relaxing fractionally before he rose and slid the condom down his length. Kole's mouth watered—he'd get his mouth on that soon enough.

He lifted his gaze. "*Now*, Beck. I'm fed up of waiting."

"Yes," Beck breathed and rested the head of his shaft at Kole's entrance.

Kole hooked his ankles at Beck's lower back and pulled him in, lodging the head in his ass, and they both groaned. His ass was stretched beyond what he'd ever remembered it being before, and the heat from him was exquisite torture. Beck paused, and Kole's eyes snapped open, glaring at him.

"Move," he demanded, and Beck swallowed hard and slid deeper, so much deeper. Kole's jaw dropped and his eyes rolled back in his head. "Fuck."

Beck paused again, but Kole didn't complain that time. The man was as deep inside him as he could be, and it was fucking delicious. Kole slid his arms around Beck's neck and nipped at his lower lip.

"Fuck me, Beck. I'm yours."

Beck's eyes darkened more than they already had, the bright blue having bled into a deeper shade as the pupils took over. He kissed him, needing that connection again, and as their tongues slid alongside each other, Beck moved, slowly at first and then harder and faster. Until all Kole could see, feel, hear, smell and taste was Beck.

His orgasm crashed down on him with no warning. One moment, he was riding the wave, and the next, he was tumbling over the surf into the water headfirst.

"Fuck, Kole."

Beck dropped his head into Kole's neck, cursed again, and held himself still, but Kole could feel the pulse of his climax deep inside him. Kole tightened his hold, never wanting it to end.

When Beck finally relaxed, Kole still kept hold, his fingers raking through his hair as his breathing slowed. Kole stared at a point on the ceiling and prayed that his heart could lock itself away before Beck lifted his head. Their coupling had been way more than he had ever expected, and he was worried he wouldn't be able to hide his feelings. Though what those feelings were, he wasn't entirely sure, but he knew they weren't suitable for what they'd just shared.

As Beck moved, Kole locked the internal box and managed a smile when their gazes met.

"I had plans to take you to dinner, but when I got back from Cornwall, it was like I was a junkie. My entire body shook with the need to get to you. Sorry. I promise I'm usually more romantic than this."

Kole chuckled and cupped Beck's cheek. "You don't need to worry. It was probably good to get that out of the way. We would've combusted before we finished dinner at that rate." Beck's cheeks flushed, and Kole pressed his lips to the reddened area. "Besides, we can order pizza."

Beck moved, and his cock slid free, making Kole wince slightly. "Sorry."

"You feel bigger than you look, and you look big enough as it is." Kole wasn't complaining.

"Sorry."

Kole chuckled. "You don't need to be sorry. About anything. We needed that. I needed that."

Beck rose and looked around, holding the used condom. "Bathroom?" he asked, meeting Kole's gaze again.

He gave directions, and while Beck cleaned up, he did the same in the kitchen and pulled his briefs back on. What would happen now? Would they eat and chat, or would Beck make an excuse and leave? Kole didn't want him to, but he wouldn't push the guy to stay if he didn't want to. While the thoughts prowled his mind, sending his stomach into a spin, he opened the drawer he'd already dedicated to takeaway menus, but the arms that slid around his waist settled his nerves as nothing else could have at that moment.

Beck's lips pressed against his neck, something he seemed to do a lot, and Kole leaned back into him.

"Any preference?" he asked.

"I could go for a pizza, but anything goes for me."

His lips distracted Kole for a few seconds, but then he blinked and cleared his throat. "You prefer Chinese if I recall?"

"Yeah, but I love pizza, too."

"Okay, pizza it is." Beck's hands wandered while Kole tried to input the order, asking Beck questions about his toppings and receiving hums in agreement, but his tongue was more distracting than his lips.

Finally, he managed to place the order. "Forty-five minutes, it says." He turned in Beck's arms and slid his hands to his neck. "Would you like a drink while we wait?"

Beck crowded closer. "How about a shower first?"

Kole smiled. "Sure. I'll show you where it is."

Beck tightened his hold. "And I hope you'll join me."

The words were soft, a little unsure, and that would've been more than enough for him to say yes, but it was the need in Beck's eyes that floored him. This need wasn't heat. It wasn't arousal. It was something deeper. A need to just be, maybe. Kole couldn't identify it, but he wouldn't let him down if that was what he needed.

"Wouldn't miss the chance to be with you," he whispered against Beck's lips.

They shared a soft, explorative kiss—so different from what they'd shared when Beck turned up earlier than planned, but no less devastating. Kole's head spun when they pulled back.

Beck took his hands and pulled him towards the bathroom. "Come on. Maybe I can make you come again before the pizza gets here." He winked.

It was certainly a mutually beneficial shower, and they had towels wrapped around their waists when there was a knock at the door. Kole checked the peephole and opened the door, smiling at the delivery driver. "Thanks."

"No problem."

Kole didn't miss the lingering glances he received, but he ignored it, in favour of trying not to shiver from the cool air coming from outside his apartment. He liked his creature comforts, which included central heating. Beck pressed up against his back, his arms banding around him.

"Thanks for the food, man," Beck said to the delivery driver and nodded before closing the door.

Kole chuckled and shook his head, carrying the pizza to the coffee table. "Drink?"

"I got it," Beck said, so Kole settled on the sofa, enjoying the warmth seeping into him. He probably should have dressed, but he liked being half-naked with Beck. He opened the pizza, but before he could grab a slice, Beck was back, nudging him forward so he could settle behind him, his legs bracketing Kole's body. He'd never thought of the position as anything but sensual until that moment, but even with the towels separating them, he was branded by Beck's heat. And when the man lifted a slice of pizza, encouraged him to rest his head back on his shoulder and held the slice to his lips, Kole was overwhelmed. His brain misfired, his stomach held a swarm of butterflies, and he wanted nothing more than to devour Beck instead.

But he bit off a piece of pizza, chewing slowly, and contained his sigh when Beck took a bite of the same slice—after all, they had shared spit, so what was sharing a slice of pizza? Kole rested his hands on Beck's thighs, his thumbs brushing the hairy skin, and tried to regain control of his emotions.

It had been the first time he'd let himself get carried away with anyone since Andrew, and although there still was a random bumblebee amongst those butterflies when he thought about their "relationship," he was more relaxed about it. He'd known from the beginning that they weren't going to be a couple, and if the sex helped him to recalibrate so he could go out and find someone, then he wasn't going to be upset about that.

Beck fed him bites of pizza until Kole shook his head, his stomach complaining, and then he ate the rest in short order—a perfect gentleman.

Kole swallowed and brought up the one thing he had been unsure about. "You said you don't have work tomorrow. Does that mean you can stay?"

Beck's face was expressionless as he stared down at him, and Kole had maybe pushed too far, but then Beck's smile spread across his face. "If you're happy to have me here, I'm happy to stay. Besides," he cupped Kole's jaw, "I haven't finished with you yet. And if I stay, I can wake you whenever I want and make you sing."

The slight edge to his voice had Kole studying his face, but he gave nothing away. "Stay," he whispered.

Beck's mouth curved, and he lowered his head, brushing his lips across Kole's before pressing harder in the brief caress. "I'd love to."

They tidied away the food, took their drinks to the bedroom after refilling them, and climbed into bed. Kole was too sore for a repeat of earlier, but they still played—he'd forgotten how much fun it was to frot, but the moment he climaxed again, he was done. Tiredness overwhelmed him, but he managed to climb from the bed before Beck and grab a wet towel. He cleaned the man who had made him remember what it was like to have a nice time without a countdown to when they would leave. And as he wiped Beck down, he ignored what he thought might have been tears in Beck's eyes because he didn't want to pry—even though he did—and he understood the need to keep things to himself.

If Beck wanted to talk, he'd be there, but until then, he'd keep his questions to himself. Mostly. Because he wanted to know everything. Which was dangerous.

He had a feeling Beck was hazardous to his balance.

9

BECK

B eck kept his body as relaxed as possible as they lay wrapped around each other, and he felt the moment Kole drifted off. He barely refrained from exhaling in a rush; he wasn't sure how long he could have kept up the pretence of being fine. He was, but he also truly wasn't.

What they'd shared was...way more than Beck had expected, and he wasn't sure what to do with it. When Kole had made his demands, Beck had submitted automatically, doing exactly what Kole had told him to. His hard-won restraint had snapped, and he would've done everything Kole asked. It was a dangerous situation because he couldn't let go. He couldn't allow himself to be vulnerable again.

What the hell was he doing still in Kole's bed? He should've left the moment the man had fallen asleep, but Beck couldn't get himself to move. Instead, his arms tightened, as if someone threatened to remove him. The two sides of him were warring, and he wasn't sure which would win. No, that wasn't true. He knew which would win because it had no choice. He'd allow Kole a few hours' sleep, and then he would take him as he should've done the first time.

Decision made, he closed his eyes and mentally relaxed every muscle in his body before succumbing to sleep.

He was woken by exquisite pleasure streaking down his spine, and he arched his back and inhaled, pressing his head into the pillow beneath him. A strong suck had the air punching from his lungs, his eyes snapping open to see Kole's dark head bobbing up and down, his tongue doing eye-crossing things to him. He threaded his fingers into Kole's strands and gripped, his hips thrusting forward with a mind of their own.

"Fuck," he breathed.

Kole's gaze rose, and the look in them was enough to throw Beck over the edge. Black dots fought to cover his vision, but he stared hard at Kole's hollowed cheeks, and his orgasm continued far longer than usual, his balls straining to release more and more. Finally, its grip left him, and he slumped to the bed, chest heaving.

Kole wiped the corners of his mouth with his fingers, and Beck grabbed those fingers and slipped them into his mouth, sucking on them like he might taste a remnant of his release. He swirled his tongue around the digits, and Kole's pupils dilated, his tongue peeking out to skim across his lips. Sliding the fingers free, Beck tugged gently on Kole's hair until Kole crawled up his body. Once he was close enough, Beck fastened their mouths together in a slow exploration.

"Your turn," Beck rasped when he pulled away for air.

Kole's cheeks darkened, visible even in the limited light. "Already done." He looked away and then back again, rolling his lips inward before saying, "You're far too sexy for me to contain anything." His teeth left a white streak across his lower lip.

Beck couldn't help it. He kissed him again, this time a little more forcefully, and when they came up for oxygen again, he rested their foreheads together. "Thank you."

Kole smiled, his eyes squeezing shut when there was a rumbling noise. "My stomach is saying it's time for breakfast, even though it's..." he glanced at the clock and exhaled, "five in the morning."

"I could eat."

Kole dropped a kiss on Beck's mouth and rolled away, leaving a wash of cool air to replace the warmth they'd created. He watched Kole drag on some joggers and smile before leaving the room.

Beck stared at the ceiling for a few long seconds. He needed to rein in whatever it was bubbling in his stomach—nothing at all to do with food—because he didn't want Kole to get hurt. And he would if Beck played with his feelings. He wasn't a man to do so, but if he didn't take a step back, he might not be able to stop it from happening.

Blinking away the thoughts, he climbed from the bed and pulled on his trousers, wandering to the kitchen. Kole stood before the cooker, the frying pan already heating. He glanced over.

"I thought we could have bacon, eggs and toast. Replenish some energy."

Beck grinned. "I think we need it." Heading for the fridge, he asked, "What are you drinking?"

"Apple juice, please. There should be a carton open. Help yourself to whatever you want. I can make coffee, too, if you want."

"Apple juice sounds good to me."

He poured two glasses of juice, set them on the breakfast bar that separated the kitchen from the rest of the apartment and returned to Kole's side.

"Need any help?" he asked.

"You can put the bread in the toaster for me."

"Sure."

It was all very domestic, and Beck tried not to enjoy it too much. After all, he wasn't going to experience this often, so he better not get used to making breakfast side by side with someone else.

Once everything was plated, they carried their plates to the breakfast bar and settled next to each other. Neither said anything as they started eating, and Beck wracked his brain, trying to think of something to break the easy silence. Not because he wanted to but because he *had* to.

"I never asked if you had plans for today. I just assumed you didn't. Sorry about that."

Kole sent him a brief smile, chewing as he was. When he swallowed, he said, "I don't have plans. Other than you all, I don't know anyone else around here yet."

"I wasn't sure if you were going to go sightseeing."

Kole scoffed. "I've been to London enough times to not need to rush out and view the tourist attractions."

Beck chuckled. "I didn't mean that. I meant the area." He waved his hand around. "As you said, you don't know anyone yet, but you could get to know the area you live in. Corner shops and takeaways are a man's best friend."

"And you know this how?"

"Because I regularly run out of things and have to race to the corner shop to get them. Plus, I don't always cook, but I still need feeding." He refocused on his plate. "I'm sure there are other places you need to know where the closest one is as well."

He tried not to think about his need to know the closest hospital or men's shelter to where he was and would take his last breath before he admitted to already having searched the internet for the ones closest to where they currently were.

"You're right. But not today."

They dropped into silence again until they finished their early morning breakfast.

"Thank you. That was delicious," Beck said, gathering the plates and taking them to the sink. "Do you have a dishwasher or do you wash by hand?"

Kole stood. "I can do them—"

"No. You cooked, so I'll clean."

Kole opened his mouth as if to argue, but then snapped it shut again. He pointed to a cupboard door, and Beck opened it, finding the dishwasher. He made light work of putting the dishes away and then wiping down the counter and the table. When he was done, he found Kole leaning against the wall, watching him.

"What?"

Kole's mouth kicked up to the side. "Nothing. I like a man who knows his way around a kitchen. It's sexy."

Those last words whispered across the space between them, and Beck, finally feeling back on solid ground, smiled and stalked towards him. As focused as he was on Kole, he saw his breath hitch the closer he went. He didn't stop until his bare chest rested against Kole's, the slight scratch of their chest hair rubbing together, and he dropped his head, inhaling when his nose reached the base of his neck, where his scent seemed to be strongest. He nuzzled his nose against his skin, rising up the strong column, along his jaw to his ear, which he nipped with his lips.

"Where were we?"

Kole's hands were warm on his bare skin, sliding over his shoulders and down his back before lifting off and slipping beneath Beck's arms to wrap around his back once more. Beck wondered why the change when Kole's hands squeezed his ass cheeks. He thrust his hips forward, his cock already liking the route they were going.

No words were spoken as their hands touched and roamed, their lips nibbled and kissed, their tongues tasted and tangled. Cock hard and leaking, Beck pressed Kole into the wall, needing the friction but also never wanting it to end.

Kole broke away from the never-ending kiss to moan. "Fuck, Beck. Need you. Suck me. Now," he demanded.

And like the submissive Beck truly was, he listened. He dropped to his knees on the hard, unyielding floor, dragging Kole's joggers with him, and fastened his mouth around his dick without preamble. The taste of him, slightly musky from sleep, had his eyelids fluttering closed, and he focused on the feel of him inside his mouth, along his tongue, in the back of his throat.

Kole's fingers threaded into his hair a few times before gripping tighter than expected, and a groan rumbled in his chest as arousal speared through him. He doubled his efforts, halting when Kole's grip held him still. His gaze darted up to Kole, and his eyes widened at what he saw. Darkened with lust, Kole's eyes held his as his free hand wrapped around Beck's nape, holding him captive. Without a word, Kole canted his hips, sending his cock deeper into Beck's waiting mouth. Pleasure flooded Beck's body, and despite his usual need to control all sexual situations, he found he couldn't. He didn't want to. He wanted what his body had always told him he needed.

Someone to take him instead of him taking them.

He didn't have time to panic at the direction of his thoughts because Kole took his complete focus and as Kole came down his throat...Beck came hands free, shooting his load into his trousers, his gaze still on Kole's face.

As Kole's cock slipped from his mouth and his breathing returned to some semblance of normal, a band tightened around his chest. He dropped his gaze to the floor but couldn't find the energy to move from his submissive position.

"Beck?"

The band tightened further, and he gasped for air, scoring his nails through his skin to get to his lungs.

"Beck!"

Black dots swam across his gaze, and he closed his eyes, trying to swallow but finding his mouth as dry as a desert.

"Shit. Beck!"

Hands rested on his back, warming his chilled skin, and pushed his head down towards the floor. Beck didn't resist. He listed to the side, falling against something immovable, and he tried to breathe, tried to remember what he was supposed to be doing, tried to think.

"Breathe for me, Beck. Inhale, one, two, three, four, and exhale, one, two, three, four. Inhale, one, two, three, four, and exhale, one, two, three, four. That's it. Keep following my words."

The continued instructions helped him to focus, and he found his chest easing, his head clearing, his eyes focusing again. Eventually, he came back into his body proper and found himself curled up against Kole's body, his arms around his waist while his face was buried in his lap. Fingers carded through his hair, and he focused on the sensation and the soft words rather than anything else.

"Are you back with me, Beck?"

"Mmhmm."

A heavy sigh from above him. "Thank fuck."

Despite not wanting to move, he needed to because as the numbness of his body retreated, the aching from how they were positioned slowly made itself known. He opened his fists, which had gripped onto the waistband of Kole's joggers, and hissed at the pain in the joints.

"There's no rush," Kole said, but there was.

He pressed his aching hands into the floor, pushing his body up and off Kole's legs, grimacing with each movement. His legs were a pincushion of pain, and he tumbled to his ass when his legs protested. Kole caught him before he hit the wall behind him, but then he rested slowly back against it and sighed. He needed to explain, but he couldn't look at Kole right then. He saw when Kole rose on unsteady feet, and Beck wanted to stop him from leaving, but it was what he deserved. He was a burden to everyone he met. Always had been. It was why he'd kept himself to himself and never slept with anyone more than once.

A glass appeared in his line of vision, and his mouth watered. He took it with shaking hands, and with Kole supporting his hands, he took a drink. The more he drank, the calmer he felt. When the glass was drained, he sighed again, knowing it was time.

"I'm—"

"Shall we have a shower? I could do with warming up. You coming?"

Kole held out his hand, and Beck couldn't stop his gaze from darting up to his face, eyes taking in every nuance. Nothing in his expression said he was upset or angry or confused or...anything negative, actually. It was inviting, a small smile on a beautiful face.

Beck nodded slowly, slipping his hand into Kole's, the man helping him stand when his legs still didn't want to support him as well as they usually did. Without making any comment on it, Kole slipped his arm around Beck's waist and guided him towards the bathroom, where he settled Beck on the closed toilet seat before turning on the shower.

"After our shower, I was thinking we could settle under the covers and watch a movie. Or would you prefer some trash TV? I'm not usually one for that, but I could make an exception if that's your cup of tea." He winked. "Or coffee."

He gestured for Beck to stand, which he did, and then dragged his trousers down his legs without preamble, ignoring the mess coating Beck's skin, even as he grimaced at the dried come on his skin. Kole undressed himself and held out his hand again. Beck slipped his hand into Kole's warm grip and climbed over the edge of the bath and under the spray. Kole followed, flicking the shower curtain around them to enclose them. Kole grabbed the shower gel, squirted some into his palm and rubbed it over the tattooed wings of Beck's chest.

Beck swallowed hard and lifted his head so the water dribbled down over his face, hiding the tears leaking from his eyes even as he hyper-focused on Kole's ministrations. When Kole turned him, the tears fell harder, and he tensed to stop the sobs from breaking free completely. He worked hard to get himself under control by the time Kole reached his feet, and when Kole turned him again, he was fine. Well, as fine as he could be.

"My turn," he croaked.

Kole smiled, his eyes lighting up. "I'll never say no to that."

Beck took his time, enjoying the experience of smoothing his soapy hands over Kole's delectable skin. He couldn't quite meet Kole's gaze, but his body relaxed with each passing moment.

When they were both cleaner than they had probably ever been, Kole flicked off the shower and dragged the curtain back so they could climb out. Drying off was another testament to his willpower, when Kole dried him and he returned the favour. Wrapping the towels around their waists, they headed to the bedroom. Kole grabbed the TV remote from the bedside table and climbed into bed, dropping the towel to the floor without a care in the world, so Beck did the same, though he put the towel over the back of the wooden chair near the bed.

Kole snuggled up to his side, and Beck lifted his arm over his shoulder, allowing Kole to rest against his chest. "Any preference?"

"Whatever you want." Beck's voice was like gravel, his emotions held tightly in check. He stared at the screen, not seeing what Kole was doing. Instead, he was reliving everything they had done in the kitchen. It was everything he had ever wanted, and nothing he could have because he couldn't give just anyone that amount of control, and he refused to ruin Kole by giving it to him without knowing how Beck could react. There was no telling what could happen if he did. The one and only time he had allowed someone that close, that deep, had ended with the guy in the hospital. He wouldn't—couldn't—do that to Kole. But how could they go back to the way they'd been before?

"This okay?" Kole asked, rubbing his soft cheek against Beck's chest.

Beck barely glanced at the TV. "Yep."

Kole threw the remote to the side and snuggled in further, resting his hand on Beck's stomach with a sigh.

Beck waited for the questions, the delving into what happened, the inquisition. Because it would come. How the hell was he going to explain away his reaction without telling the truth? There was no way he was doing that. He'd buried the secret for twenty-seven years, and he wasn't planning on breaking that streak.

10

KOLE

Kole didn't say a word. He had questions, of course he did, but he knew from experience that whatever Beck had been through, he wouldn't want to discuss it until he was ready to. When neither of them spoke, he felt Beck's body release the tension. It had taken everything in him not to respond to anything that had happened when all he wanted to do was take Beck into his arms and take away all the pain. And when he broke in the shower... Kole had felt his own tears building, but he refused to let them go. No one had the right to push someone to explain their actions, especially when they weren't ready. But it killed something inside him that Beck had been through anything that had caused that reaction.

As the episode progressed, though he had no idea what was going on because he was focused on Beck, his mind whirled, needing answers but not wanting to ask. His brain supplied so many versions of what could've happened to him, and he didn't like any of them.

When the episode finally ended, Kole let it run onto the next one, but he moved around to rest his hands on Beck's chest and his chin on his hands, looking up at the gorgeous man who deemed him worthy of sharing a bed with.

The corners of Beck's mouth twitched. "What? Have I got drool on my chin or something?"

Kole chuckled. "No. I was just reminding myself you were real and not a figment of my imagination."

Beck brushed his finger across Kole's cheek. "I'm real."

They spent more time in bed, watching TV and switching between shows and movies depending on their mood, and mid-afternoon, Kole made what he called a "picky" lunch, which was basically a picnic-style lunch but on individual plates instead of a spread across a blanket. They took that straight back to bed, and once the plates were cleaner than they probably had been after being in the dishwasher, Beck dragged him into a searing kiss, and he promptly lost his mind.

Mutual handjobs followed, and Kole fell into a dreamless sleep.

He woke, smiled and stretched like a cat rising from a nap in the sunshine. Glancing over to the other side of the bed, his smile dropped when Beck wasn't there to greet him. He checked the clock, seeing it was just after five o'clock—he'd only slept for around an hour—and strained his ears for any sound from the apartment.

Nothing.

He inhaled and let it out slowly, vacillating between getting out of bed to check and see if he'd left or staying where he was to hide from what he knew was the truth.

Beck had left.

Being the big boy he was supposed to be, he climbed from the bed and dragged on the joggers he'd thrown to the floor after making lunch. Inhaling once more, he left the room and scanned the place, but no one was there. Not sure how to feel—though he understood their arrangement had been one night and nothing more—he swallowed hard and went to make himself a cup of tea, and that's where he found it. Beside the kettle was a note:

Thank you. B

Kole couldn't help the smile that spread across his face. It didn't change the outcome—Beck had left, and they didn't have any plans for a do-over—but it settled something inside Kole to know that Beck had thought enough of him to leave him a note before he'd gone home. With that in mind, he filled the kettle, flicked it on and headed to put some more clothes on. It wasn't particularly warm in his apartment when he didn't have someone's arms to warm him, but he didn't dwell on that fact.

When he was better dressed, he made his tea, flicked a lamp on to fill the space with a soft but warm light and settled onto the sofa with a drawing pad and pencil. His mind was awash with images, and he needed to get some down. His hand moved across the empty page, filling it with swirls and dots and lines until there wasn't an inch of space left. And then he flipped to the next page and continued. He'd never had so much energy and so many ideas needing to be extricated.

He only stopped when his hand cramped and he had to shake and stretch it out, and he spat his tea back into the cup when he received a mouthful of cold liquid. Checking the clock again, he'd been sitting there for three hours. No wonder his tea was cold. He put the drawing pad on the coffee table and made himself another cup of tea before returning to his warmed seat. He didn't pick up the pad again until he'd drunk the tea, not wanting a repeat of the cold version, but once he was done, he swapped the cup for the pad and went back to the beginning.

Eyes widening, he stared at the designs. He'd never designed such intricate—and large—designs before. There were designs within designs on the page, and he could see a little of Beck in each one. Nothing that could be identified as relating to him, but Kole could see it as the artist. His emotions laid bare on the page. Kole swallowed hard and closed the book, unsure if those designs would ever see the light of day again, especially at Life in Ink.

His phone rang, jarring him from his staring match with the darkened sky through the window. He reached for it, smiling when he saw Christi's name.

"Hey, you," he said.

"Hey, yourself. How are you doing?" Christi asked, the noise of subdued music in the background.

"I'm good." And he was. "Where are you?"

"Where do you think on a Sunday evening?"

Kole shook his head. "You really need to get more sleep before a Monday morning."

"I get enough sleep, thanks. What I don't get enough of is seeing Di singing her heart out at karaoke."

Kole laughed. "You're smitten."

"You will be, too, when you find your match. How's that going, by the way?"

Ignoring the need to divulge and dissect what had happened with Beck, he huffed a laugh. "I'm happy to just find my feet in a new city for now. I'll consider looking for my soul mate in a few months. Is that okay with you?"

Christi sighed. "I suppose. I just want you to be happy."

"I know, and I am. I promise. This move, while unexpected, was the best idea I think I've ever had."

"What about that time you—"

"Nope. We're not doing memory lane. We all have plenty of things hidden in our closets, Christi. No need to unlock those doors." He laughed, setting her off.

"Well, if you insist." She snorted.

"How's the salon?" he asked once they'd calmed.

Christi and Di were working on getting the perfect location for the salon they wanted to open together. It was an inspired idea, what with their unique skill sets and abilities, and clients would beat the door down as soon as they opened.

"We've just found a space that might work," she gushed. "We're going to look at it tomorrow."

"That's great. Just remember not to sign on the line before you've gone away and thought about it first."

"Yes, Dad," she sassed.

They spoke for a few minutes more before Christi rang off when Di got the microphone. Apparently, Di couldn't persuade Christi to go running, which Kole was not surprised about, and she also couldn't get her to sing with her. She wasn't remotely into getting sweaty anymore, as she called it, but give her yoga, Pilates or meditation, and she was there for it. She used to go to the gym all the time, but recently, she had changed what she had enjoyed previously. Kole thought something might've happened, but he had no proof, especially as Christi had never seemed scared or anything remotely unsure or unhappy. Maybe he was looking for answers where there weren't any, and Christi was just fed up with what she had been doing and wanted a change. He hoped so, anyway.

Despite the still fairly early hour after he'd said goodbye to one of his best friends, he got ready for bed and slid between the clean sheets. The scent of Beck had gone, although he could lie to himself, but the memories hadn't. And they are what kept him company during the dark hours of the winter's night.

It was three days before he saw Beck again. The guy had been sent to cover Dallas in Scotland, and because they loved taking their own equipment, he had driven himself up there early on Monday morning. Kole wasn't sure why he had gone in Dallas's place, but it wasn't his place to ask.

When he did catch a glimpse of him, Beck was running down the stairs to reception, but by the time Kole got there, he had left the building for lunch. If Kole had been a worrier, he'd have thought Beck was avoiding him, but there was no reason for him to do that. They both knew what they'd had was a fleeting one night—all right, one night and one day—but they'd agreed that it wouldn't affect their working relationship.

Hadn't they?

Kole thought they had, but what if Beck didn't want to see him anymore? Even as a friend? What if it made things too difficult for them both to work there? Kole would have to leave. After all, artists were a dime a dozen, whereas a tattooist was a different matter. Especially one as talented as Beck was.

"Everything okay?" Ani asked, and Kole realised he'd stopped at the desk and was staring out into the rainy day. He shook himself.

"Yeah, sorry. My mind is a little frazzled."

"You should go for a walk. Staring at the same four walls can drive everyone insane at times. Have you had lunch?"

Kole shook his head. "I brought stuff." He tilted his head towards the stairs.

"Even so. If you hurry, you might be able to catch up with Beck. He's gone to get his and my lunch. He won't mind you tagging along."

But would he?

"Thanks. I just might do that. Be nice to get some fresh air, even though there's a little shower with it."

Ani chuckled. "Well, British people could never be said to stay indoors when it's raining. We'd never be out of the house."

Smiling, he left the shop, even as those pesky butterflies in his stomach tried to fly out into the rain-soaked streets. He pulled his hood over his head and headed down the street to where Ani said Beck was heading. He wanted to see him, to make sure they were okay, that there weren't any issues between them. Seeing Beck's eyes was the only way for him to know the truth. And when he stepped inside the sandwich shop, Beck's eyes lit up, and all the tension Kole had been carrying disappeared.

"Hey." Beck's smile was contagious. "You want something?" He pointed at the chiller cabinet.

"I'll get it. It's fine."

"No, my treat. What are you having?"

Kole tried to focus on the chalkboard behind the counter, and in the end, picked the first thing that sounded half decent. He didn't have the brain power to do much more right then.

"How was Scotland?"

Beck blew out a breath. "It's a fucking long drive."

"Wouldn't it be easier to have some equipment stashed across the country, so that you could fly to these places and just pick up the kit along the way? If you had the stuff close to the airports you mainly use, you could easily pick them up before continuing to your destination."

Beck stared at him, mouth gaping. "Why the fuck didn't I think of that? Or any of us, for that matter? We're so fucking stupid."

A ball of fire lit inside Kole. "No, you're not. Sometimes, it takes someone from the outside looking in to see what you're too close to. You're not stupid at all." And he wouldn't have anyone saying so, even themselves.

They stared at each other for a moment, Kole entranced by the eyes that seemed to be a different shade of blue each time he looked, before Beck huffed a laugh and broke the spell.

"You're dangerous," he murmured. "Tell me what you want to eat, and I'll tell you about Scotland."

Kole tried to pay but Beck was having none of it, and when they settled on the stool by the window to wait for their order, he tried not to stare, focusing on the raindrops sliding down the glass instead. But he wanted to stare, wanted to look at the man who had caused him to have less sleep than was optimal since their night together.

"I rarely do the Scotland visits, mainly because Dallas has family up there, and it gives him the opportunity to see them. I'm normally in Wales and in the south-west of England. I say usually because all of us have made contacts throughout the country, and therefore, we'll go wherever we're asked, but we have certain areas we like best. I love Wales. One day, I might retire there."

"Retire? You? I don't believe it. But then I don't believe Joey will retire to Italy either, so I'm probably not a good judge."

Beck chuckled, and Kole wanted to roll around in the sound, feel it against his chest or back. "Yes, it does seem a pipe dream right now, but that's the plan. Anyway," he waved his hand, "Scotland was unexpected, and as such, when word got around that I was visiting instead of Dallas, well, I had a list of people who wanted my style. I was only supposed to be gone for an overnighter. Ended up staying a lot longer to get through everyone. Ani had to reschedule my other clients because there was no point in me coming all the way home to do that trip again later."

"Makes sense."

"I did use a few of your designs. I've let Ani know so she can keep track."

"How did you..."

A flush coloured Beck's cheeks, and he rubbed at it in a move Kole was sure he would have no recollection of. "I took some photos before I left. Showed them around while I was preparing." He smiled and nudged Kole with his shoulder. "You're popular already."

It was Kole's turn to hide his heated cheeks by ducking his head. "I drew some more intricate designs this week."

He hadn't meant to say anything.

"Yeah? Can I see?" Beck's voice held a note of excitement.

Kole hummed, unsure, because he hadn't wanted to show anyone. He'd wanted to keep them a secret, but Beck had a way of making him spill what was on his mind without even trying. And without even meaning to. It had been Kole who had blurted it out.

"I'm not sure..."

"That's okay. I know some designs are private. It's no problem. I love your work, though, so if they ever see the light of day, I want first pick."

Kole stared at him. "You want my designs on you?"

Beck licked his lower lip, his tongue rolling over the mound and his teeth following the path. He wanted that over his body again, the feel of those sharp points scraping his nipple and the rough but slick tongue soothing the ache afterwards. He exhaled quickly but quietly, trying to get ahold of himself when Beck started talking again.

"Hell, yes. I've already decided about one, but I'm waiting."

Kole frowned. "For what?"

"For you to learn to tattoo. You're the artist, and I want you to ink it as it should be inked. Right here." He tapped the back of his neck, just before his hairline.

Was it a coincidence that the place was Kole's favourite? A place he spent many hours touching, sliding his fingers over the skin, mesmerised by the softness.

"But what if I never learn?" he managed to say.

"Then I'll just keep the design with me. It'll still be mine." He leaned closer, lowering his voice. "But you want to, don't you? I've seen you watching, your eyes sparkling."

Kole met his gaze and couldn't do anymore than tell the truth. He nodded slowly. "Yes, I do."

Beck grinned, the crinkles around his eyes and mouth deepening. Kole wanted to kiss them or run his fingertips over them. Instead, he stared, taking everything in so he would remember it forever. Because he'd stopped kidding himself at that moment. He wanted Beck with a fire he'd never known before, but like a scrap of fabric that was soaked in fire retardant, he couldn't catch him. Wouldn't. Because Beck didn't want him the same way, and he refused to lock Beck into something he didn't truly want. He could deal with the pining if it meant he would still see Beck often at work, but if their friendship got ruined because of Kole's wants, he'd never forgive himself and would slink back to Whitby with his tail between his legs.

He'd rather hide his feelings away than lose what he had with Beck.

After all, no one would blame him for not finding someone straight away. It would bide him some time. At least until Ethan or Christi set in on him again. They meant well, but they were like alligators after fresh meat when they wanted to be.

"Beck?"

They turned to the voice, and Beck flinched beside him. The only reason Kole knew was because their arms were resting close and he felt it. Ignoring the slightly overweight man for a moment, he focused on Beck, and what he saw he didn't like. His usually warm skin had leeched of most of its colour, and his hands had turned into fists of stone. He stared at the man, his breathing increasing until he broke the spell and smiled.

"Hey, D. Long time. How have you been?"

Kole knew at that moment he wouldn't be leaving Beck alone with whoever this guy was.

11

BECK

While Beck had an outwardly calm demeanour, inside, he was a mess. He'd never thought he'd ever run into Drake again, especially as the last time he'd spoken to him, he'd said he was moving out of the country. Beck had celebrated that news by getting considerably drunk and finding someone to share the night with. He'd thought he was free and clear. It was too much to hope for, he supposed.

He swallowed hard and kept the smile on his face as Drake began to speak.

"I'm good, thanks. Great, actually. Just got a promotion with work after spending a few years in Dubai, so I'm taking a holiday before that starts up in a few weeks. I thought I'd come back and touch base with some friends." He grinned. "Didn't think I'd see you here."

There was something in his voice, the same something that had always been there, the same something that had the hair lifting on the back of Beck's neck and his forearms.

"Congrats on the promotion. Are you heading back to Dubai again or is it back here?" *Dubai, Dubai, Dubai.* The chant started in his head—or rather, the prayer. Beck wasn't a religious man, but he would pray with the holiest people on the planet for the rest of his life if Drake said he was going back to Dubai.

"Dubai. Such a beautiful place. Best decision I ever made was to take that job, even if it meant I couldn't see my family anymore.

The price of plane tickets is crazy." Drake grinned again, his eyes flicking to the side.

Beck wet his lips and swallowed again. "You still see Roger and Erika?" He wasn't sure he truly wanted to know the answer, but in some ways, he did. Roger and Erika Price had been the foster parents he'd shared with Drake until they'd told the social worker to find another placement for Beck. It had been completely out of the blue, and Beck had no idea why.

Beck entered the room, eyes darting around at the four adults seated on the sofas and chairs in the small space. Two of them, Roger and Erika, his foster parents, wore slight smiles on their usually cruel faces, and the other two had pursed lips and annoyed expressions.

"Come on in, Beck. We need to have a chat," Roger said. "Sit down."

Beck dropped into an empty chair, the words, while quieter and softer than usual, still holding the demand they usually did. He had questions, of course he did, but he was twelve, and he wasn't supposed to ask.

"Good morning, Beck," the unknown woman said. "I hear there have been a few issues with your stay here. We would like to find out what those issues are so we can find you a better fit with a new family."

The woman sounded harsh and, in all honesty, fed up, but if she had to deal with this shit all day, Beck wasn't surprised. What he was surprised about was the so-called issues he was having. What issues?

He glanced at Roger and Erika, who smirked at him, and it was then he realised what she'd said. New family. He was leaving. And while he was half grateful for the opportunity to leave this awful place, which had far too many children for the space and far less love and support he had hoped for, it had been his home for three years. He'd believed—wrongly, it seemed—that he wasn't going to stay there until he aged out after all.

"Tell us about the forest. Why did you hurt those children?"

Beck frowned. "Hurt who?"

Roger scoffed. "You know who. Daniel got his arm broken and Lisa sprained her ankle. Not to mention the scrapes and bruises littering their bodies and the nail scratches on your body."

Beck shook his head. "Daniel tripped over a log as we were playing chase, and Lisa fell off a stone as we walked across the stream. The scrapes and bruises, including mine, were from running through the trees." He paused. "I don't understand."

"I told you he wouldn't admit it, but he needs somewhere with no other kids, I believe," Roger said. "He might be a danger to them if this behaviour increases."

The unknown woman scratched a few notes in her book. "Are you willing to keep him for a few more days until we can find a suitable place?" she asked Roger and Erika.

"We are. At least we know what to look out for."

The conversation continued without his input, and he blocked them out, trying to figure out what the hell was going on. He hadn't been there when Daniel and Lisa had hurt themselves, only turning up when he heard them shouting for help. In both instances, he had carried them on his back to the house so they could get some first aid. Never had he believed his actions would come back to haunt him—especially as he'd done nothing wrong.

Had Daniel and Lisa complained he had, or had Roger and Erika finally decided they were sick of him? It was most likely the latter because he believed he had wonderful friendships with Daniel and Lisa.

He tuned back into the conversation when the two unknown people, who he now believed were from social services, stood.

"We'll be in touch as soon as possible. In the meantime, I would suggest keeping an eye on him and keeping him away from anyone else as much as possible."

Beck's denials stuck in his throat. He couldn't be left alone. He couldn't. He enjoyed being around people and hated it when he was alone. Alone was when the problems happened. Alone was when he got hurt. Alone was when... He blinked and shook his head. He just had to survive the next few days. Maybe they'd send him to a nice family, one who actually took care of the children they looked after.

"Don't worry, Beck. We made sure to tell them you preferred being alone," Erika said with a grin. She patted his head in mock sympathy. "Now, go to your room and stay there. You don't leave for any reason other than using the toilet. If you do, you don't want to know what will happen."

Beck swallowed hard and followed her instructions. He was going to be alone. All day. Every day. Until he left this place.

Scared didn't even cover what he felt.

"Yes, I do occasionally," Drake said, bringing Beck back to the question he'd asked. "We talk on the phone all the time."

Beck wasn't at all surprised. They were like peas in a pod. It was no wonder they had taken to Drake and not to Beck. They saw the same personality in Drake that they had themselves.

"That's...good." He stood. "I'm sorry to cut this short, but I have to get to work."

Drake didn't give an inch, and even though Beck was taller and more muscular than Drake, he was still that trembling child inside, wishing Drake would go away.

"Who's your friend?" Drake asked, tilting his head behind Beck.

Beck frowned, glancing behind him, surprised to see Kole sitting there. That's right. He'd come to the sandwich shop to get some food, and Kole had turned up. How had he forgotten?

But now he remembered, he didn't want to introduce them. He wanted Kole as far away from Drake as he could get.

"Hey, I'm Kole, and sorry, but we need to get these back to our colleagues." Kole stood, picked up a bag Beck didn't remember seeing before and nudged Beck's arm. "Come on. We'll be late."

It got Beck moving, his eyes on the floor as he put one foot in front of the other. The closer to the door he got, the more his breathing increased.

"I hope to see you around!" Drake called, and it took everything in Beck not to burst into tears at the thought.

"A little further," Kole whispered, and Beck held his breath until they turned a corner. "Now breathe."

Beck didn't breathe. He hyperventilated. He dropped his hands to his knees and bent forward, his lungs screaming for air. A hand rested on his nape, and he tore himself away, putting several feet between him and his assailant. His eyes darted around, only seeing one person with him, but he didn't feel safe. He felt alone.

"I have...I...go," was all he managed before he ran.

He ran and ran, arms pumping, heart pounding, legs screaming, but still he ran. And when he finally collapsed in exhaustion, he sank to the floor near a tree and closed his eyes to stop the world from spinning. Then he lay down, cushioning his head with his hand and pulling the other over his head, blocking out the world.

And there he stayed.

He wasn't sure how long he'd been wherever he was when he finally moved his muscles and uncurled himself, his entire body screaming at him from being in the one position for so long. He sat upright and rested his forearms on his knees, his hands hanging free, while he let his head settle. He let his eyes wander around him, taking in the darker skies—which wasn't any help with telling him the time because it was winter, and therefore, it became darker earlier—and the surrounding trees.

He wasn't entirely sure where he was, but he could rectify that easily enough by checking his phone. He didn't want to, though.

Stretching his legs out in front of him, he groaned and then sighed, knowing he had to look. The phone beeped as he pulled it from his pocket, and he unlocked it. Several feelings flowed through him at the sixteen missed calls and twenty-one messages staring back at him. He was grateful to have people who cared to check up on him, scared that they would ask questions he wasn't ready to answer, and tired. Just goddamn bone tired.

He took himself to his feet and stood there while he checked the messages. Ani had sent the most, Joey the second most. There was even a couple from Kole.

He dropped his chin to his chest. Damn it. Kole. He'd disappeared on him and left him at the shop, which was a shitty thing to do. Hopefully, he'd remembered his lunch.

What if Drake had done something? Would he have followed Kole once Beck had left?

Stomach somersaulting, he dialled Kole, talking the moment he answered. "Are you okay? Did you get back okay?"

"I'm fine, Beck. I'm fine. I promise."

Silence descended, and he waited for the inquisition. It didn't come.

"Have you eaten?"

Beck swallowed against the lump in his throat. The lump that wanted to climb up through his eyes and out through his tear ducts. Through his churning stomach came a growl that reminded him he hadn't eaten.

"I'm okay," Beck said. "I just wanted to check on you because I left...quite abruptly."

"As long as you're okay. I'm cooking lasagne for dinner if you would like to join me. No strings. No questions. Just a hearty dinner."

The sincerity in Kole's voice was easy to hear, and Beck agreed when he really should have said no and holed up in his house by himself. But he wanted to check on Kole in person. At least that's what he was admitting to himself.

"Okay. I'll see you whenever you get here."

Beck stared at his phone when the call ended, knowing he needed to let others know he was all right, but he couldn't find the energy. Instead, he pulled up the maps and found he was around eight miles from Life in Ink. With no energy left to walk back, he called a taxi, giving the woman Kole's address when she arrived. She tried to start a conversation, but Beck couldn't reply.

He had nothing left to give.

And when Kole opened his door for him, it took every ounce of his willpower to not burst into tears when he saw him.

"Come on in. It's almost ready."

And that was it. That was all he said. Beck crossed the threshold and closed the door behind him, waiting for something...anything. He wasn't used to feeling so out of sorts, and he wanted to say something to explain, but if he did, it would open an enormous box of snakes. A box he wasn't sure he could close again.

"Do you want to get the drinks ready and I'll dish it up?" Kole said.

Beck nodded and did his chore on autopilot, silence following them through the motions. When they sat at the table with a steaming plate of lasagne with a side salad, Beck tensed. Would Kole bring it up now?

"The shop was really busy this afternoon. I sold a few pieces, which is great. Oh, Joey has decided to get another tattoo done. He said he was going to let Ethan have a go, but Ethan started complaining, saying he wouldn't trust himself to do it." Kole chuckled. "Joey tried arguing the point, but I don't think he'll win. Well, unless he agrees to have it done in a really obscure place."

Beck ate small pieces of the food, chewing a hundred times before he swallowed it felt like. But the more Kole talked about his day, the more Beck relaxed. And when the tension finally released its hold, he ate ravenously. Kole stood to get him a second portion with barely a pause in his talking. How he was eating and talking was beyond Beck's comprehension right then.

When his second helping disappeared, he rested his hand on his stomach and groaned. "That was fantastic. Thank you, Kole."

Kole beamed. "You're welcome." He gathered up the dishes. "Would you like a coffee?"

Beck exhaled. "Actually, I probably shouldn't. I need to get some sleep."

With those words, the tension crept back. Getting some sleep would mean going home, and going home would mean being alone, and being alone would mean he wasn't safe. He shook his head, frowning. His home was safe. He'd made it that way. Even so, his stomach wouldn't quit.

"You're welcome to stay here instead of fighting with the traffic if you like," Kole said from the kitchen area where he was putting the plates in the dishwasher.

The sight brought Beck's manners to the forefront. "Let me do that." He took the plate from his hand and nudged him from the kitchen. "Rest."

Kole dropped into silence while Beck finished the chore, and then he wiped his hands and realised Kole was waiting for an answer from him. Checking in with himself, he decided he wasn't ready to be alone, even if he knew his house was safe. Drake's visit had shaken him enough to need company.

"If you're sure, I'd love to borrow your sofa."

Kole tilted his head. "You're welcome to the sofa, but you're also welcome to share my bed." He held up his hands, palms facing outwards. "No strings attached. Just a slightly more comfortable sleeping arrangement."

Beck nodded, but a yawn startled him. Covering his mouth, he wiped at his eyes and apologised. "I won't say no to somewhere comfortable."

Kole smiled. "Come on. Let's get ready for bed then. I could do with an early night myself."

Stepping into Kole's bedroom again, Beck saw things he hadn't taken the time to notice the first time around, like a lone photograph on the shelf opposite the bed. He moved closer, leaning down to see it more clearly. What looked like a teenage Kole was standing in front of his parents with huge grins on their faces at the beach.

Kole came to stand beside him. "I had just turned sixteen, and my parents thought a beach trip would be a good birthday celebration." He chuckled. "It's not like I saw the beach every day. Auntie Ava took this photo, and she'd just said something funny enough to make us all laugh."

Beck had few and far between beautiful memories like that. He took one last glance and turned to the bed. "Thank you for..." He waved his hand towards the bed.

"Well, I'm being selfish, really." Beck raised his eyebrows and waited. "You're like a furnace, so I won't need the extra blanket I often do."

Beck chuckled and shook his head, tension leaving his body again, and suddenly, his body felt so heavy, like he couldn't lift his limbs. Kole must've seen some change in him because he led him to the bed, unfastened Beck's trousers and dragged them down. They stopped at his shoes, but that didn't deter Kole. He pushed Beck to sit on the bed and took off his shoes, socks and trousers.

"Do you want to take your shirt off, too?" he asked.

Beck nodded, unable to make his tongue work. Kole lifted the shirt from him, yanking it over his head.

"Come on. Lay down." He lifted the covers and encouraged Beck backwards. The covers fell over him, and Beck turned to his side, punched his hands into his pillow and was gone.

12

KOLE

As Beck's breathing deepened, Kole's heart broke all over again. He had so many possibilities floating through his head about what had happened to Beck, but unless he was willing to talk, Kole could do nothing. But at least he could offer his bed, even if it was for comfort rather than sexy times.

Needing a minute, he left the room and headed for the kitchen to grab a glass of water for them both. He drank one while he stared across the apartment, not really seeing anything. Where had Beck been all afternoon? Why had he run? They were questions no one could answer. Kole had messaged Joey and Ethan when Beck had called him to let them know he was okay, but he hadn't sent any other updates. What could he say? Beck was physically all right, but that was about it. He wasn't sure how much anyone else knew, and he refused to break confidences by asking, so it was a case of leaving it as it was and seeing what happened when Beck woke.

It certainly gave Kole a level of reassessment of his own situation. Even though he didn't know what happened in Beck's past, Kole's mind went to abuse of some kind, which, in his opinion, was significantly worse than just being hit a few times. He wasn't undermining what he'd been through, but it was a lot easier to push it aside when he had Beck to focus on. Was that healthy? Maybe not, but he wouldn't stop it from happening. If he could, he would forget all about that asshole and never think of the incident ever again.

He wandered to the doorway of his bedroom and rested his head against the frame while watching Beck sleep. Letting out a long, soft sigh, he allowed his heart to voice its wants.

It wanted Beck in his bed from that moment forward.

He wanted Beck in his bed from that moment forward.

Kole and Beck fell into a routine of sorts. They would work and then Beck would leave, eventually turning up on Kole's doorstep, where they would share a late dinner and fold themselves into bed. And every time, Beck would disappear before Kole woke, leaving a "Thank you" note behind. It didn't worry Kole as much as it had the first time. He would see him again. Nothing else sexual had happened between them, but Kole found it reassuring to have someone else not only in the apartment but in his bed, and it both worried and eased him.

Then three weeks later, Beck didn't turn up. Kole put a movie on and settled on the sofa, obsessively checking his phone every few minutes in case he hadn't heard the notification of a message or call, even though it was in his hand. His gaze darted between his phone, the door, the TV and the window as the sky darkened further until the film ended and he sat in the glow of the screen wondering whether Beck was all right.

Did he have the right to call and ask him if he was coming? It wasn't something they'd discussed; it had just started happening. Would he push Beck further away if he did call? Had something happened to him? Was he in a hospital somewhere and no one had told him?

His mind went through every potentially bad thing that could've stopped Beck from getting to his house, and by the end, his hands shook and his breathing came in ragged spurts. When he noticed, he clenched his hands into fists and closed his eyes, working through the breathing exercises the therapist had told him to do until he calmed. Then he grabbed his phone again and messaged Ethan.

KOLE: Hey, do you know where Beck is?

He didn't expect a message straight away, so he set about cleaning the apartment, and even though it wasn't exactly dirty, he made good use of his scrubbing brush against the wooden floors—something he'd been saying he needed to do and had never had the energy to do.

When his phone chimed, he jumped for it, almost knocking the bucket of water over, and checked his messages.

ETHAN: He's gone to Paris. Annabelle requested another appointment. Is everything okay?

The air left his lungs in a rush, and he dropped his chin to his chest. Beck was fine. He was working. After a moment of regaining his equilibrium, Kole replied, trying to tactfully say he was just wondering.

KOLE: Yeah, everything's fine. I just hadn't heard from him. Sorry to message you so late.

A few seconds later, Ethan's name flashed up on his screen, and Kole groaned and then answered.

"Hey."

"First, you don't need to apologise for messaging late. You know I don't mind. And second, are you ready to tell me what's going on between you two?"

Ethan's no-nonsense tone sent Kole's pulse spiking, but he couldn't lie to him. Not when they were talking; he'd hear it in Kole's voice.

"Not really. But only because I don't know what's going on if I'm honest."

Ethan said nothing for a moment. "Is this something we need to talk out face to face?"

Was it? Kole needed someone to talk to, but was bringing Ethan into it the best option?

"I'd be happy to discuss some things, but I can't tell you everything."

"I understand that. If it won't help you, I'll leave it alone, but you sound like you need an ear."

"I do," Kole answered honestly.

"You order the pizza. I'll bring the vodka."

Before Kole could argue, Ethan had hung up. Resigning himself to a long night—but also inwardly grateful to his best friend—he ordered their usual food, despite being unlikely to be able to eat it.

Half an hour later, Ethan was at his door, and the man pulled Kole in for a hug straight away.

"I was wondering how long it would take for you to need to talk about it." Ethan pulled back and gave a lopsided grin. "Whatever it is."

Kole pushed him away with a laugh. "You're nosey, that's your problem."

"Oh, honey. I have so many problems I wouldn't know where to start." Ethan snorted and headed for the sofa, placing the bottle of clear liquid on the coffee table. "I couldn't decide what juice to bring, so I brought apple juice, orange juice and some coke. The drink, not the drugs."

Kole handed Ethan two glasses and settled beside him, tucking his legs beneath him and resting his elbow on the back of the sofa. "I can always rely on you to make me laugh."

"Not just me." Ethan side-eyed him, and Kole exhaled, staring at Ethan's hands as he made their drinks.

"There is a lot I can't tell you, Ethan."

"And that's fine. But just know, whatever you tell me will never go further than these four walls if you say it can't."

"I know. But it's not my story to tell."

Ethan nodded, handing him a drink. "Understood." He leaned back, meeting Kole's gaze. "How are you?"

Kole sighed. "Tired." He frowned. "Worried. Unsure." He stared into his glass. "Scared," he whispered.

Ethan's hand dropped onto his forearm. "Scared of what? Is someone bothering you? Is Beck bothering you?"

Kole shook his head quickly. "No, not Beck. Never Beck." He licked his lips. "I'm scared of falling in love with him."

"Oh, Kole. It's a little too late to be scared of *falling*, don't you think?"

Kole closed his eyes and swallowed against the lump in his throat. He opened his eyes again and gave a wry smile. "Let me rephrase. I'm scared of *being* in love with Beck."

Ethan squeezed his arm and let go. "He's not Andrew. He would never be Andrew, I can almost swear to that."

"I know that. I truly do. My brain keeps flitting between knowing that and being scared."

"What is scaring you the most?"

Kole considered the question while sipping his drink, wincing at the strength. "Giving it a go and realising we're bad for each other."

"I doubt that would be true, but I can see why it might be a worry." He scraped his teeth over his lip. "I know nothing about Beck's past, but I know Beck, and so does Joey. If he wasn't a good guy, he wouldn't be working with them."

"It's not his character I'm worried about." Kole scratched his fingernails against his scalp as he tried to explain without explaining. "We both have issues, and I'm concerned that we might...hold each other up, so to speak. That we'll begin to rely too heavily on each other and won't...heal properly."

Ethan nodded slowly. "You're already in love with him, Kole. Whether you admit that to him or not, you're already in deep. I don't know how Beck feels because I don't know him as well, but even if you don't trust your own instincts, I trust you. I know you will do what you believe is right."

And wasn't that the conundrum?

Kole tossed back the vodka and orange and gestured for another. "It's Friday, and I'm not working tomorrow. I plan to get drunk."

Ethan frowned. "I thought you were going in tomorrow?"

"Only because I had nothing else to do. Instead, I'm going to sleep off my hangover."

Ethan chuckled. "Understood."

And by god did he have a hangover. When his body brought him to consciousness, he didn't even need to move to know his head hurt. The jackhammers and steamrollers were playing in their playground, also known as his head, and when he tried to peel his eyelids open, he realised the gritters had also been out doing their job. He felt like he had a year's worth of grit sliding across his eyeballs. And don't get him started on his mouth. The inside of his hoover was probably cleaner.

Finally opening his eyes, his blurry gaze landed on his bedside table, and despite the weird angle advertising he was probably diagonal across his bed, he could just about see the outline of a glass of water. As carefully as he could, he crawled himself forward until he could reach it and found two tablets beside it as well.

"Thank you, Ethan," he whispered.

Shoving them into his dry mouth, he grabbed the glass, sipping it sideways so he didn't have to move his head any more than he already had. He spilt half of it into his pillow, but he didn't care. Putting the empty glass on the floor—because he had used all his energy and couldn't reach up again—he pulled the duvet over his head and went back to sleep.

He jolted awake at the sound of a bell and groaned when the movement hurt. The bell sounded again, and he realised it was the doorbell, the annoying buzzing something he really wanted to change but had never got around to it.

"Go away," he whispered.

The swarm of bees continued, and Kole finally dragged himself from the bed, using the walls and doors to keep him upright. He opened the door without looking to see who it was and came face to face with the person he'd least expected, but it woke him the fuck up.

"Can I help you?" he asked.

Drake smiled that fake stretching of his lips, and Kole's stomach rebelled, but he swallowed it down. He tightened his hold on the door handle, wondering if he could get away with slamming it shut before the guy said anything, because Kole was sure he didn't want to hear it.

"Yes. I'd like to talk to Beck."

Over my dead body. "He's not here right now. He's out of the country, in fact."

Drake's smile turned to a sneer. "Is that right?"

That was the moment Kole realised he'd said the wrong thing, and a shiver went down his spine.

"Okay. Thanks for letting me know. I'll come back another time."

Kole opened his mouth to say the apartment wasn't where Beck lived but thought better of it. He watched Drake wander down the corridor to the lift. The man winked at him as the doors closed behind him, and Kole slammed his door closed, leaning back against it.

"How the hell did he know where I lived?" he muttered to the empty apartment.

Brushing the thought aside, because trying to think when he hadn't recouped all his brain cells yet was impossible, he headed for the shower. Might as well try to clean up while he was on his feet.

Once he'd showered and dressed, he dropped onto the sofa after collecting some snacks and a drink—the non-alcoholic kind—and put on some crappy TV show. He didn't have enough energy to figure out what else he could watch. But as the food and drink soaked into his body, giving it the nourishment it needed, he began to feel better. Well, better, but sleepier.

His front door opening had him jerking awake, but this time without the groan of pain. Darkness had fallen over the room, and he could see there was a person by the door.

"Beck?" He lifted himself to sit and rubbed a hand over his face.

"No, sorry to disappoint."

The voice had Kole freezing in place. "How did you get in?"

"I was very persuasive with the landlord," Drake said, moving forward more into the light of the screen.

"What do you want?"

"So many questions. I want answers of my own, so you'll shut up and answer them."

Kole swallowed hard and didn't reply. He had no idea what to do. His phone was on the coffee table, and he was sure he wouldn't be able to go for it without consequences. There wasn't necessarily menace in Drake's voice, but he hadn't broken into his apartment for fun and games. Well, not the kind Kole thought was fun, he was sure.

"Beck doesn't live here, does he?" Kole didn't answer, and Drake stepped forward and slammed his hand on the breakfast bar. "Does he?" he yelled.

Kole shook, visions of Andrew's attack flashing through his mind, but he shoved it down. "No."

"Well done. Where does he live?"

No way in hell was he answering that question.

Drake chuckled. "You're going to make things worse for yourself."

"I won't tell you. No matter what happens," Kole said, sitting up straighter, finding strength from somewhere.

Grinning, Drake stepped forward, each step a slow, methodical approach, and though Kole's newfound strength faltered, he held his ground.

"That's no problem. I like it when my partners fight me."

Hands sweating, Kole eyed his phone. It was too far away, and Drake was too close. He readied for an attack, but nothing came.

"One more question...for now. When does Beck get back?"

"I don't know," he answered. Drake raised his eyebrows. "I actually don't. I didn't even know he'd gone."

Drake frowned. "I thought you were his boyfriend? How can he not tell you?"

Kole ignored the hurt pressing on his chest when the asshole echoed what had been in his head the previous day. "We're fuck buddies, not boyfriends."

The smile that spread across Drake's face was nothing short of terrifying. Kole must've said something that helped Drake in some way.

"You must be good to keep Beck coming back. From what I know about him, he never usually visits a bed more than once." Drake's hand ran over his crotch. "Maybe I need to get a taste."

He stepped close enough for Kole to surprise him with a kick aimed at his balls, but he missed and rolled to the floor, scrambling on hands and knees to get away. Drake wrapped his beefy hand around his ankle, slamming him to the ground. His chin hit with a thud, sending a rattling ache through his jaw. Heart pounding, he got his hands beneath him again, kicked his free leg back, connecting with something, and crawled forward. A weight crashed into his back, taking him to the floor again and pushing the air from his lungs.

"I don't think so, Kole. You're my ticket to proving a point," Drake said into his ear before licking a stripe up his cheek. Kole jerked his head away and bucked. "Hell, yes. Keep doing that, and we'll get along just fine."

Drake's groin rubbed against Kole's ass, and for a split second, he froze. Long enough for Drake to wrap his hand around his neck and keep him in place.

"What shall I do with you now?"

A boom sounded, and then voices. Lots of voices. But Kole's gaze was narrowing, his lungs screaming for air that Drake was keeping from him. He scratched at his neck, at Drake's hands, trying to get him to let go, but then the weight was gone, the hand was gone, and his head slammed to the floor. He dragged in a lungful of oxygen and coughed it out again, repeating it until his head cleared enough to hear a commotion behind him.

"He invited me here! He likes it rough, for god's sake!"

"If I were you, I would keep your mouth shut until you have a lawyer, Mr Price," someone else said.

"Mr Peterson? Kole? Can you hear me?"

Kole blinked, his vision swimming. Finally, a strange man came into view, but as he wore a police uniform, Kole's mind automatically deemed him the safer option.

"Mr Peterson?"

"Yes," he croaked. He winced at the pain of talking.

"Good. I'm Officer Bryant. We're going to get you to hospital for a checkup. Your throat is severely bruised. Is there anyone you'd like to call?"

"Ethan," he rasped, pushing to sit with help from the police officer.

Kole's landlord handed him his phone when he gestured to the coffee table, and Kole glared at him. The man held his hands up.

"I'm sorry. As soon as I gave him the key, I called the police. I tried calling you but you didn't answer. I didn't get here quick enough. I'm so sorry."

Kole didn't have the energy to argue with him at that point. He dialled Ethan.

"Kole? Is everything okay?" Ethan's sleepy voice made him realise exactly how late it was.

"No," he croaked and winced again. He swallowed, but he couldn't say anything else. It hurt too much.

"Kole?"

Kole held the phone out to the police officer, who took it and told Ethan what was happening. He tuned out and stared at the front door. He couldn't hear or see Drake anymore, but that didn't mean he wasn't around.

"Ethan is going to meet us at the hospital," Officer Bryant said and handed him the phone again.

Kole nodded slowly. Surprisingly, he was calmer after this attack than he had been with the first one. Andrew had been a nice guy until he had proven himself to be deluded. Drake had never pretended to be anything but creepy. Maybe that was why. Didn't stop him from closing down, though, and as the officer helped him to his feet, he stayed quiet, only answering when he was asked direct questions.

The major difference between the attacks was, that time, Kole wanted Beck to be with him. Whereas the last time, he'd wanted to be alone. To not be touched at all. At that moment, all he wanted was for Beck to fold him in his arms and never let go.

But that would never happen. Not now.

Drake had effectively ended any chance of him and Beck having a relationship. Because now Beck would blame himself and wouldn't touch a hair on Kole's head ever again.

13

Beck

Beck was watching a repeat of *The Late Show with James Corden* when his phone rang, and considering it was almost four in the morning, it had him on instant alert.

"What's wrong?" he asked Joey.

"You might want to come down to the hospital, Beck. Kole's been hurt."

Beck shot upright, hitting his toe on the coffee table but barely feeling it as his stomach churned. "How? What?" He paced in front of the windows, his heart pounding as he waited for Joey's answer.

"Some guy convinced the landlord to give him the key to Kole's apartment and then attacked him."

Beck stopped still, his entire body turning into a solid block of ice. Joey's voice wavered in and out as his eyes glazed over and the past and present merged. He couldn't tell which words were from Joey and which were from years ago until a short, sharp crack of his name slammed him back fully into the present again.

"What?" he croaked.

"Fuck," Joey muttered. "I said, I'm coming to get you. He's asking for you."

"No! I'll...I'll get there. Just...give me a few minutes, yeah?" He wasn't in any fit state to drive right then, but he didn't want Joey seeing him like he was at that moment.

"Not a chance, Beck. I'm almost at yours, anyway. If you're not there when I turn up, there will be hell to pay. You feel me?"

Beck swallowed and knew his friend would keep his word. "Sure." He wasn't at all sure, but he had to talk the talk.

"Do I need to keep you on the phone while I drive the last few streets?"

That made Beck crack a small smile. "No. I'll be here."

"Good. Have a drink and get dressed in something other than those threadbare joggers, okay?"

"Yes, boss."

"And leave the sass at home." Joey ended the call.

Beck gave himself precisely thirty seconds to let the panic and pain wash through him before he raced off to get dressed, and being the exemplary employee that he was, he drained a glass of water before the doorbell rang. When he opened the door, Joey looked in about the same state as Beck probably was, with a creased T-shirt, jeans and a hoodie beneath a worn, thick leather jacket and bloodshot eyes.

"Come on."

With no other information or words, they headed to Joey's car. Beck had so many questions but wasn't sure which to ask. Luckily, Joey knew him well enough to start talking once they were on the road, and Beck gripped his hands together to stop them from giving away just how hard he was shaking.

"I know you might not want to hear the details, but I think you need to, and Kole has given me permission to explain." Joey's hands tightened on the wheel, his white knuckles visible on the passing streetlights. He let out a tremendous sigh. "Kole had fallen asleep when the guy let himself in. When Kole realised, he tried talking the guy down, but he wasn't interested. He had a point to make, apparently. He got Kole on the floor with a hand around his throat. Kole can barely whisper right now, and the doctors have advised him not to talk too much. His throat needs to heal."

"Did they catch the guy?"

"Yeah. Kole knew him. Drake something."

For the second time that night, Beck froze. His lungs burnt, his heart pulsed, and his head throbbed. *No. He wouldn't.* But he couldn't bring himself to believe his thoughts. Drake could and would and...had.

"Jesus, fuck. Breathe, Beck. Fucking breathe."

His body slammed forward and then back again, and then Joey's hand rested on his nape and his head was thrust between his knees. Soothing circles were drawn over his spine and he found his lungs easing.

"You scared the fuck out of me, asshole." Joey exhaled. "You okay?"

"Nope," he croaked.

"You ready to tell me what the fuck is going on?"

Beck's brain fired up, and he rose. "You ready to tell me why you're swearing so much tonight?"

"Because my fucking boyfriend had the scare of his life tonight, and then we find out his best friend was almost fucking killed, and then you're having fucking panic attacks on me, and I just want to know what the fuck is going on."

Beck couldn't help it. Despite the seriousness of the situation, he burst out laughing. And then suddenly, he wasn't laughing anymore and tears streamed down his cheeks. Arms slid around his shoulders and pulled him into a warm cocoon.

"Whatever the fuck this is, Beck, we're in it together. You got it?"

Beck nodded against Joey's chest, but he couldn't form any words. He just sat there clinging to Joey and crying like the baby he apparently was. That brought him up short. He was stronger than that. He had to be. Kole wanted to see him, and therefore, he needed to be in one piece. For however long it took him to make sure Kole was all right, he would keep it together. He pulled away from Joey and wiped his face, sniffing hard to unclog his nose and throat.

"Better?" Joey asked, and Beck could almost feel his need to get going.

"Yep."

"Liar, but I'll let that go for now."

Joey started driving again, and Beck tried to get his head around the information Joey had told him. How had Drake even known where Kole lived? But then he rolled his eyes. It wouldn't be the first time his ex-foster brother had stalked someone, but it would be the last if had anything to do with it.

Keeping himself together for the rest of the journey, he gave himself two precious seconds after Joey had parked the car to breathe, and then he climbed out and followed Joey into the hospital.

The medicinal scent of the place had always turned his stomach, but with the number of times he'd ended up in a place like that, he was used to ignoring it. The fake niceties of the staff still rubbed him the wrong way, but that was a him problem. They were just doing their job, however strained it seemed to him.

"He's this way."

Joey led the way. Beck kept his eyes on the distance, turning when Joey did, stepping into the metal death trap that was the lift when he was told to, and finally, Joey stopped outside a door.

"Ethan managed to get him into a room by kicking up a fuss with the staff. His argument was about us being well known, which isn't wrong, and so Kole has some privacy."

Beck swallowed and nodded. "Okay."

Joey stared at him for a long minute and then knocked softly before opening the door and poking his head around the edge. For those few seconds, Beck held his breath, tightening every muscle in his body to keep his feet planted right there instead of tearing him away from the very place he didn't want to be. But he did it. For Kole. But it would be the last time because Beck had brought pain and disaster to Kole's door, and he refused to do so again. They were over, even though they had barely begun.

Joey stepped through the door, leaving it open for Beck to follow, which he did. And then he had to lock his knees again so he didn't hit the floor when he met Kole's gaze. Despite them both knowing why Kole was there—because Beck had brought Drake into their lives—Kole's eyes were, as ever, trusting, kind and patient. It made Beck want to howl with the unfairness of it all.

Kole held out his hand. "Come," he rasped, and Beck almost broke at the pain in those words. Pain, not from emotional hurt, but from physical hurt.

His gaze dropped to Kole's neck, which was free of clothing and bandages and anything else, and saw the already formed dark bruises marring his perfect skin. His nostrils flared to keep his emotions in check. He had never been this blatantly emotional before. Or had he?

"Come." Kole's rasp accompanied his waving fingers, urging him closer, and Beck moved, drawn by the order. "Not...your...fault."

Beck placed his hand over Kole's mouth. "Stop talking," he said, his voice far shakier than he intended.

Kole grabbed his hand and squeezed, and Beck could see the words he wanted to repeat, but no matter what Kole said, it *was* his fault. If Drake hadn't been part of Beck's life, however short a time, he wouldn't have focused on Kole. Though why he did was still a mystery to him, but one he intended to figure out. The one redeeming factor was that Drake was in jail, which meant it was trickier for Beck to get to him, but even harder for Drake to get to Kole.

Kole pointed to the chair beside the bed, and Beck sighed and sat down when Kole wouldn't let go of his hand. Beck glanced at Joey and Ethan, the two having their arms around each other. Ethan looked wrecked, but he managed a smile when he saw Beck looking.

The room dropped into silence, and eventually, Kole fell asleep. Once he was sure he was gone, Beck slipped his hand free and stood, heading for the door.

"Don't turn your back on him, Beck," Ethan said.

He stopped with his hand on the door. "I will always be there if he needs me, but I'm no good for him. He'll be better without me."

And with that, he walked out of the room, down the corridors, down the stairs instead of the lift and out through the automatic doors. He barely felt the cold seeping through his thick jumper. He barely registered the puffs of air leaving his mouth as he strode down the street. He barely acknowledged whenever he bumped into someone he hadn't seen. He just kept walking, his mind a tangle of memories, nightmares and lies.

He finally slowed to a stop, his mind flickering with knowledge of the present, the past receding, and he glanced around.

"Hyde Park," he murmured.

Under normal circumstances, he wouldn't have been storming through the large, semi-deserted park at that time of night, especially without a coat. He turned in a full circle and got his bearings before slogging his way to the nearest taxi stand. He could've called someone, but he didn't want to talk to anyone. He just wanted to go home and lock himself away. But before he could do that, he had to speak to the police officers who had arrested Drake, and there was no way the police station would let him do that at that hour of the morning, looking like he did.

When he reached home, he showered under the hottest spray he could, hoping it would bring the feeling back into his body, but that type of cold wasn't so easily washed away. Instead, he dressed in warmer clothes and rode his bike to the police station, waiting in the car park around the corner until a reasonable hour. He didn't want to do what he was about to do, but it was the only way to make sure Kole was safe. If that meant he had to break his silence after all this time, he would.

Taking a deep breath, he walked into the station and up to the desk.

"Good morning," an older man said. "What can I do for you?"

"Is there a time limit on when someone can report a..." He swallowed hard and took another breath. "A rape?"

The man blinked and then shook his head. "No limit at all. Is that what you'd like to do?"

The images, already beginning to bombard him, froze for a second with his indecision, but he straightened his shoulders and looked the man in the eye. "Yes."

Within seconds, he was taken to a room with comfortable chairs and beige walls and given a cup of coffee he immediately forgot about and told someone would be with him shortly. He settled into a chair and stared at the neutral wall, trying to stem the flood of his past. It wasn't to be. After all, he was there to bare his soul. Because even if some people didn't believe men could be raped, Beck was living proof they could. And hopefully, by giving the detectives this new information, Drake would be kept behind bars for a very long time.

The door opened, and two officers entered. "Beck Cavanaugh?" one said.

Beck nodded. "Yes."

"Do you mind if we sit?"

"Not at all." He repositioned himself from his slouch.

"I'm Detective Conrad. This is Detective Haynes. Can you tell us about what you want to report?" the second said, and Beck focused on the softer-spoken officer.

Steeling himself, Beck said, "I was raped from the age of eleven by a man you currently have in custody. His name is Drake Price."

The officers glanced at each other before Haynes spoke. "Are you willing to give us all the information you can? No matter how small?"

"I am. I remember every detail." His voice cracked on the last word. "I will be upfront and say Drake just attacked someone close to me, but this is not retaliation. Not truly. I want my boyf—my friend to be safe, and if this means I have to talk about what happened to me to ensure Drake stays behind bars, then I will. I'll tell the world if I have to."

"Knowing who you are as I do," Haynes said, "you'll have no choice about the world finding out. You need to be ready for that."

Ice-cold fingers raked down his spine. "I am. I have to be. I will not let him hurt anyone else."

"Okay. Let's get some information down," Conrad said.

Beck frowned. "Are you not going to record it?"

Conrad tilted their head. "We thought that might be too much for you."

Beck shook his head. "No. Please record it. I want to get it all down."

Haynes reached inside their pocket and produced a recorder, and Beck told his story. Every sad, demeaning, painful word of his past. Every threat, every encounter, every...touch. Not once did he break down because he was doing it for Kole, and he needed to be strong.

He wasn't sure how long he had been there before the detectives called a stop to the interview.

"Go home and get some rest. We'll start investigating, but it'll take a while. Reporters will get wind of it sooner rather than later, so prepare yourself and those around you. It won't be pretty."

Beck huffed a laugh, the first tendril of amusement working its way through him since that brief burst of laughter in Joey's car. "None of this has been pretty."

Haynes stood and held out a card. "We suggest you talk to a counsellor. Not only to help yourself through the process but also to help us with more information if you're willing to allow them to discuss your sessions with us. It's not mandatory, but we recommend it."

Beck stared at the card. "Will it help the case?"

"It certainly won't hurt the case."

That hadn't been an answer, but he'd do anything to protect his family. "Okay."

"Drake Price won't be leaving jail right now. With this new information you've given us, we can hold him for longer. I can't guarantee it will be indefinite, but we'll do what we can."

Beck stood, fingering the edge of the card. "Can I ask one favour?" Haynes nodded. "Will you let me know if he's released?"

"Absolutely."

Beck nodded slowly, his body beginning to feel the emotional upheaval of the last few hours.

"Get some rest, Mr Cavanaugh. We'll be in touch soon."

The winter sun had him squinting as he exited the station, but he breathed deeply of the frigid air. He didn't feel any lighter for sharing his story, but he had to hope it would be enough to protect them. Beck wasn't powerful enough to do it alone, even though he wasn't an eleven-year-old anymore. If it took every penny he had, every item he owned and the clothes off his back, he would stop Drake from hurting anyone ever again.

He just wished he'd done it sooner because then Kole wouldn't have been hurt, and Beck might've been able to look himself in the mirror. He also wished the world wouldn't find out, but it was what it was. One day, he would look Drake in the eye and smile as he got sent to prison. One day, he could put it all behind him. One day, he might even be able to love someone.

Maybe.

14

KOLE

As Kole had expected, Beck wasn't there when he woke, but he still hadn't shown up when Kole was released the next afternoon. What he wanted to do was storm around to his house and demand Beck see him, but that wasn't the way to go. Knowing Beck as Kole did, the man would freeze him out—if he hadn't already. No, what he needed to do was get advice. The question was, who did he ask? Joey might've been the best person, but he wasn't sure he should break Beck's confidence in case he hadn't told him about their relationship.

Well, whatever type of relationship they had. Or would've had.

He needed to figure out how to approach Beck and make him understand it wasn't his fault. The fault lay in Drake's hands and always would.

Kole sighed in the back seat of the car as Joey drove him home. Ethan was chattering away as he usually did, and Kole tried to ignore how Joey kept flicking his gaze towards him. Ethan had been there for him after his first attack had happened, but Joey hadn't. Neither of them was hiding how unnerved they were. It wasn't like Drake was going to come back for him. He was in jail at the moment, and when he got out, it was highly unlikely he would be stupid enough to try something again, not with how much security was now in place.

When they stopped at Life in Ink instead of Kole's apartment, he frowned. "What are we doing here?"

135

Joey cleared his throat in an unusual show of uneasiness which instantly had goosebumps rising on his arms and neck.

"Beck wants to talk to all of us."

"About what?"

Joey scratched his chin. "I don't know." He climbed out of the car, leaving silence behind.

Ethan turned in his seat and met Kole's gaze. "He honestly doesn't know what it's about, but he's worried Beck is leaving."

Kole's chest constricted, but he pushed open the door and climbed out, barely wincing with the ache in his body. His throat still hurt, but at least he could talk properly now. He didn't care what he had to do, but he would stop Beck from leaving. Beck's family was there, and if he left, he'd lose his support network. The Life in Ink crew wouldn't turn their backs on him, but he would turn his back on them, which would be worse.

They entered the tattoo shop and headed to Beck's studio. With every step Kole took, he felt the heaviness in his limbs, the rapid pace of his heart and the scrambling of his mind as he tried to find a solution. He still hadn't come up with anything when they stepped into the tidy space. Beck paced in front of the window until Joey closed the door behind them, Dallas, Finn and Ani having already arrived.

"What's this about, Beck?" Joey asked.

Beck clasped his fingers together and raised them to the top of his head, his elbows stretched wide as he finally stood still. His gaze was rooted to the floor, and Kole's heart ached for him. No matter what he was about to say, he was in pain, and Kole wanted to soothe him.

"When I was eleven years old, I was...raped repeatedly by my foster brother." Beck crossed his arms over his chest as Kole froze. "Drake was the son the Prices had always wanted. Someone as twisted and vile as they were. Neither of them believed me... No. Neither of them *cared* when I told them. They told me to stop whining and get on with my chores. I thought if I just kept quiet, he'd leave the others alone." Beck sighed and faced the window, his back a stretch of muscle tightened to the extreme. "He threatened many times to start on one of the others if I didn't do what he said, so I let it happen. At least until they found an excuse to make me leave. After, I was so worried about the others, but none of the social workers listened to me either. They didn't want the *headache* a rape allegation would bring them."

Kole would've been able to hear a splash of ink hit the tile floor at that moment. He could feel everyone holding their breaths, either with sympathy or fury, at what had happened to their friend. But they all seemed to realise Beck wasn't finished, and Kole braced himself for the rest of his story.

"I'm only telling you this because I went to the police today and reported him."

Kole couldn't help the gasp that left him, and Beck turned to face him, locking gazes.

"It was the only way I could think of to protect you," he continued. "Drake is mean and unforgiving and unrelenting. He would never give up if he was released. It's why he's back. I was the one who got away, but you're paying the price. I can't have that."

Kole stepped forward, but Beck blanched, so he stopped.

"The media will have a field day with this when they get wind of it. I wanted to make sure you have the real story before they start hounding us with their made-up versions. I'm sure the Prices will get their fifteen minutes of fame soon enough."

He faced the window again but said nothing more.

"You better not be thinking of leaving," Dallas said.

Beck turned and rested back against the windowsill, arms still tightly bound across his chest. "There's no point. The police will need to keep talking to me, and wherever I go, someone will find me. I may as well face the music here."

"I, for one, am fucking glad for that." Joey stepped forward and dragged Beck into a hug, despite Beck not returning it. "You're family, and we'll all be here for whatever comes." He stepped back and into Ethan's arms.

Dallas clapped his shoulder. "Whatever you need, just name it."

"Don't need anything. I was just warning you of the hurricane coming our way."

Finn stepped up as Dallas dropped back and murmured something too low for Kole to hear, but Beck nodded slowly. Kole couldn't do anything. After all, when he'd tried to approach before, Beck's body language had warned him off. Glancing at Ethan, his best friend tilted his head towards Beck, but Kole shook his head.

"Well, I'll get back to work," Dallas said, clapping his hands together and making Kole jump.

Beck's gaze snapped to him, but he lowered his head again straight away. Finn followed Dallas out, and Joey, Ethan and Ani copied, leaving just him and Beck. Kole swallowed again the pain, both in his throat and his heart.

"Beck, I—"

"It's fine. It is what it is."

Kole sighed. "Don't shut me out, Beck. I definitely haven't been through what you have, so I can't begin to understand, but I'm here. I want to be here, and I *will* be here whenever you want me. I'm not leaving you."

Beck's gaze met his, and the emptiness inside his eyes was almost too much for Kole to bear. "You should. There's nothing worth staying for." He turned to face the window again, effectively dismissing Kole.

As much as he wanted to argue, Beck had already been through so much—and *for* Kole—so he did what Beck wanted and left. For now.

Closing the door softly behind him, he swallowed against the tears fighting to be set free from everything Beck had been through and wandered to his own studio. He grabbed a pencil and pad and tucked himself into the armchair in the corner of the room and let his emotions run free.

Time ran away, but it seemed less than a few minutes when Ethan came to see him.

"How are you doing?"

Kole sighed and closed his sketching pad, holding it close to his chest. "I don't really know." He coughed, his voice rough from not being used for long and the rough treatment it had received. "I can't say I'm surprised by Beck's news."

"Me neither." Ethan settled onto the stool that had come with the room, spinning it side to side almost subconsciously. "I had hoped I was wrong. Bloody hell, though. He has balls of steel to walk straight into the police station and offer up that info."

Kole stared at him. "What?"

Ethan paused his spinning and cocked his head. "Beck waited until this morning, then walked into the police station to give a statement against Drake."

Kole's chest ached, the band that had already been constricting his lungs tightening further. "Why?"

Ethan rolled his eyes. "Beck said why, but even I can figure out the answer to that without asking. To protect you. And others. I dread to think how many people Drake had got to over the years."

"But it's going to cause so many problems for him. For you."

"The only problem it will cause is giving us more advertising. There is no bad advertising, remember?"

Kole shook his head. "This is different. This is Beck's life."

Ethan sighed. "We have no choice in this, Kole. It was Beck's decision to make, and he made it. We have nothing to say about it, and neither should we. He's the bravest son of a bitch in the world in my books."

"And in mine," Kole whispered, turning his head to stare out of the window. "I just wish he hadn't had to go through it all—in the first place, and now, all over again."

"Same." Ethan sighed. "Come on. Let's get you home."

Kole didn't argue, and before he knew it, he was back at the scene of the crime, crossing the threshold into his newly repaired apartment. Surprisingly, he had no issues with being there. Ethan had been with him when he entered, but Kole held no bad feelings towards the place. The landlord, however, was another matter.

"We've had new locks put on, and the landlord has agreed to not have keys for the moment. He might change his mind, but for now, he doesn't want us to cause problems, so he's willing to forget that he doesn't have them."

"Good job, too. I'd hate to have to apartment hunt because he's an asshole." Kole settled onto the sofa and rested his head back. "Go on. Head back home. I'll be fine."

"You sure?"

"Definitely."

"Ring me straight away if you have any problems."

Kole smiled. "Yes, Mum." He reached for the remote.

Ethan put his middle finger up at him and closed the door behind him as he left. When silence descended, Kole took a breath. And another. And another. There, in his apartment, behind locked doors, he could let all his feelings out, but what he found was that anger was the most prevalent. How dare Drake hurt Beck? How dare he take that innocence from him?

A crack sounded, and he glanced at the remote in his hand. The remote that now had a lovely crack down the middle of it. He put it down and stood, shuffling to the bedroom. As much as he didn't want to, he needed sleep. Unafraid of nightmares relating to his ordeal, he was more worried about nightmares about Beck's because he wasn't sure he could stand watching even hypothetical images of what happened to him. But then,

Beck had been through it. The least Kole could do was weather the imagery.

Four hours later, he rethought his idea. Having woken from nightmares five times already, he wasn't sure he could withstand much more, so he climbed from the sweat-soaked bed, stripped the sheets and shoved them in the washing machine before making himself a hot chocolate. Caffeine was not a good idea, and though chocolate held some, it wasn't enough to bother him. Maybe the heat of it would help him sleep again but on the sofa that time.

Putting the drink on the coffee table, he picked up the cracked remote and aimed it at the TV, hoping it wasn't broken enough not to work. Luck was on his side—for once—and he chose a black and white film he had no idea the title of, wrapped a blanket around his shoulders and another over his legs, and cradled the mug in his hands.

He wasn't sure how long he'd stared at the screen before a beeping drew his attention. It stopped almost as soon as he heard it and then started again. Putting his empty mug on the coffee table, having no idea when he'd drunk it, he wandered into his bedroom and unplugged his phone. He checked the screen to find several messages.

BECK: *I hope you can forgive me.*
BECK: *I may have had a little too much to drink.*
BECK: *Ignore me.*
BECK: *You don't need to forgive me.*
BECK: *I wasn't there to protect you, but I'll make sure you never go through that again.*

Kole's heart skipped several beats as he read the messages. As far as Kole was concerned, Beck rarely drank a lot, but he must've drunk a fair amount to be messaging him. Was it wrong for Kole to be considering messaging back while Beck was under the influence? Maybe. But was he going to do it, anyway? Hell, yes. He'd take Beck whichever way he could have him.

KOLE: *There is nothing to forgive. You didn't do this. Drake did. Don't take his responsibilities onto your shoulders.*
KOLE: *Now, tell me, what do you need?*

He waited. Would Beck reply or not? When the dots danced across the screen, he held his breath.

BECK: *I have everything to be sorry for. If I had told sooner, Drake wouldn't have done that to you.*
KOLE: *You said you did tell, and no one believed you. That wasn't your fault.*

He tucked himself into bed, dragging the cover over him as he waited for the next message.

BECK: *I could've tried harder.*
KOLE: *Do you really think it would've worked?*

He waited, then followed it up with another.

KOLE: *Really?*
BECK: *I want to believe it would have.*
KOLE: *The world is cruel sometimes. A lot of times. But we can survive it all. With family. With friends. With partners. With anyone who means something. If we have that someone, we can fight our way through to the other side.*
BECK: *How did you get so wise?*
KOLE: *I blame my mother.*

There was a long few minutes where Kole thought Beck had fallen asleep or something, but the dots appeared again.

BECK: *I'm sorry.*
KOLE: *You only have something to be sorry for if you pull away, Beck. I'm here. Don't push me away.*
BECK: *I'll try.*
BECK: *I'm going to try to sleep off this alcohol. Night.*
KOLE: *Night, Beck.*

Nothing else appeared, so Kole set his phone on the bedside table and slid onto his back, staring towards the ceiling. His entire being felt lighter after their conversation, but whether Beck would remember anything the following morning was the question. It depended on how drunk he truly was. He'd seemed fairly sound of mind.

Kole rolled over to his side, tucking his hand beneath his pillow. The next thing he knew, his body was protesting the need for more sleep when it needed the bathroom as well. He dragged himself to the toilet before splashing his face with cool water to help the discomfort of gritty eyes. When he sat on the edge of his bed to check his phone, he found another message waiting for him, but he startled as the current time caught his eye. He hadn't slept until eleven in the morning for years. Clicking on the message, he grinned at Ethan's words.

ETHAN: *I'm assuming you're asleep, and that's why you're not at work, and that's a good thing. I'm also a little worried that something else has happened, but Joey has told me to stop being a mother hen, as did you last night. I'm trying. So I'm not tearing around to your apartment. Yet. If you're not in touch by noon, all bets are off.*

Kole snorted and typed a message back, letting Ethan know he was alive and would be in after lunch. Then he scrolled through the messages he and Beck had shared and chewed his lip. After a few minutes of deliberation, he sent one.

KOLE: *Hope your head doesn't hurt too much this morning. Let me know if you need any paracetamol. Or breakfast.*
KOLE: *Or rather brunch at this time of the morning.*

Once he was satisfied that he'd kept the conversation open, he went for a shower. His body still ached from what had happened, but it was easier to move around than it had been the previous day, even if his bruises belied that thought. After his refreshing shower, he checked his phone again, shaking his head at how much he used the damn thing, but then that thought flew out of his head at a reply from Beck.

BECK: *I'll be at The Cuckoo if you'd like to join me for breakfast/brunch/lunch all rolled into one. Say half twelve?*
KOLE: *I'll be there.*

And though he tried to shove it all down, he couldn't help the ache in his cheeks as he dressed and headed for the door. Maybe things would turn out okay after all.

15

BECK

When Beck had checked his phone after he'd woken from an alcohol-induced sleep, he'd been mortified to find the messages he'd sent to Kole. He'd promised himself that he'd step back from him, giving him the chance to find someone else, but his drunken self obviously had other plans. So when Kole had checked on him that morning, it had taken him a good fifteen minutes to decide whether or not to keep the bridge open between them.

In the end, it hadn't been something he could deny, no matter how much he told himself he should.

Waiting at The Cuckoo for Kole to arrive was a lesson in patience he didn't know he needed. He ordered a cup of coffee because he was half an hour early and didn't want to sit there without buying something while he waited.

The cafe was a small, family-owned business on a side street Beck had found during one of his long, wandering walks when he'd first started working at Life in Ink. He'd known a bit of London and had wanted to explore in the early hours of the morning and hadn't felt like using his bike was the best choice. Nothing like upsetting the neighbourhood with a roaring engine to dispel the serenity. He'd been visiting the cafe ever since and had come to know the owners well.

"Anything else, B?" Miko asked. He was the son of the owner, barely eighteen but already raring to take over.

"Nothing at the moment, thanks. I'm waiting for someone."

"Okay. Give a yell when you do."

"Will do."

Miko wandered off, and Beck immediately transferred his gaze back to the window, stomach somersaulting as his gaze scanned the street for the face he couldn't wait to see. And when that face appeared, his entire body locked into place. He barely remembered to breathe.

There was nothing plain about Kole. Despite his skin being a tattooist's dream—because there was so much skin to ink memories into—Beck couldn't imagine anything making the man more gorgeous than he already was. He loved ink on a person, but Kole was magnetic without it. Would he be just as alluring with patterns of black or splashes of colour? He might have to do some temporary inking to find out.

"Hey," Kole said, slipping into the seat opposite him.

Beck's palms dampened against the coffee cup, and he licked his lips. "Hi. Sorry about last night. Alcohol is not always my friend."

Kole smiled, and Beck's breath caught. "I don't mind. I'm glad we could do this." Kole grabbed a menu. "Do you have any recommendations?"

Beck studied him while his attention was on the plastic sheet. Kole seemed to be favouring one side of his body, and the banked fire in Beck's stomach simmered a little hotter. "The paninis are good. So are the baguettes. Everything is freshly made to order."

Kole raised his eyebrows at him. "You come here often?"

Chuckling, Beck relaxed more and sipped his now-cold coffee, grimacing a little. "A time or two."

"You ready to order now, B?" Miko said, reappearing again.

Kole cleared his throat, and Beck's cheeks heated as he focused on the server. "I'll have—"

"A barbecue chicken and bacon melt panini and a coffee?" Miko said. "Yeah, I know."

Kole chuckled. Beck leaned towards Miko. "If you want to keep customers, I would let them order for themselves."

"But it's a sign I know you! Mum said I needed to get to know customers," Miko said, frowning.

"I think it's an excellent trait to have," Kole said. "Might I make a suggestion?" Miko nodded. "If you know their order, just say it without the attitude. It'll come across much more sincere and respectful."

Miko tilted his head, then nodded. "Yeah, okay. I can see how that might sound bad. Sorry, B." Miko stood taller. "Would you like your usual, B? The barbecue chicken and bacon melt panini?"

Beck nodded. "That would be great, thanks."

"And for you?" Miko turned to Kole.

"I think I'll try the same. Can I get a glass of water, though, please?"

"Absolutely. It won't be long."

Kole gave Miko the thumbs up and the guy wandered off. "A time or two, huh?"

Beck got trapped in Kole's gaze and found himself beginning to talk. "It wasn't too bad at first. Drake pretended to be friends with us all. Played up the big brother role, and we loved it. But then he changed. Either something happened or he was always that way and had hidden it, but he became meaner. Upsetting people—except our foster parents—was his favourite pastime. I took on as much of it as I could because the other kids were smaller than me. It wasn't fair to them."

Beck looked out of the window again, the street disappearing to be replaced with the memories of the house and the woods...and the bedroom.

"At first, it was little touches that could've been considered accidental. But then one day, the Prices were out with the younger kids." He swallowed. "It was the first and only time I cried," he whispered. "I never gave him the satisfaction of hearing it again. But I allowed it, time and again, so he wouldn't turn to the other kids. I wanted them to have happier memories. But he used it against me. He'd threaten to go after them if I didn't do as he said. When they sent me away, I was so scared for them, but no one would listen. I never heard anything, so I was forever hopeful he hadn't done anything to anyone else."

He met Kole's gaze, and the non-judgemental look settled him.

"I want to say thank you on behalf of all those people you have saved by going to the police. Even if it turns out he has been an asshole for years, you've saved countless future victims."

Beck's throat closed up, and he couldn't say anything. He turned his gaze to the window, swallowing convulsively while trying to get his emotions under control. He had thought being out in public would be easier for him. Apparently not.

He wanted to be able to reach for Kole, but his body wouldn't let him. Touch was something he only thought he needed when he was sleeping with someone, but Kole was a whole other ballgame when it came to Beck's feelings and needs. He wanted to let go of everything he ever knew, everything his mind was telling him, everything he'd ever learnt for survival, just so he could let Kole into that part of him he hadn't thought he needed anyone in.

Clearing his throat, he linked his fingers. "The police rang me to say Drake was not leaving jail right now. They are going to investigate his life to see if anything crops up."

"It's good that they're looking into it and not brushing it aside. They might find something that helps their case."

"I know that would help, but I also hope they don't. If they do, it means someone got hurt."

Kole covered his hands with his own. "I know. But the priority now should be getting Drake off the streets."

Miko arrived with their drinks, causing Kole to pull back, and Beck immediately felt the loss.

"Your food will be here soon."

"Thanks, Miko," Beck said.

Silence fell between them as they both played with their cups. At least until Kole pushed his drink aside and leaned forward.

"Look, Beck. I'm going to sound harsh, but life is shit sometimes. I'm not saying what you, or anyone else, went through isn't terrible. I'm truly not. You couldn't have stopped Drake from doing anything. But if he has done things, they are going to make him more likely to never be able to do this again."

When Kole had started talking, Beck's throat had closed, his insides churning as he thought Kole was showing his true colours. As he continued, Beck wanted to weep. He swallowed hard, trying to let his words sink in. Understanding what Kole was trying to point out was easy, but it still left a sour taste in his mouth. He wouldn't wish the pain on anyone, even if it meant it would help Drake stay in jail.

"I know what you're saying, but I still don't like it."

"I know. It's shit," Kole agreed.

Their food arrived while he was still contemplating Kole's words, and it gave him the chance to recentre himself and breathe for a few minutes.

They didn't talk again until their plates were almost empty.

"Are you ever going to tell me why you're keeping a spce on the back of your neck?" Kole asked before taking another bite.

Beck licked his lips and smirked. "Nope."

Kole rolled his eyes, pointed at him with his fork and said, "This food is amazing. I'm glad you showed me this place."

Beck nodded as he finished his mouthful. "It's the worst kept secret around." He grinned, feeling decidedly lighter than he had. He opened his mouth to say something else, but his phone interrupted him. Pulling it from his pocket, he frowned at the private number. Usually, he wouldn't answer, but when the police called him, it said the same—though why they would be calling again, he didn't know.

"Hello?"

"Mr Cavanagh, it's Detective Conrad. We'd like you to come to the station. We have some new information that's come to light."

"What is it?" He stared at Kole, his stomach doing somersaults.

"I'd prefer to talk in person. There's no rush, though. Just whenever you can."

Beck licked his lips. "Okay. I'll be down shortly."

"Thank you. See you then."

The call ended, and Beck stared at the screen. Had they let Drake out? No, surely they would've said that on the phone if that was the case. Had he escaped? No, again, he was sure they would've told him. What could they need him for? He'd given them everything he had and more. The only thing that was left was his blood and sweat. They already had his tears.

"Are you okay?"

Kole's words brought Beck back to the present, and he blinked. "Yeah. I think. The police want to see me again. Apparently, they've found something."

"That sounds like good news...in a way." Kole put his cutlery down. "I can pay for this if you need to go."

Beck shook his head, scraping his teeth across his lower lip. Did he have the courage to ask? He met Kole's gaze. "Will you come with me?"

"Of course. But only if you're sure. I don't want you to feel like you have to ask me because I'm here."

Beck let out a long breath. "No. I want you there." He reached across and rested his hand on top of Kole's. "I think...I need you there."

Kole twisted his hand until they were palm to palm. "Then here I'll be until you no longer need me."

"I think that'll be a while," Beck whispered.

Kole smiled, the corners of his eyes crinkling. "I'm glad to hear it."

Miko interrupted them before Beck could make even more of a fool of himself. "Would you like anything else?"

Beck pulled back and cleared his throat. "Just the bill, please."

"Alrighty." Miko disappeared as quickly as he arrived, returning faster than anyone Beck had ever known. "Here you go."

Handing him a card, Beck said, "Add a ten-pound tip for yourself."

Miko's jaw dropped. "I can't do that!"

"Yes, you can. Ask your mother."

Miko glanced over his shoulder at the counter, and Beck grinned when Sofia waved at them. Beck signed the question to her, and she beamed back at him, signing her response to Miko, who turned back to him. "Wow, I didn't realise that was allowed."

"As long as you don't go asking for tips, I think you're all good."

"Thank you," Miko said and signed. "Have a great day."

When the brisk, cold air filled his lungs, Kole nudged his shoulder. "I didn't know you could sign."

"Yeah, I learnt it on the road. One of my clients is deaf, and I wanted them to not have to pay for a translator every time they came to me. It's amazing how many people you bump into who are deaf that you wouldn't have been able to talk to otherwise."

"You're a man of many talents." They stopped at Beck's bike, and Kole's gaze darted from him to the bike and back again. "I can get the bus or a taxi."

Beck chuckled. "I have a spare helmet if you're okay with riding behind me."

Kole swallowed, his Adam's apple bobbing deeply. "Sure."

He retrieved the helmet, helping Kole to buckle it on before he swung his leg over it and kicked off the stand. The engine roared to life, vibrating through his body and calming him. A similar feeling to how Kole made him feel. He glanced at him and held out his hand. Kole slipped his hand into his, and Beck helped brace him as he climbed onto the back. The warmth seeped into his legs and back immediately, and he exhaled slowly as Kole slid his arms around his waist.

"Ready?" Beck asked.

"Always."

Despite knowing the bike still made Kole a little uneasy, Beck roared off, delighting in the tightening of Kole's arms and the slight noise he heard before the wind whipped it away. Beck kept to the speed limit through the streets of London, weaving his way to the police station. The closer they came, the more his stomach churned and his chest ached. What had they found?

It took every ounce of stubbornness to stop the bike in the car park and not carry on until he reached the ocean. Breathing deeply, he turned off the bike, holding it steady while Kole climbed off, and then kicked the stand into place. He gripped his helmet tightly, feeling the sturdiness of it beneath his leather gloves, before locking it and Kole's to the bike so he didn't have to carry it.

"I'm here, Beck. Whatever they say, I'm here."

Beck stared into Kole's eyes, immediately feeling grounded. He cupped Kole's jaw, brushing his thumb over his cheek. "I will never understand what I've done to deserve you giving me your time," he whispered.

"You must've been a saint in a previous life."

It took a second for his words to sink in, but then Beck snorted a laugh. "I must've been." He dropped his hand. "Thank you."

"You're extremely welcome. The bill is in the post."

Beck shook his head, unable to stop the smile from spreading across his face. It was so much easier to face the police with Kole by his side. Why had he not done it before? He shoved that down, grabbed Kole's hand and strode for the doors. His heart skipped a beat when he entered, but he ignored it and stopped at the counter.

"I'm here to see—"

"Mr Cavanagh, this way."

Beck looked to the side where Detective Haynes stood. Tightening his hand around Kole's, he led the way. Haynes paused outside a door, glancing at Kole.

"He's staying," Beck said before the officer could object.

Haynes hesitated but nodded, opening the door and gesturing for them to enter.

"Give us a couple of minutes," Haynes said.

The detective closed the door behind them, leaving Beck standing in the centre of a windowless office. Again. Not for long, though.

Conrad entered before Haynes and closed them in again. "It's good to see you again, Mr Cavanagh."

"Beck, please." Conrad nodded. "What is this about?"

"Have a seat. We have a bit of information to share and then a request."

Beck swallowed and let go of Kole's hand. They settled into chairs, and he said, "What's happened?"

Conrad leaned forward, elbows resting on the table. "As I mentioned, we were going to look into Drake Price's past. Well, we did, and what we found was a trail of people. Some of whom are also willing to testify."

Beck covered his mouth, staring at Conrad. He wanted to ask who but knew that was confidential. The only other thought that kept going around his head was, "How many?"

Conrad's expression softened, as much as it could. "Seven."

"But we think there has been more," Haynes added.

"Don't forget, if you tell anyone about this, I'll find a new playmate. Maybe Rebecca or Sarah. Maybe even Allan, if I'm feeling

generous," Drake sneered, his face too close for Beck to focus on fully.

"I won't," Beck said, swallowing the sob that wanted to escape. If that happened, Drake would make things worse.

"Good. Now be a good boy and turn over."

Beck returned to the room with a shaky inhale to find Kole rubbing his back and a glass of water clasped in his hands that he didn't remember reaching for.

"How are you doing?" Kole asked.

"Just peachy." He coupled it with a small smile to show he wasn't as far gone as they probably thought he was. "How did you find so many so fast?"

"He wasn't quiet about his conquests."

"You said there was also a request."

Conrad nodded slowly. "Obviously, everyone's details are confidential, but one of the women has asked if you will meet with her."

Beck frowned. "Why?"

"She knows you."

He tried to think who it could be, and horror flooded his veins. "Who?" he croaked.

"Rebecca Straith."

Beck dropped his head into his hands. *Rebecca.* He didn't recognise the surname, but if it was who he thought it was, he hadn't been able to protect her at all. Everything he had done was to keep them safe from Drake, but there was one part of his story he hadn't wanted to think too much about—when he was told to leave. Because that meant there was no one to protect the other kids once he was gone. And it seemed that Drake might've focused on Rebecca.

"Yes. I'll meet her."

"She's willing to come in today to see you if that's okay?"

Beck exhaled. "Does it have to be here?"

Conrad shook their head. "No. I thought it might be easier here, but you're welcome to meet up anywhere. I just had to get permission from you beforehand."

"It won't mess up our testimonies if we talk before the trial?"

"We have your testimonies already on file and recorded, so we will be fine." Conrad handed him a piece of paper. "This is Rebecca's phone number."

He stared at the scribble, wondering if he was doing the right thing. Would it hurt or help each other if they met up and talked about the past?

16

KOLE

K ole could see the indecision on Beck's face from the moment he was handed the paper; he took it as if it was made of glass, resting it on his shaking palm. Wishing he could make everything better, Kole nodded at the police officers and led Beck out of the station. They didn't talk until they reached the bike.

"Are you going to call her now?" he asked carefully, not wanting to push Beck too far.

Beck scraped his lower lip with his teeth, a tick he was showing more and more recently. "I don't know if it's a good idea."

"How come?"

Beck exhaled roughly and rested back against his bike, still staring at the slip of paper. "What if she blames me?"

"I don't think she would ask to meet you—or that the police would allow it—if she blamed you. But, if she does, you deal with it. You can't control other people's opinions. You know this more than the average person, being in the spotlight already."

Beck tilted his head as he stared at him, making butterflies swarm in Kole's stomach. "Thank you," he murmured. He dropped his gaze to the paper again, but then he pulled his phone free and pressed the screen several times. Inhaling deeply, he put the phone to his ear and met Kole's gaze once more.

Kole had no idea how the conversation was going to go, but if Beck needed to stare at him to get through it, then he would glue his feet to the ground for as long as he needed him to. He couldn't begin to imagine what was going through Beck's mind. Having people he had lost contact with years prior just turn up, out of the blue, was a difficult scenario.

"Um, hi," Beck said, his voice strained. "Is that...Rebecca?"

Kole couldn't hear what the other person was saying, but Beck blinked a few times, his nostrils flaring.

"Yeah, yes. That...would be nice." He listened a bit more. "Um, there's a pub called Forest Tavern in Stratford. Two hours? Okay. See you then." He paused and then pulled the phone from his ear.

Kole watched him swallow as he slowly put the phone in his jacket pocket and waited him out, knowing he was processing the conversation.

"Is it bad of me that I specifically chose a place I rarely visit to meet her? I didn't like the idea of..." He exhaled and frowned. "I suppose, souring is the right word. I didn't want our meeting to sour the places I like to go. That sounds awful. I'm sure she's lovely."

"I'm sure she is, too. But I completely understand that. You need to be able to have a safe place. A place you can keep free from issues. It was a good choice."

At that exact moment, the hair stood up on the back of his neck, and it took everything in him to not react. He clenched his jaw and every muscle in his body to keep his fight-or-flight response from kicking in. Every time it happened, he swore it felt like someone was watching him. Previously, he would've studied his surroundings and walked away, but he couldn't leave Beck alone.

"What's wrong?"

Kole blinked, bringing Beck back into focus, and found the man on his feet and looking around. "Nothing."

"Kole."

The voice that brooked no argument was back, and while Kole appreciated the return of some normalcy, he wished it wasn't at the expense of his mental health.

"I think I just need to get out of here. Are you okay to head out now?"

Beck stepped closer, lowering his head to look directly into his eyes. "We're good to go, but talk to me."

"Later. Please." He wasn't sure he had enough air in his lungs for a full conversation right then.

Beck studied him for a long moment, then nodded. "As soon as we get back."

But he knew Beck would let it go if Kole said no. It didn't take them long to get on the bike and back home. He felt awful for wanting the ride to last longer so that he could not have the conversation he knew Beck would want to have. How could he explain his issues? That he saw and felt things that weren't there? That he was scared of his own shadow some days? It made him feel weak and defenceless, and he hated that. He was able to acknowledge that he was a lot better than he had been, and he truly believed that was due to his new home and the amazing people he worked with. Plus Ethan, he supposed. That thought brought a small smile to his face as they entered Beck's house.

"Are you feeling better?" Beck asked as they removed their coats and hung them up.

Kole inhaled and let it out slowly, relaxing his body in the familiar space. "Yes, thanks."

Beck stared at him for a long second and then headed for the kitchen. "Would you like a drink?" He rounded the counter and met Kole's gaze again. The corners of his mouth lifted. "A hot chocolate maybe?"

"I'd never say no to that." Kole settled onto the stool and watched him putter around. After a few minutes, he started talking. "I feel someone watching me sometimes. It raises the hair on the back of my neck, and depending on my mood, I either run or freeze." He huffed. "Or breakdown." He wrung his hands, rubbing some warmth into them. "There is never anyone there, but it feels like it. I hate it. I hate that I have no control over it. When it happens, I mean."

"How do you know?"

Kole frowned, going over his words to figure out what he meant. "Know what?" he asked when he couldn't.

"How do you know no one is there?"

"Whenever I look around, I can't see anyone."

Beck poured the milk into the hot chocolate, the clink of the spoon against the mug soothing in its monotony. "People are good at hiding," he murmured, sprinkling a small handful of marshmallows over the top. "I know that far too well."

Kole stared down at his hands, thinking back on the earlier times. He couldn't remember exactly when they first started happening, but there had been no one there. At least...he thought there hadn't been. Bringing up the night of the event, the night Beck had helped him, he walked himself through the memory. It was dark, and people were walking past him. Laughter, conversation, until...there wasn't. It had gone quiet. He hadn't remembered that. It was as if someone had blocked his ears or turned down the volume. He remembered the feeling of unease, the tingling on the back of his neck, skating down his spine. How his hands started to shake.

He closed his eyes, sinking himself further into the memory. The hotel hadn't been too far ahead; the lights seemed to glare bright. He looked over his shoulder, tracing the shadows with his gaze. Nothing stood out.

Swallowing, he paused. No, that wasn't true. He didn't want it to stand out. Warmth covered his hands, and he turned them over to grip tightly as he looked closer at the shadows. A figure disentangled themselves, stepping free. Someone with broad shoulders, hands in pockets with a baseball cap on.

His breathing increased. Who was it? His hands trembled as his heart pounded with knowledge. He snapped his eyes open.

"No."

Beck tightened his hold on him. "I'm here."

The words Kole had previously said to Beck settled him more than he expected. He took a breath. "Someone was there." He met Beck's gaze. "How did you know?"

Beck shrugged. "Your body's responses don't lie. If something is telling you to run, then there's usually some reason for it."

"But who?" Beck stared at him, and Kole realised he knew the answer but hadn't wanted to. "Andrew."

"Is it?" Beck asked.

Kole brought the image to the forefront again. "I think so."

"Maybe we can talk to the police about it."

"I don't think there would be any point, would there?"

"Why not? It seems he's still following you. They should be able to do something about it. Even if it's just to warn him away."

Kole thought about it as Beck put a mug of hot chocolate in his hands. The heat burnt his palms, but he didn't move it. He needed the grounding it gave him.

"Drink," Beck ordered from beside him.

Kole did. Pushing aside his own issues, he asked, "How are you feeling?"

Beck licked his lips, staring at his mug. "Weird. I still don't know if it's her, but I think it is. I'm hoping she doesn't hate me."

"She won't. You weren't to blame for what *he* did."

Beck nodded slowly. He didn't believe him, but Kole would do everything he could to make him believe it one day. Maybe not that day. Maybe not the next day, but eventually, he would help Beck to understand it wasn't his fault what Drake did.

"Finish your drink. We'll have to leave soon."

Kole didn't push, so he let them drop into silence and drank his drink. And when Beck dragged himself from his stool, Kole followed suit. The silence lasted through the journey to the pub, and when they paused beside the bike, studying the building, Kole slipped his hand into Beck's and squeezed. He heard Beck's inhale and exhale before he stepped forward, Kole staying beside him.

Unsure what to expect but having a feeling it would be an emotional time—because Kole was certain this was the Rebecca from Beck's past—he kept quiet, trying to be as much of a rock as he could. Beck had been so helpful to him, especially with his most recent revelation—something he'd think about another time.

The pub wasn't very busy, and as soon as they entered, a woman with long, dark hair stood from a stool at the bar. She stared at Beck, and Beck stared back. Kole squeezed his hand again, not only to show solidarity but to break the moment enough to not cause too many heads to turn their way.

Beck stepped closer. "Rebecca," he whispered.

The woman licked her lips, one side of her mouth curving up. "It's just Becca."

Beck huffed a laugh. "You used to tell us off for calling you anything but Rebecca."

"I had to put my foot down about something. There were far more boys than girls." She cleared her throat. "Would you like a drink?"

"A lemonade would be great, thanks." Beck turned to him. "What would you like?"

"A glass of water would be good, please."

Becca ordered for them, and when she turned back to them, Beck said, "This is Kole, my boyfriend."

"Nice to meet you," Kole said through a closed throat. He hadn't expected such an introduction, but he couldn't deny he was pleased.

"You, too," Becca said. She gestured to a table. "Shall we sit?"

They headed over and settled in, the gentle conversation humming around them, the music only just loud enough to mask their words. It had a homey feel to it, kind of rustic, and Kole liked it.

"I asked to speak to you because I had so much to say, but now you're here, I can't think of any of it." She sighed. "I'm so sorry, Beck."

Beck played with the condensation on his glass. "You have nothing to be sorry for. If anything, I am the one who should be sorry. I thought he'd stop when I got sent away. I don't know why I thought that. Maybe I just needed to believe it, but I need you to know... I tried to tell them. I tried several times, but they didn't believe me." He huffed. "Or if they did, they didn't care."

"Oh, they knew," Becca said. "I heard them talking weeks after you went. I didn't really understand it at that age, but thinking back now, I know what they meant. You weren't the first, either."

"I wish I had been the last."

Becca leaned forward. "What happened to me was not your fault. Drake's an asshole. He always has been."

"I hope he goes away for a long time."

Becca tilted her head, her hair slipping over her shoulder to cover her arm. "What made you say something now? If you don't mind me asking, that is?" she added quickly.

Beck looked at Kole, his eyes roaming his face and making Kole feel hot all over. "He hurt the man I love."

Kole's heart pounded painfully. He could barely breathe. Where had the guy who didn't want attachment gone? Not that he wanted that, but Beck seemed to be jumping through so many relationship hoops very quickly. If Kole didn't want it so much, he might've been concerned. Well, he was concerned, but that was up for discussion another time.

"Aww, you two are so cute together. But I'm sorry to hear that you got hurt, too. As I said, he's an asshole."

"How long did you stay with the Prices?" Beck asked, taking the spotlight off their relationship.

"Another four years." She stared at her glass, though her eyes were unfocused. "They only sent me away when I started making too much noise about what they were hiding."

"Did social services not do anything?" Kole asked.

Becca snorted. "They wanted nothing to do with it. If they could pretend it wasn't happening and that I needed moving for a different reason, they would." She met his gaze. "Less paperwork, you see."

Kole shook his head. "I sometimes wonder how these people keep their jobs."

"Well, if they're still doing them now, they won't be for long."

"Why?"

Becca smiled. "I'm a social worker myself now. They wouldn't look too kindly on people who hurt one of their own, even if it was before my time. I guarantee, if those workers are still doing the same role, they'll be out on their asses before the end of the week. Even if it's just to cover the higher up's *asses*."

"Do you know how many people he hurt?" Beck asked.

Becca bit her lip. "I have an idea, but some won't come forward."

"How many?"

She stared at him for a long minute, then sighed. "You were number two. I was number four. Including Kole as his most recent, I believe the number is around twenty-four."

Beck inhaled shakily and panted, pushing his chair back as he rested his hands on his head. Kole rubbed his back, encouraging his head further down to help with his breathing.

"It's okay, Beck. I'm here. Breathe for me. Just breathe. In. And out." He repeated the mantra into his ear, hoping that at least some of his words got through to him.

When Beck lifted his head, tears stained his face. "I should've fought harder. He has darkened many lives. I should've stopped him."

Kole opened his mouth to answer, but Becca beat him to it. "You couldn't. They wouldn't let you. It wasn't that you weren't loud enough, Beck. It was that you were too loud. They silenced you the only way they could. Labelling you a troublemaker. You did the right thing. You *lived* to tell the tale."

Her words brought tears to Kole's eyes. She was so right, and although he could see how Beck could feel about not having been able to stop Drake before, the fact that he lived his life to the degree he had was amazing.

"I'm waiting for the Prices to get their fifteen minutes of fame with this," Becca said. "Although, hopefully, they'll stay hidden if they know what's best for them."

"I need to go," Beck said but made no move to leave. "Can we do this again?"

Becca smiled. "Absolutely. You have my number. Call me anytime."

"Thank you for the drinks," Kole said as they stood.

"It was nice to meet you, Kole. Take care of this lug." She grinned, and Kole had a feeling they would be seeing more of her. In fact, he might make it a demand. She might be a good influence on Beck's mental health.

Becca gripped Beck's arms, and they stared at each other in silence for a moment before she pulled him into a hug. "Take care."

Beck nodded, and they headed for the door. At the bike, Beck dropped his head back and exhaled roughly. "That happened."

"It did."

Beck glanced at him. "I'm guessing you didn't black out some of what I said back there."

Kole's stomach somersaulted. "You're guessing right."

The man he was madly in love with stepped closer, pushing Kole back into the bike seat and caging him with his arms. His gaze traced his face again, something Kole noticed he was beginning to do a lot. "Bloody hell, Kole. How did you happen? How did you become so important in such a short time? How have you fit so seamlessly into my life? As if you've always been there."

Kole swallowed. "Must be talent," he whispered.

Beck cupped his jaw and kissed him. Kole let him. After all, who in their right mind would say no? He was lightheaded and weak-kneed by the time Beck finished devouring him.

"I need you, my love," Beck said, and if Kole hadn't already been in love with him, those words would've cemented it.

"You have me."

"Let's go home."

As they wound their way through the streets, Kole wondered if he was strong enough to be what Beck needed. Could he provide what he was almost certain Beck needed in the bedroom? Could he dominate Beck fully? At the end of the day, they would find their rhythm, he had no doubt, but he wanted to be able to give Beck everything. And though his lover was unlikely to admit it—even then—Kole needed to be that person for him. He needed to be Beck's haven. He *wanted* to be it. The question was, how?

17

BECK

D espite feeling emotionally, mentally and physically wrung
out from the meeting with Rebecca—Becca—Beck also had
an itch inside him. He needed what he always needed when he
felt like this. Sex. But not with just anyone. The idea of sleeping
with anyone who wasn't Kole sent a shiver up his spine. He
needed Kole in a way he had never needed someone before. And
he needed him right away.

He barely gave Kole enough time to safely climb off the bike
before he'd turned it off, grabbed Kole's hand and dragged him
into the house. The swarm of ants feasted on his body as he made
himself wait until they were in the bedroom before he faced the
man he loved and paused. His chest heaved, and he could taste
the sweat on his upper lip.

Kole tilted his head, his mouth curving at the corners, and said,
"Take your clothes off, Mr Cavanaugh."

And with those six words, Beck's world narrowed to where
there was only him and Kole. His hands were already unbuttoning
his trousers by the time his mind checked in again, his shirt
already gone.

"That's it," Kole breathed. "Show me everything."

And boy did Beck want to. It wasn't what he usually
did—listening to someone else call the shots—but he pushed the
thought away and focused on Kole and his words. It was so much
better than drowning in his own mind.

When he was naked, Kole stepped closer, lifting his hands and skimming his fingertips across Beck's skin. Goosebumps followed in his wake, as did Beck's gaze. Kole left no area untouched, and by the time he returned to his starting point, Beck's knees shook.

"Lay down on the bed."

Beck licked his lips at the order, swallowed hard and obeyed. The second his back hit the bed, it was as if his body understood. He sank into the mattress, letting his limbs stay where they fell, and let out a long exhale.

Kole towered over him. "Are you okay?"

He nodded. His throat had closed enough to require some heavy swallowing before he could talk. "Yeah."

"Do you want me to stop?"

That made him smile. "Not even a little."

"In that case…" Kole smirked and crawled onto the bed, caging him in with his arms and legs. As he looked down at him, Beck stared into his eyes, knowing exactly where his heart lay—at Kole's feet.

"Why has it taken me so long?" he whispered, mainly to himself.

Kole seemed to understand. "Because you weren't ready. And neither was I. We both needed each other but didn't know it." He brushed his fingers across Beck's cheek. "I never believed I could trust anyone. Until you."

"But I'm broken."

Kole shook his head, grabbing Beck's jaw with his fingertips. "You're not broken. You're bruised. As am I. But bruises heal. They might leave a mark behind for a while, but they heal. As will we. Togcthcr."

"I love you," Beck said, unable to keep it in.

Kole smiled. "I love you."

Beck lurched up, fusing their lips in a kiss as soft as it was harsh. Kole responded in kind, and they tangled for a while, slowly decreasing the intensity while increasing the fire. Kole manoeuvred him onto his back again, and the feeling of Kole being fully dressed against his nakedness sent fuel through his body. He wanted that man with a burning he couldn't explain, but his body knew, as did his subconscious. His conscious mind was beginning to catch up. Finally. Although...

"Get undressed," he said when he pulled away for air.

"Soon."

Beck shook his head. "Now. I feel like..." He paused, shaking his head, not wanting to explain, but when he glanced at Kole, he saw patience. "I feel like you're ready to leave."

Kole dropped a kiss on his lips and lifted from him, standing beside the bed. Beck instantly missed his warmth, but that fire roared when Kole's fingers went to his buttons. It didn't take long, and Kole didn't take his eyes off him the whole time. Then, not even three minutes later, Kole was back, the warmth of his skin sliding over Beck's as he returned to his previous position.

Cradling Beck's face in his hands, Kole said, "You can always ask for anything you want or need. No matter what it is, don't be afraid to ask. I will never curb your ability to choose the best option for you. I might ask you to do something, but I will never make it an order you can't disobey if you need to. Do you understand?"

He did. Kole was giving him the control, even as he was taking it from him. Something Beck had never thought he could allow anyone to do. Drake had taken his control away from him, and he hadn't been able to stand anyone else having that again. Until now.

He told Kole as much.

"Thank you for giving yourself the chance," Kole said. "You are the bravest man I know."

Beck shook his head. "You make me feel brave."

"I'm glad I could help." Kole stared at him for a second and then lowered his head.

The kiss started slow but soon heated. Kole's fingers were everywhere, skimming across his skin. A sea of goosebumps followed, making him shiver. As their lips separated, Beck dropped his head back, giving Kole room to reach his neck. His kiss-swollen lips continued the path down his body, focusing far too briefly on each of his nipples before moving lower. Beck's cock loved the attention, twitching and leaking with every nip and lick, and he raked his teeth over his lips to contain his groans. At least until Kole met his gaze and said, "Let me hear it, Beck. I want to hear everything."

Beck gripped the sheets by his sides, fisting the fabric to keep himself from grabbing Kole by the hair and putting him where he wanted him. The place weeping and aching for him.

And the place Kole wrapped his hand around.

"Holy fuck, Kole." He repeated the refrain when his lover's mouth encased his cock head but couldn't keep his eyes away from him. Watching his dick disappear into his mouth was one of the hottest things he'd ever witnessed, and feeling it at the same time was mind-blowing. He was right on the edge almost immediately. He panted to keep as much control as he could, but what Kole was doing with his tongue should have been illegal.

When Kole lifted his head, Beck dropped his back to the pillow, his chest heaving.

"You okay?"

Beck swallowed and nodded. "Yeah. Bloody hell. Where did you learn that?" He glanced at Kole. "Actually, don't answer that. I don't want to know. I'm just glad you did."

Kole grinned. "Glad my experience has helped." He licked his lips. "Where is your lube?"

Beck reached for it and handed it over, barely moving from his position. "Kole..." He inhaled deeply, then met his gaze again. "I just want you to know... I want this. I know what I've said before, about not wanting to lose control, about having to be in charge, but I don't...like it as much like that."

"I know, Beck. And if you'll let me, trust me, I'll make it good for you."

Beck rose until they were almost chest to chest and cupped Kole's jaw. "I know you will. That doesn't worry me one bit."

"But what does worry you?"

He exhaled, mapping Kole's face with his gaze. "That I won't be enough for you. That I'll freak out." He closed his eyes and shook his head. "And now I've ruined the mood."

His hands were shoved off Kole's face, and his eyes snapped open. But before he could apologise, Kole's hands copied Beck's gesture, sliding across the skin of his jaw. "You haven't ruined anything. If anything, it has made me want you even more." Beck frowned, and Kole hesitated before continuing. "I love having control, Beck. I love being able to give you everything you need, especially when you can't articulate that you need it. I love being the one responsible for making you cry out because I've found something you didn't realise you loved. I want to be that for you. I *need* to be that for you."

Tears filled Beck's eyes, and he blinked rapidly to stop their fall, to no avail. "Thank you," he croaked.

Kole kissed him, pushing him backwards onto the bed again. And then his mouth left his and detoured down his body once more. Encasing his cock in wet heat again, Kole went to town, taking Beck right to the edge. But then he pressed against Beck's pucker, his wet finger massaging the area before pushing more forcibly. Beck bore down, hissing when it slid inside his channel for the first time in far too many years. The sensation, while not foreign, sent his brain spinning. Or was it the pleasure racing through him? He hoped for the latter.

"Talk to me, Beck," Kole said, having paused in his ministrations.

"I'm okay. It's just...a lot."

"Do you want me to back off?"

"No!" Beck glanced down at him. "No. Please. Keep going."

Kole stared at him for a moment before he curled his finger and pressed against the spot inside him, sending his brain spinning once more, but for slightly different reasons. He'd never experienced that, though he'd known about it.

"Holy shit!"

Kole chuckled around his cock, and it sent more vibrations through him. Beck closed his eyes and let himself feel everything Kole was doing to him. A second finger joined the first, the initial burn something that tried to send him back to when he was younger, but he refused to let it. It helped that Kole was sucking his dick because Drake never did that. A third finger. A fourth, and Beck was right on the edge of coming. Kole must've realised it, too, because he removed his mouth.

"Ready for more?" Kole whispered.

Beck opened his eyes. "Always with you." And it was at that moment that Beck realised something he'd always known but hadn't realised he'd known—Beck had the control. Being a bottom was all about control regardless of what he'd thought before. Kole had the power to force him, but he wouldn't. Beck had the ability and the right to say no, and Kole would obey him. With that epiphany, every muscle in his body relaxed, and Kole's eyebrows rose.

"I love you," Beck said. "You'll never hurt me."

"I won't. Not intentionally."

Kole pulled his fingers free and sat upright, his cock ready and willing to take Beck. He slicked it well, Beck watching his every move, and then Kole braced himself on one hand while pressing the head against Beck's hole. Beck slid his hands up Kole's body until he reached his face and cupped his jaw.

"I trust you. I love you."

"I love you, too."

Kole pressed in, and Beck's breath caught at the welcome intrusion. The heat, the uncompromising pressure, the stretching. The *pleasure*. It was everything his previous times had never been.

When Kole was fully seated, he caged Beck in with his arms, and Beck wrapped his legs around his waist, needing the full-body connection for just a moment. Beck kissed him and slowly built the intensity of it until all he could feel, hear, taste, see and smell was Kole. He was all around him. And when Kole finally started moving, it was everything.

Tears overflowed as their movements increased, the push and pull of their bodies indicating a frenzy was oncoming. Beck unhooked his legs, resting his feet against the bed so he had more leverage and for Kole to go deeper, but Kole had other ideas. He grabbed Beck's legs and lifted them to his shoulders before slamming into him. Beck's eyes crossed at the pleasure, the heated flush working its way through his nerves, his muscles, his skin, everywhere. All he could hear was their panting breaths and the slap of their skin, and it was beautiful music.

He wrapped his hands around his cock and stroked, his other hand reaching above him to brace himself on the headboard.

"Fuck, yes." Beck gritted his teeth, unable to look away from Kole, sweat dripping down both their faces. "Give it to me."

"Jesus, Beck. Don't talk like that if you want me to last."

"Fuck me, baby. Come on. Give it to me."

Kole's rhythm faltered, his grip tightening on Beck's thighs, and Beck increased his stroking. "Fuck, fuck," Kole chanted and held himself deep inside Beck.

Beck helped himself over the edge at the same time, his head dropping backwards as his climax rushed through him, wracking his body with contractions. With the rushing in his ears, he couldn't hear anything except Kole's cursing, and he couldn't help smiling.

He let out a long exhale when his body finally stopped and caught Kole as he slumped forward.

"Holy shit, Beck," Kole panted.

"That's my line."

Kole chuckled and kissed him briefly. "That was..." He didn't finish, just shook his head, and Beck grinned, feeling much lighter than he had before, almost as if a weight had been lifted from his shoulders.

They stayed that way for a long while, even as their skin cooled, and goosebumps covered them both. It was only when a shiver wracked Kole's body that Beck's instincts had him rolling them over so he could climb off the bed and start a bath. He put in some lavender bubble bath and headed back to the room. Kole hadn't moved an inch, although he was awake, but his eyes tracked Beck's movements.

"What?" Beck asked.

Kole smiled. "You're amazing."

A warmth heated his body, nothing to do with arousal this time, and he cursed silently as his cheeks flushed. He knew they had because he felt it. "You're not too bad yourself."

"High praise." Kole sat upright. "You're running a bath?"

Beck nodded. "We could do with a relaxing soak, I think."

"Sounds like a plan." He stood. "I'll grab some nibbles for us." He slipped on Beck's robe and disappeared after another smile in Beck's direction.

Alone, Beck expected some of his previous thoughts and images to bombard him, but nothing showed its head. For the first time in such a long time, he was completely at ease. Completely and absolutely and undyingly content. And it was weird. Wonderful, but weird. Wonderfully weird.

Shaking off his crazy thoughts, he aimed for the bathroom again and checked the water level, how many towels he had and anything else he might need before Kole appeared, which he did just as he turned off the taps.

"I thought we could do with something to drink, too."

He held up two small bottles of Appletiser and a large plate filled with nuts, cheese and other picky foods. Beck chuckled. "I'd forgotten about those drinks."

They climbed into the bath, and Beck leaned against Kole's chest, his head resting back on his shoulder. Closing his eyes, he breathed deeply, enjoying the scent hanging in the room.

"How do you feel?"

Beck inhaled and held it, then let it out slowly. "Really good. I had thought talking to Becca would terrorise me or something, but I think it actually helped."

"I'm glad."

"I don't know where we're going from here, but I feel positive about the future for the first time in a long time."

"And what does your future hold, Beck?"

"Tattoos, friends, family, fun and fu—"

"I get the picture." Kole laughed, covering Beck's mouth with his hand.

He snorted and moved until his hand dislodged. "I was going to say *full stomach*. Someone has a dirty mind!"

"Yeah, sure you were, Casanova."

Beck chuckled and closed his eyes again. "What are your plans, Kole?"

"Tattoos, friends, family, fun and...giving you everything you want."

Beck's heart pounded as he met Kole's gaze, and he slid his arm around Kole's neck and kissed him. "You already have."

18

KOLE

They had met up with Becca twice more since their initial meeting three weeks prior. Kole could see the difference in Beck since that first one, and he was so proud of what he'd achieved. In that time, he'd also received a message from his friend, Donovan, to say he was involved with the case, too. Donovan had been the only person Beck had kept in touch with from his foster days, and that was only because he hadn't taken no for an answer when he'd originally found Beck when they were older.

Unfortunately, Donovan had also had a run-in with Drake but had been rehomed quickly. From what Beck told him, Donovan had been Drake's first victim, their time at the Prices only overlapping by a few months. Despite not knowing what had happened to each other, they had shelved the past and pathed a future as friends, even so much so that Donovan had introduced Beck to Prince Christian, who regularly received tattoos, too.

But there had still been a slight pall over them—Drake. He'd been remanded in custody without bail being allowed, but the police had been in touch to say they had wrangled a quick hearing. That was good news in some ways, but not in others.

Beck had taken the news in his stride, but the strain was showing as the time drew nearer. He'd been to see a counsellor several times to help with the process of being on the witness stand and reliving everything for everyone to hear, and they'd spent every night wrapped around each other.

Kole wouldn't admit it, but he had been sure that Beck would pull away from him as the date arrived, but he hadn't. If anything, he'd pulled Kole closer, which he hadn't argued with. If he could've wrapped Beck in cotton wool and kept him from having to go through the process, he would've. He was certain Beck would have said the same thing about Kole's previous situation, too.

They had the full support of the Life in Ink crew, as expected, and when the morning of the hearing dawned, Beck had received messages from all of them, confirming they would be there for him. That was another thing Kole had thought Beck would disagree with—having his friends listen to every sordid detail, but Beck surprised him once more. When they'd told him that, he'd thanked them and nothing more. Kole had wanted to discuss it, but he'd refused to make Beck explain himself, so he'd left it.

"Are you ready to go?" Kole asked, stopping beside Beck.

Beck faced him, and though the strain was there, there was also determination in those beautiful orbs. "Absolutely."

The bike ride, despite being a frosty morning, was beautiful as the sun glowed in the cloudless sky. Kole held tightly to Beck's waist until he parked. Before Kole even climbed off the bike, he could see the crowd of people waiting outside the nondescript building, but he couldn't see who they were. His mind, however, wandered a little when he felt the hair rise on the back of his neck. He tried to ignore it.

Beck stopped beside him and exhaled. "Let's go." He slipped his hand into Kole's and squeezed.

As they drew closer, Kole raised his eyebrows and sucked in a breath. There were loads of people. "What is this for?" he muttered.

Beck stopped walking, and Kole glanced at him. "Holy shit," Beck breathed.

Joey came towards them before Kole could find out what that expletive was about. "Hey. I would ask how you are doing, but..." He pulled Beck into a hug and clapped his back. "We're here for you all the way."

"Thanks." Beck looked around. "I wasn't expecting so many people to be here."

Joey nodded, his gaze going to the crowd. "Ryker heard along the grapevine about this and insisted on being here. Naturally, the rest of them came with him. After all, this is part of what they do and who they are."

"Yeah. Never expected it to be me, though," Beck said.

Kole squeezed his hand, even though he didn't understand the dynamic with the legion of bikers he could see mixed in with the other people. Becca separated herself from the mass and headed towards them. Joey clapped Beck on the shoulder again and headed back to Ethan.

"Hey," Becca said.

"Good morning," Beck replied. "Are you okay?"

Becca tilted her head from side to side. "So-so. I'll be better when this is over. As will the rest of them."

"Rest of who?"

Becca pointed to a small group of people slightly separate from the rest. "Who he hurt."

Kole counted. Sixteen. *Sixteen* people, not including Beck and Becca, were standing there waiting to give evidence against Drake and send him to prison. *Sixteen*. That asshole had a lot to answer for.

"I didn't realise there were so many," Beck said.

"I didn't either. It's only when I spoke to Detective Conrad yesterday that I thought to ask how many others might come. I couldn't believe he'd found so many."

Kole glanced at Beck to see how much of a toll the news had taken on him, but Beck's eyes narrowed, focused as he was on the group, until he straightened.

"Let's send this fucker down." Beck grinned at Becca, resting his hand on her shoulder.

"Abso-fucking-lutely."

"Beck!"

Beck turned at his name, a smile Kole hadn't been sure he'd see tagt day spreading across his face. "Donovan." They hugged, eyes wet when they released. "I'm so sorry."

"You don't need to be sorry. This has been a long time coming. I'm ready for it." He tugged at the man beside him. "This is Wally, my boyfriend."

"Sorry about meeting under these circumstances," Wally said.

"We'll arrange something lighter soon."

"Definitely," Beck agreed. "This is Kole, *my* boyfriend."

Donovan beamed. "It's so nice to meet you. I'm glad you caught this lug."

"Hey!" Beck said.

"I can't imagine not having him."

"Time to go," Becca said, interrupting gently.

They all shared determined gazes and squared their shoulders. They headed for the building, Beck never once removing his hand from Kole's, and joined the mass of people. Breaking through after several greetings, they climbed the steps and entered, the warmth from inside not even touching the ice Kole held inside. The feeling of being watched had never abated, but he couldn't concentrate on that right then. He had other things to focus on.

It didn't take them long to be guided to the room used for the hearing. The audience, so to speak, entered the court room, while the witnesses—and the person supporting them—headed for another room. They wouldn't be allowed in the main room until they had given evidence, and right then, they didn't know who would be called on first. They had a police officer in the room with them, ensuring they weren't talking about anything they shouldn't be, but Kole internally laughed at that. If they had wanted to talk about it, they would've done it before then.

Surprisingly, it was barely half an hour before Beck was called in. Kole settled into a chair next to Ethan in the front row while Beck continued through to the witness chair. What followed was an hour of excruciatingly painful details about what Beck went through. He gave every detail they asked him and didn't lose his cool when the defendants tried to paint him in a poor light.

Once Beck was done, he settled beside Kole and grabbed his hand, squeezing hard and shaking so much that Kole wasn't sure how he was still sitting on the chair.

And on it went. Person after person, account after account, a list as long as some of the most prolific bad guys Kole had ever heard of. Not everyone who Drake had hurt had come to court that day, but it wasn't necessary. The Prices had gone on the stand but told complete lies from Kole's point of view.

"The court finds Drake Price guilty of eight counts of rape of a minor, twenty-three counts of rape, eighteen counts of coercion of a minor and eleven counts of aggravated assault. He is sentenced to fifty-two years to be served consecutively," the judge announced. He turned to Drake. "You are a horrible man, and it's my great pleasure to ensure you will not be released for the foreseeable future. Take him away."

Kole watched Drake as the guards came up to him. His face was pale, but he hadn't lost the smirk that had always been present whenever they had been in each other's company. Unfortunately, he also turned to look at Beck, and that smirk turned into a grin. "See you in your dreams, Beck," he called, winking before the guards dragged him off.

"Asshole," Ethan muttered from beside him.

Kole focused on Beck. "Are you okay?"

Beck faced him and smiled, surprising him. "I'm great. Because, do you know what?" Kole didn't need to reply. Beck cupped his jaw and brushed his thumb over his cheek. "He's wrong. It's not him I'll see in my dreams. It's you." Beck kissed him chastely before pulling back.

Kole chuckled. "See? You're a charmer. Always have been."

He wasn't delusional. He knew it wouldn't be as easy as Beck said, that he would need help to get through what would continue to be a difficult time for him, but he also knew Beck wouldn't give up.

As they exited the court, Ryker waited for them. "We're happy to escort anyone who would like the extra support. Just let me know so I can divide us up."

"Thanks, Ryker," said Joey. "Let me ask."

Joey disappeared, leaving them with the biker. Although Kole's initial reaction had been stereotypical—a reaction he was going to try to stop happening—he could see the concern and affection the man had for the crew. How that came about, he wasn't privy to at that moment, but he was certain they would tell him, eventually.

"I haven't experienced what you went through, Beck, but if you need anything at all, any of you, please don't hesitate to let me know. Okay?"

Beck held out his hand. "Thank you, Ryker. I will."

The man disappeared into the crowd—an amazing feat for someone who towered above others—and Beck exhaled. Kole slid his arm around his waist.

"What do you want to do now?"

"Sleep for a week." Beck smiled down at him, the exhaustion evident.

"Come on, then. I'm told I'm a good tucker-in-er." Kole grinned, ignoring the goosebumps rising on the back of his neck again.

Beck chuckled. "I can believe it."

"If you need anything at all…" Ethan said.

If Kole could've offered to drive them home, he would have, but he didn't know how to ride a bike. Beck got them home safely, and when they entered his house, he stopped in the centre of the room. Kole stepped carefully around him until he faced him. The blank expression didn't fool him. He slid his hand into Beck's and tugged him towards the stairs without saying a word.

It went to show exactly how exhausted Beck was that he didn't argue with anything Kole did. He undressed him to his boxers and encouraged him to lie down, pulling the covers over him before crouching beside him.

"I'll be here if you need anything."

Beck nodded slowly, his eyelids already closing. His eyes snapped open again. "I didn't say bye to Donovan."

Kole shushed him gently. "He'll understand. You can call him later."

Kole remained there until Beck's even breathing showed he was asleep, and then he headed for the kitchen, needing a drink. A hot one, not an alcoholic one. As the kettle boiled, he scrubbed his hands over his face and hair, with the feeling of needing to stretch from being confined for a long period. Maybe it had something to do with how long it had taken for them to get to that point. He couldn't imagine what people went through if they'd had to wait months or even years before they got a result. He'd be eternally grateful to the police officers for expediting the court case. He didn't want to envisage how emotionally unstable they would've been if they had to wait much longer.

The kettle clicked off, the steam filling the space above the counter and warming him slightly. He poured the water into his cup and doctored it the way he liked it before wrapping his hands around it and aiming for the living room. He ignored the need to sit in the armchair in Beck's room and watch him sleep because even he wasn't that creepy. Well, not always.

Settling into the sofa, he flicked on the TV and scrolled for far too long, settling on *Gilmore Girls*. He had seen them before, but they were still good, and he wasn't sure he could concentrate on anything heavier.

His phone beeped.

ETHAN: *Hey, how is Beck doing?*
KOLE: *He's out cold. Understandable, really.*
ETHAN: *Definitely. He's so fucking brave, recanting everything that happened to him. I don't know if I would've been able to do that.*
KOLE: *Me neither.*
ETHAN: *Everyone at the shop is overwhelmed with everything they heard, especially Joey. He's been sitting in front of the TV since we've been home. Just staring at it.*
KOLE: *It's a lot for people to hear, especially when they're so close-knit. I can imagine it must be horrendous to actually know the minute details about what happened.*
ETHAN: *How are you doing?*
KOLE: *I've been better. I don't want to imagine what he's been through, but it's hard not to.*
ETHAN: *Yeah, and with you being together now, it's that much harder for you. Anyway, let me know if there's anything we can do. I can imagine you want to hide away for a few days, so I'll try to keep everyone away.*
KOLE: *I'll check with Beck, but yeah, probably.*
ETHAN: *You rest up, too.*
KOLE: *I'll do my best.*

He saw another message, this time from Christi.

CHRISTI: *I hope you're all okay. I know I'm a long way away, but if you need anything, please let me know.*

KOLE: *Thank you. We will.*

Kole placed his phone face down on the arm of the sofa and wrapped his hand back around his drink, the warmth seeping into him once more. He tucked his legs under him and leaned back, staring at the TV but not really seeing it.

Beck stirred, and Kole checked his watch as he stood, placing the mug on the coffee table. It had been three hours. No wonder his body screamed at him when he moved.

Heading for the bedroom, he found Beck on his back, staring at the ceiling.

"Hey," Kole whispered.

Beck sniffed and rolled his head towards him. "Hey." He gave a small smile. "Sorry for—"

"If the next words out of your mouth are anything but *not sleeping long enough*, then I don't want to hear them," he said, settling onto the bed beside him.

Beck huffed and rolled his eyes, returning his gaze to the ceiling. Kole let the silence stretch, waiting for whatever Beck needed to say or do. It took five full minutes—and he knew that because he'd counted—for Beck to say anything.

"I feel lighter but also heavier. It's weird."

"You've let your past come out, which makes it easier on you, but you've taken in what everyone else has been through as well. It's bound to be a strange balance for you."

Beck swallowed, his Adam's apple bouncing several times. "If I had just spoken out more forcefully, he would never have hurt them."

That was what Kole had been expecting. As Becca had said and the police had confirmed, Beck had been the second child Drake had done anything to. Kole, however, wasn't so sure. From what Beck had told him and what he'd heard in the courtroom, there was no way Drake hadn't done it before. How many was anyone's guess. Which, while horrifying, alleviated some of Beck's burden. Not that he'd tell him that.

"They wouldn't have listened, Beck. You know that. You tried, and they didn't listen. That's on them, not you. You are not to blame for others being hurt. That lies with the social workers and Drake. No one else." He fisted the duvet, knowing what he was about to say would receive a rebuttal. "I think you need to keep seeing the therapist. To help you sort through everything in your mind."

Beck said nothing for a moment, but then he looked at him. "I agree."

Kole opened his mouth to argue his point but paused when his words registered. "You do?"

"I might not like sharing a lot of things, Kole, but I understand when I've made a mistake. I should've spoken up, and with a professional, long, long ago. In fact, I have already asked the therapist if she had any spaces. I have an appointment next week."

Kole smiled and reached out for the first time, brushing his fingers across Beck's cheek. "Look at you, being all grown up."

Beck grinned, the shadows, though not gone, banked for the moment. He lifted and grabbed Kole around the waist, and before Kole could even blink, he was on his back with Beck above him.

"You'll pay for that," Beck growled, poking at Kole's sides and underarms. Tickling was one thing Kole hated. Well, not *hated*, but it made him laugh so much he sometimes peed a little.

"Stop!" He laughed, closing his eyes and squirming to get away, but Beck wouldn't let him. "Oh, my god! Stop, stop!" He got his arms down to his sides, making things trickier for Beck, but not impossible. "Ha ha! Fuck, stop!"

"Nope. You deserve this for talking back to me."

Beck was relentless, but Kole tried to sidetrack him by lifting his hips towards him, and it immediately stilled him. Their gazes clashed and locked, both panting hard. Kole lifted his hands to Beck's face.

"I love you so damn much," he murmured.

Lowering to his elbows, caging Kole in, he said, "Right back atcha."

Their kiss was slow and explorative, with neither of them pushing to go further. Just a reconnecting. He let his body and mind sink into it, needing the connection more than he realised. When they pulled back, Beck's lips were swollen and bright red, his cheeks flushed and his eyes bright. If Kole could keep him looking like that for the rest of their life, he'd die a lucky man.

"What?" Beck said.

"You're gorgeous."

Beck's smile lit up the room. "You're not so bad yourself."

Kole laughed. "Thanks. I think."

Dropping a kiss on Kole's mouth again, Beck pulled back. "Are you hungry?"

"Actually, yeah. Didn't realise how much until you mentioned it."

Beck pushed off the bed, adjusting himself as he stood there. "Come on, then. I'll cook something."

"You don't have to. We can order in."

"Nah. I'm in the mood to cook." Beck shrugged. "Not sure what I have, though, so might need to do a shop run."

"Why don't you get sorted, and I'll check the kitchen?"

"Deal."

Beck disappeared into the bathroom, and Kole lay there for another minute before getting up. He wasn't naïve enough to know that Beck was okay, but he would be. Especially if he'd already thought about and organised additional therapy sessions. Kole would've never believed he would do that without one hell of a push. Just went to show how much someone could surprise another when they didn't know each other fully yet.

He checked the cupboards and fridge, seeing they had enough ingredients to create a stir-fry but not much else. While he was there, he grabbed two glasses of water and drained one, handing the second to Beck when he entered the room.

"Thanks. So what are the options?"

"Stir-fry, but not much else available."

Beck grimaced. "Not really in the mood for stir-fry. I'll nip to the shop to grab something more palatable."

"I'll come with you."

They dressed for the weather, and when they got outside, he linked his arm through Beck's as they set off down the street.

"Oh, I forgot my phone!" Kole said.

"The shop is only a few streets away. We won't be long."

As long as they didn't go mad and buy the shop out, they should be able to carry it back. They didn't rush, and Kole enjoyed the conversation and choosing the food Beck would make—and maybe let Kole help with. They couldn't hold hands on the way back because both had two bags each, but at least it wasn't the entire shop.

"You could do so much better."

Koel glanced at Beck. "What?"

Beck looked at him, frowning. "What?"

"What did you say?"

"I didn't say anything."

Goosebumps rose on his arms, and he inhaled deeply before looking over his shoulder, almost dropping the bags when he saw a man standing extremely close to them. How he hadn't felt him before then, he'd never know, especially as he usually felt it when he was being watched. He stared at him, taking a few small steps backwards, away from him.

"Andrew..."

"Kole?" Beck said.

Kole snapped his gaze to Beck and immediately back to Andrew. "Beck, this is Andrew. From Whitby."

He saw the grimace on Andrew's face when he looked at Beck, the top-to-toe glare of someone who didn't like what they saw. Andrew turned back to him.

"You could do so much better. You don't want him."

"Andrew, you need to leave. You shouldn't be here," Kole said.

"Yes, I should. I'm saving you! He's tainted."

Beck's breath caught, and Kole wanted to reassure him, but he couldn't. He had to stop this before Andrew blew up further.

19

BECK

Beck tried not to let the words hurt him—after all, the guy was unstable—but it hurt all the same. "Let's just calm down here."

"You're tainted. You shouldn't be with him! Kole, please, listen to me!"

Andrew went to grab Kole, but Beck dropped his bags and gripped the man's wrist. "Unless you want to be in even more trouble with the police than you already are, you need to leave."

"Kole! Listen to me. I can give you everything you need. Everything you could ever want. Listen to me!"

"Andrew, I'm sorry, but I just don't think of you that way. I enjoyed what we had, but I'm with Beck now." He put the bags down.

The placating tone was obvious, but it didn't seem to get across to the man.

"You can enjoy it again! All you need to do is get rid of *him*," Andrew shouted, beginning to draw attention to them from the passersby.

Kole held his hands out, palms forward. "Andrew, I need you to leave."

"No! Not without you!"

Before Beck could blink, a searing pain went through his left hand, the one holding Andrew at bay. Reflexively, he let go, hissing as the pain increased and then cursing when he saw the pocketknife sticking out of the back of his hand. He jerked his hand away when Andrew went to yank it out, knowing, somewhere in the back of his mind, that if he did, he'd end up losing a lot of blood.

Andrew went feral, but it didn't last long. Within seconds, he sprinted away, lost in the growing crowd.

"I've called the police," someone said to them. "They're on their way."

"Fuck, Beck! Are you okay?" Kole cradled his hand, and Beck tried not to move it too much.

"Yeah," he said, although he could hear the pain in his own voice. "Good job it's my left hand and not my right. At least I can still tattoo. Though it's going to make it a lot harder."

"Bloody hell," Kole said, glaring in the direction of where Andrew disappeared. "He's even more unhinged than I thought."

"And a stalker to boot."

Kole scraped his teeth along his bottom lip. "Yeah, I guess only time will tell."

"You'll have to be more careful now. He's pissed. He'll be up for revenge."

"We'll both have to be careful." Kole leaned closer to the knife. "Does it hurt a lot?"

"Just a bit." Beck played it down, but it hurt like a fucker.

Sirens wailed towards them, and a police car and paramedic car pulled up beside them. Beck could honestly say he'd had enough of the police by that point, but he could hardly tell them to piss off. He would press charges against Andrew—if they ever found him—and hopefully, it would give them extra to add onto whatever stalking charges they could pin on him.

They explained everything to an officer while the paramedic tended to his hand. When Beck interrupted to ask about taking the knife out, the paramedic shook her head.

"It would be better to keep it in place until you get to the hospital. They will probably have a surgeon look at it before deciding how to remove it. They won't want to do more damage than necessary." So, she bandaged it up, with the knife still reaching for the sky. "I'll take you in." She turned to the officer. "You'll have to finish getting his statement at the hospital."

They settled into the back of the paramedic's car after securing their shopping bags in the back. It was a quiet ride. The paramedic, Stacy, tried to make conversation, but neither of them was forthcoming. He couldn't speak for Kole, but Beck was tired. Bone-tired. Sick and tired. Just bloody, fucking exhausted from it all, and he didn't want to take it out on anyone.

When they finally arrived, they were sent directly into a room, with one bed and one chair, neither looking very comfortable. Beck settled onto the bed and Kole took the chair and still they didn't speak very much. Kole must have got the message that he didn't want to talk because he went silent, but the look he kept giving him spoke volumes. Beck knew he was being an asshole, but he couldn't help it. He was pissed at the world.

Surprisingly, it didn't take long for a doctor to arrive—or several—and they had the bandages off his hand, in complete gory detail, being examined by several people.

"We definitely need to get some tests done on this to see where the knife is."

"In my hand?" Beck said.

"Beck…" Kole warned.

The doctor laughed, his mouth and eyes crinkling, showing that he laughed a lot in life. "Yes, it is definitely in your hand. We need to just make sure it's not touching or severed anything vital before we try to remove it, so we need to take some pictures to do that. Once we've done that, we can get it taken out all being well."

"How long is this likely to take?" Beck asked.

"We'll call down to get the test done now. It shouldn't be too long."

The doctors disappeared, and Beck exhaled, long and loud. "In other words, we're going to be here for hours."

"We'll be here for as long as necessary to ensure that your hand is in the best condition possible when we leave," Kole said, leaning forward and pointing a finger in Beck's face. "And you'll grin and bear it. Understood?"

Beck tried to ignore what that tone did to him, and instead, just stared at the ceiling.

"Understood?" Kole's tone brooked no argument.

"Understood," Beck murmured, closing his eyes.

He would give the doctors their due, it didn't take them long to get him down for a test. It could have been an X-ray, or it could have been something else, he wasn't sure because, with the knife in his hand, he wasn't certain what test could be done without causing problems. But he did what Kole had asked of him. He grinned at the right points; he bore it as much as he could, and by the time they were back in the room, there were already some people waiting to discuss the next steps. The doctor who had spoken previously to him, who was called Dr Stevens, stepped closer and held up the photo. It looked like an X-ray, but Beck still wasn't certain.

"This," Dr Stevens explained, "is your lucky day. The knife has missed everything vital and has cleared the most important parts. It will be a fairly easy surgery to remove it, and although I know you'll want it to just be pulled out now, I don't recommend that because taking it out that way could cause problems. The slightest wrong movement as we take it out could cause lasting damage. So, we are going to get a room prepped for you and get his knife out as quickly as possible."

"Thank you, Dr Stevens," Kole said. "We appreciate how quickly you're doing this for us."

Dr Stevens chuckled. "It's the least we can do."

With that cryptic message, the doctor jerked his head to the side, a clear message to his coworkers that it was time to leave. Beck wanted to ask what that sentence was about, but he assumed it had something to do with them knowing who Beck was.

"That's all I need," he said. "I hate being a celebrity sometimes. Although Joey says we're not celebrities. We're celebrities' acquaintances." Beck huffed. "Can't see what the difference is, really."

Kole smacked his feet to the floor, clapped his hands on his thighs and stood, glaring. "You should be grateful they are doing this for you. It doesn't matter why they are doing it. There are people who probably had a knife in their hand who've waited for days before they got it sorted."

"Don't be so dramatic," Beck said.

"I'm not being dramatic," Kole replied. "It's the truth. Not everybody is lucky enough to get top-notch treatment, and I am so grateful that you do. Especially because…" His breath hitched, and he covered his mouth with his hand.

Finally, Beck took his head out of his ass and realised. "Oh, fuck. Come here." He held out his good arm, and Kole collapsed onto him, sobbing.

"I'm so sorry he did this to you. I didn't think it would be anything. I didn't think he would be like that. Even with him attacking me, I never actually thought it would go further. My brain obviously did because that's why I needed to speak to the therapist, but my mind never caught up to that fact until now. I was so scared he was gonna hurt you, and he did!" Kole broke off on another sob.

Beck held him, pressing his lips against his temple and making shushing sounds like a mother would to a baby—not that he was saying Kole was a baby, but the universal sound calmed most people.

It took a few minutes, but Kole eventually calmed enough to wipe his tears.

"Are you okay?" Beck said.

"Not particularly," Kole replied with a laugh. "I guess I was more upset than I thought I was.

"Maybe just a little," Beck teased.

"Hey, if you're not careful, I'll pull that knife out myself," Kole warned.

Beck laughed. "Think you might be in trouble with the doctors if you do that."

"Yeah, I think so, too," Kole agreed.

Beck latched onto something to keep the conversation light, spying the carrier bags to the side of his bed. "I have a feeling several of those items are going to have to be thrown straight in the bin." His tone implied the sheer horror of throwing away what would have been good food.

"At least we can buy it again and have it tomorrow." Kole smiled.

"Think you might be doing the cooking if we did that." Beck laughed. "Not sure I'll be doing much with this hand as it is now. We did get some crisps and things, though, and I am hungry. Maybe we should eat some of it."

Kole stood. "I want to check with the doctors that it's okay first. I don't know what kind of surgery you're going in and whether or not you're allowed to eat."

"Oh, bloody hell," Beck said. "If they tell me I'm not allowed to eat, I'm tempted to walk out of this hospital because I'm starving."

Kole chuckled. "You'll do as you're told." He winked at him and disappeared out of the room.

While he was gone, Beck had nothing to distract himself, and he stared at the bloody mess that was his hand, hoping with everything in him that he'd heal nicely and have no problems with it later on. Although he was right-handed, he did use his left hand for certain things while tattooing. If it became impossible to do, he didn't know what he would do with his life. Tattooing was all he knew and all he wanted to do. It would truly devastate him if he was taken from him.

"They said you can eat just fine," Kole said when he reappeared. He went to the bags, bringing them up on the side of the bed. "So, what do you fancy? Uncooked pasta? Bacon crisps? Onion rings? Nik-Naks?"

"I'll always go for the Nik-Naks," Beck said, reaching for them.

"Good job there are two packs of them," Kole said, grabbing another from the bag. "How about something healthy, too? We've got apples or bananas?"

"All right. I'll do my duty and eat a banana first," Beck said, turning his mouth down to make him look sad.

"Those puppy dog eyes won't work on me. Eat your banana," Kole said, but the twitching of his lips gave away his humour.

They switched on the TV, and he let Kole flick through the channels to see if there was anything decent to pass the time. Beck hadn't checked his phone since they arrived, and he wasn't sure he wanted to. He had no idea the messages he would have. Though he expected plenty of 'let me know if I can do anything' type messages from his friends. He wasn't sure he could stomach them right then.

Kole settled into the uncomfortable chair but brought it right close to the bed so that they could hold hands. He'd chosen a rerun of some old murder mystery, which wasn't Beck's cup of tea—or coffee—it passed the time.

The channel had just switched over to the next programme when a nurse came bustling in.

"Hello, Mr Cavanagh. My name is Susie, and I'm getting you prepped to get this tiny, annoying item removed from your hand."

Susie was the type of nurse that Beck had always wanted whenever he visited a hospital—one that took no crap, but also had a friendly smile and a good sense of humour. They bantered a bit until she cleared him as ready to go.

"The porter will be here in a few minutes to take you up to the operating room," she said.

"Am I going to be knocked out?"

"I'm not certain," Susie said. "Possibly. It depends on if they think they can do it without, but I'll leave that to Dr Stevens to tell you. I'll see you on the other side, Mr Cavanagh."

"I think you know enough about me now, Susie, that you can call me Beck."

Susie laughed. "I'll see you on the other side then, Beck."

She disappeared, and Kole chuckled from beside him.

Beck raised his eyebrows. "What?"

"You're such a charmer. I now know how you get away with everything. You could probably get away with murder if you put your mind to it."

"Yeah, probably could," Beck said in a matter-of-fact tone, causing them both to burst out laughing. At least until Beck hissed because he'd moved his hand.

A guy knocked on his door and poked his head around. "Hello, Mr Cavanagh. Time for your taxi ride to the operating room."

"Can I come up with him, or do I have to stay here?" Kole asked.

"You're quite welcome to join us up to the floor, but you will have to stay in the waiting room until we're done. I'm not entirely sure how long the procedure will take, but the doctor or nurse will come and let you know."

"Okay, thanks."

The porter, James, took the brakes off the bed and manoeuvred it through the door. When they got into the corridors, he realised why it was so quiet. There were several guards outside his door and at the end of the halways. Beck chuckled.

"Donovan."

"What?" Kole asked.

"The guards. They must've been from Donovan."

On the journey, where possible, Kole stood beside Beck, and when it wasn't, he followed behind. Beck could feel his presence and that helped calm his nerves. He didn't know why he was nervous. It wasn't like it was a huge surgery, like heart surgery or something. Just a little knife in his hand.

When they got to the floor, James paused and pointed to a room off to the side. "That's where you'll have to wait, I'm afraid," he said to Kole.

Kole nodded and exhaled. "Okay, then. Don't cause too much trouble, Beck. I will make the doctors tell me if you become a petulant child while you're in there. And I love you."

Beck reached for him, sliding his good hand around the back of his neck and pulled him to him for a kiss. When he finished, Kole's eyes were slightly glassy and his lips red and swollen. "I love you, too. See you soon. And don't eat all those crisps."

"Wouldn't dream of it," Kole replied.

Kole stayed standing until James pushed Beck away until he couldn't see him any longer. The nerves began invading, but there wasn't much he could do about it. They entered the operating room, which was awash with people and machines. Anyone would have felt terrified. Beck wasn't scared as such, but he had wished that his night had gone in a different direction than what it was.

"Mr Cavanagh," Dr Stevens said. "We're ready to get going. I'm going to recommend a regional anaesthetic with intravenous sedation just because I don't know how long this is going to take. Are you happy to go ahead with that?"

"Yes, that's fine. How long will it be before I wake up?"

"You won't be asleep, you'll just be feeling very drowsy and relaxed. I'm hoping this won't take more than an hour or so."

"Okay, thanks. Can you ensure updates are given to Kole, please?"

"Absolutely. Take a deep breath. You're in expert hands," Dr Stevens said.

"Take care of *my* hand for me, doctor," Beck said as the medicine started working.

"Will do." Dr Stevens winked at him, and Beck smiled before a wave of exhaustion flowed over him, his eyelids feeling heavier by the minute. He felt a sharp scratch and the pain in his hand stopped bothering him. He drifted, content in thinking about Kole and how amazing the guy was. He didn't deserve him, but he wouldn't be the one telling him that. No, he'd keep Kole for as long as possible.

20

KOLE

When Beck came out of surgery, he was awake and very happy and smiley. It was amusing, to say the least. Kole sat by his side as he drifted off to sleep barely minutes after returning to the room, and he waited with bated breath for him to wake up again. Although the nurse had come out to say that everything was fine and he had nothing to worry about, it still didn't alleviate his nerves that something might have gone wrong.

Thankfully, nothing did. And as he waited, which took Beck far too long to wake up for Kole's liking, his stomach settled. He went through everything that had happened. After all, that's what he always did in those situations. He couldn't believe Andrew turned so much from what Kole had thought he was. If Kole had seen him in his rightful mind, there was no way he would've slept with him, even that one night, but a lot of people could put on a mask to make other people see them differently. After all, that's what abusers do. They make it look like nothing's wrong to the outside world; whereas inside things are completely different.

When Beck blinked his eyes for the first time since the surgery, Kole saw it because he was a creepy asshole like that, watching his face, tracing every mound, every valley, every dimple, every wrinkle while waiting for him.

"Hi," he whispered, causing Beck to glance his way. He rolled his head a little and groaned, a completely groggy noise that most patients made, Kole assumed. "How are you feeling?"

"Absolutely wonderful," Beck croaked, and Kole reached for the small cup of ice chips the nurse had brought in not that long before. Kole wet Beck's lips with the ice shard before pushing it in so Beck could get some liquid, and then settled back into his perch, watching and waiting while Beck regained his equilibrium. It didn't take him long.

Beck glanced down at his hand and said, "Is everything okay with it?"

Kole nodded. "Yeah, everything's fine. We didn't have to worry. They didn't nick anything. It's all perfect."

"Did they say how long recovery might be?"

"No. Dr Stevens didn't tell me anything else. He said that once you were more alert, he would be in to discuss the healing side of things. He said that he'd kept the pocket knife in case you wanted it as a treasure."

Beck chuckled. "Maybe not a treasure, but it would help to use it as evidence against Andrew."

Kole raised his eyebrows. "I hadn't thought of that."

"Fingers crossed it'll help. Anyway, how are you doing? And how long have I been out?"

Kole smiled at him and brushed back some of the hair on his forehead. "You've been dozing for about an hour."

"Still feels like I could sleep for a week. No, probably a month, actually."

"And I will be right there beside you," Kole said. "I feel exactly the same."

"Why does everything happen all in one go?" Beck mused, closing his eyes again. "It would be nice if these things came one at a time rather than a dozen."

"Well, they always say that things come in threes."

"And have we had three?" Beck asked.

Kole pretended to think things through. "I think we've had our fair share. That's more than enough, and it's way more than three." He smiled. "Why don't you get some more sleep? The doctor will be in soon and I'll wake you up then."

"But I've already been asleep for so long," Beck complained.

"Yes, but the more you sleep, the quicker you'll heal. I'll still be here when you wake up. Promise."

Beck grumbled a bit more before succumbing to the sleep he so badly needed. The stress on his body must have been horrendous. Kole settled back in a seat, feeling much happier now Beck had roused, even for the short time that he'd been coherent. He picked up Beck's phone, after receiving permission to use it earlier, and started shooting off messages, replying to all those friends who had sent messages to them. He had spoken to Ethan at one point, just to let him know what had happened, but he'd said, in no uncertain terms, that if anybody turned up at the hospital wanting to wait, he was going to physically escort them out himself. Beck had had enough and didn't need anybody else coddling him. That was Kole's job. He received several replies, and so it went on for several long minutes.

Susie, the nurse, bustled back in, checking the machines and writing on the notes. "He's looking good. Don't worry," she whispered with a wink before leaving them alone again.

Kole dropped his hands on his lap and took a big inhale, letting it escape slowly. It went a long way to calming him. He hadn't realised quite how concerned he had been until Susie had said that. He'd been worried, don't get him wrong, but his entire body slumped in the chair, releasing all the invisible tension.

He continued to breathe, even as his mind went to Andrew. The man had disappeared for all accounts, but he doubted he'd be gone for long. If they was right, he was the one who had been following Kole all this time, making him feel unsafe and crazy. If that was the case, he doubted Andrew would stay hidden. He'd need to get his fix.

What was it about Kole that had made Andrew target him? He was just a guy. Not that he'd wish this on anyone, but what made him stand out from someone else? He doubted he'd get answers to those questions, especially with him being in the wind.

It took until mid-afternoon the following day for Beck to be released from the hospital. And even then, it was because Beck was constantly complaining about being bored. He was, but he was also putting it on. Every time the doctors or nurses came in, he complained, but then when they left, he winked at me and laughed. He got his way, though.

"Your chariot awaits!" Dallas called when he entered the room, his towering form filling the doorway a couple of hours later. He was their designated driver, as neither had a car with them. Kole supposed he could've left Beck there to fetch his car, but he hadn't wanted to, and Dallas was more than happy to make the journey when he asked.

"Thank god!" Beck said. "What took you so long?" He climbed from the bed and stretched, his shirt exposing his midriff, and Kole couldn't keep his eyes away until Beck cleared his throat.

"Why, you're *very* welcome that I made my way all across London to bring you home!" Dallas said sarcastically, shaking his head, even as his grin spread.

Beck rolled his eyes, but said, "Thanks, Dallas. I appreciate it. We appreciate it, as I'm sure the doctors and nurses do, too."

"Don't tell me you did the complaining trick?" Dallas asked, folding his arms over his chest.

Grinning, Beck said, "Works every time."

Kole stood, hands on hips. "And just how many times have you been in this situation to warrant knowing what works and what doesn't?" He was only jesting, but he was also curious.

"Too many to count and not enough to talk about," Beck murmured, making Dallas laugh.

"Between all of us, we've had our fair share. I'm surprised they've not named a wing after us." Dallas snorted.

"I think the doctor recognised me. At least, he implied he did." Beck grabbed the shopping bags, but Kole took them from him with a glare.

"Not a chance."

"I still have one good working hand." He held it out. "I can take one at least."

"Nope." Kole shifted the bags until he could carry them without cutting off his circulation. "Let's go. The quicker we get out of here, the quicker we get home."

Kole wasn't sure which house he was referring to, but he didn't want to examine that yet. He was happy wherever Beck was, and that included Life in Ink. As far as he was concerned, it didn't matter the location, just that he was with Beck. Maybe he was too involved with their relationship, especially as he hadn't planned on being with anyone for a while after what Andrew did to him, but Beck was a force to be reckoned with when it came to Kole's heart.

He sat in the back of the car—or rather, truck—and listened to Beck and Dallas bantering. It warmed his heart how much they all looked after each other. He didn't know what Dallas's story was, but he was sure if he needed to know, he would be told. It didn't stop the man from being a gentle giant, and he deserved love, just like the rest of the crew. He couldn't thank Ethan enough for introducing Kole to them.

Kole shook his head absently at the direction of his thoughts. It was interesting the way his brain worked sometimes, but other times, he wished he could quiet it and just...be.

"What...the...fuck?" Dallas breathed, garnering Kole's attention just before the flashing blue lights did.

He glanced at the man before following where his gaze was and sucked in a gulp of air.

"What the hell!" Beck yelled, opening the car door and scrambling out. Kole followed, racing behind him as he strode for the barrier surrounding the shell that had been Beck's home. "How did no one tell me about this?" He waved his arm around, grabbing the attention of someone official-looking.

"Mr Cavanagh?" she said.

"Yes."

"I'm Detective Kirby. I apologise for not getting in contact with you. We tried several numbers, but we couldn't locate you."

They obviously hadn't checked with their own police officers who had Beck's up-to-date number. Kole almost rolled his eyes.

Beck held up his hand. "I've been in hospital."

She raised her eyebrows. "From this?" she asked, pointing towards the smouldering house.

"No. I didn't even know about this. It was fine yesterday."

"We are still trying to determine what caused the fire, but we have reason to believe it was arson."

"What reason?" Kole asked, butting in to the conversation.

"We found a petrol can in the back garden. We've taken it to see if we can get any prints from it."

Kole's stomach sank, and he glanced at Beck. "Do you think it was Andrew?"

Beck growled. "More than likely. When I get my hands on him..."

"Who is Andrew?" Kirby asked, pulling out her notebook.

"The bane of our existence, right now," Beck murmured, staring at the building, because it wasn't a home now. It was a shell.

Kole sighed. "He's an ex, of sorts. I had what was supposed to be one night with him, but he wanted more. He attacked me and was arrested, but they let him go, saying there wasn't enough evidence. This was in Whitby. I moved to London not long ago, and I thought I was free of him, but he turned up last night as we were walking home. He is who did that." Kole pointed at Beck's bandaged hand.

"Okay. Can you give me as many details about him as you can, and I'll look into him?"

Kole did as requested, keeping an eye on Beck, who stared at the remains of the house. The shell itself was still intact, but the windows were blown out, and it had black smudges all over the brickwork. The roof was half gone, smoke still rising in places.

"I can't believe this," Beck murmured.

"I'm sorry," Kole said. After all, it was his fault. If he hadn't brought Andrew into Beck's life, his home would still be intact.

Beck pulled his gaze from the wreckage and locked gazes with Kole. "*This* was *not* your fault. In no uncertain terms," he said, cupping Kole's jaw with his good hand, "you are not to blame for this. Whoever did this is." He paused, blinked and turned back to the detective. "It could also be someone else." His hand slid down to grip Kole's hand, bringing a lump to his throat. "I've recently given evidence against someone."

Beck briefly told the story, and once again, it struck Kole as amazing that Beck could talk about it with no qualms. Just threw it out there whenever he needed to. The strength of the man beside him astounded Kole.

"Okay, thanks for that. I'll get looking into it." Kirby handed Beck a card. "This is my number if you need or think of anything. I'll let you know how things progress."

"Is anything salvageable?" Beck asked.

Kirby sighed. "I'll be honest. Not a lot. You can't go in right now because the fire crews are trying to stabilise the roof, but as soon as they have and it's safe, air-wise, for anyone, I'll let you know. You'll be able to walk through it and see what you can get. I'm sorry."

Beck exhaled. "It's fine. It's only material stuff."

Kirby nodded and headed back to the fire crew.

"And my phone," Kole muttered.

Beck hissed. "Shit, yes. Damn it. Sorry."

"It's fine. I can get a new one. I'll ask Ethan to let my parents know."

"I can do that," Dallas said, making Kole jump. He'd forgotten Dallas was there.

"Thanks."

Beck blew out a long breath. "I guess we're staying at yours." His mouth quirked, but Kole could see he was upset and trying to hide it. "So much for enough bad stuff happening."

"What's mine is yours," Kole murmured with a smile.

Beck squeezed his hand. "Come on. Let's go to our other home. Dallas, are you okay taking us to Kole's, please?"

"Absolutely."

They climbed back into the car, and with one final lingering look from Beck, Dallas drove off.

"I can't believe this happened," Dallas said. "And you said something about Andrew?"

They went through it again, giving a bit more detail than what they had given to the detective.

"And he's still breathing?" Dallas growled.

"Barely," Beck said.

"What is the plan now?" Dallas asked. "Where do you go from here?"

Beck shrugged. "I have no idea. Like I said, it's all material stuff, so it doesn't really matter. There was nothing in that house that I'm worried about losing, for the most part. Nothing sentimental, thankfully."

Although Beck said that like it was a good thing, it made Kole sad. Everybody needed some sentimental items, but it seemed like Beck had never had the opportunity. If there was one thing they were going to change, Kole would make sure Beck had plenty of things that reminded him of what they'd done and where they'd been. He could understand how difficult it was, even if Beck seemed like he could easily brush it aside. Maybe it was because he was in the foster care system for so long that he believed it wouldn't stick. Kole would make him see otherwise. If it took him all the years he had in this life, he would show Beck he was important enough for people to stay around him.

Instead of snuggling up on the sofa in Kole's apartment like he had thought they would, he guided Beck to the bedroom, settling him up against the headboard while Kole pottered around getting things together so they wouldn't have to move until the following morning unless they wanted to. Beck laughed at him when he told him that after Beck enquired about what he was doing.

"You're making a nest?"

"Yep. No reason to leave this bed at all, as far as I'm concerned."

Beck chuckled. "I like that idea."

"Me, too." He climbed in, nestling himself on Beck's good side so he didn't inadvertently hurt him, and held out the remote. "You choose."

"I must be ill. It's not like you to give up the remote," he joked, then looked at the remote. "What is this?"

Kole's cheeks heated. "Don't know what you mean—it came that way." Beck raised his eyebrows. "Anyway... You might be an invalid right now, but I can still punish you."

Beck's eyes widened, and he licked his lips, swallowing hard. "Hmm. I'll take that under advisement."

Despite the sad reason behind them being where they were, Kole couldn't bring himself to be too upset. They had a roof over their heads, and they were together. Beck had lost a lot, but they would rebuild it better if that's what he wanted. Kole couldn't see a future without Beck in it, and he would do everything to make him happy. With everything that was going on in their lives—separately and together—they deserved some solace.

Hopefully, the police would do their job and find Andrew before he did anything else, either to harm them or himself. Life had a funny way of working out. He almost wished he'd never met Andrew, but if he hadn't, he might not be where he was right then, and he *didn't* wish that at all. Beck had become so important to him that he couldn't imagine life alone, despite him having sworn it after his attack. Ethan had seen through him, but at the time, Kole couldn't see the light. He was sure most people were the same. It took something amazing, something beautiful for them to rejoin the world and let themselves love.

Family was important. Friends were just as important. But it was those people they *chose* to spend their lives with that became the building block of a contented person. Beck was that to Kole, and it was as much a surprise to Kole as it was to anyone else.

As he listened to Beck's breathing evening out, he swore, to whatever deity was real and listening, that he would do *anything* to give Beck what he deserved. *Anything.*

Once he'd told his parents and aunt about what happened, Auntie Ava was on the first train down. It was lovely to see her and introduce her to everyone at Life in Ink. Especially Beck. They got on like—for want of a much better word—a house on fire. She couldn't stay long, but she promised to visit often, more so because she loved the shows. And in her words, no one does it like London.

He hadn't expected his parents to come, mainly because they didn't believe they needed to. He'd been used to it all his life, so he wasn't bothered. He had Auntie Ava, he didn't need any other family but the Life in Ink one.

21

BECK

I t took several days before they had any kind of information
from the fire crew and police about what happened at his
house, even with Donovan and Christian putting their weight
behind it. They had been able to go in the following day to see
if anything was salvageable, but what was left was nothing that
Beck needed—or wanted. They hadn't been able to find Kole's
phone, but a fire officer said it was unlikely to be easy to find in
the ashes. They said they would keep an eye out for it, though.

Luckily, the neighbours' houses hadn't been affected by
anything except the smoke, and that could be rectified easier
than fire.

In the end, he took nothing from the house. It was all
smoke-damaged and could be bought new, so there was no point.
Instead, they holed up at Kole's apartment, and if Beck was honest
with himself, he loved that small apartment as much as his larger
home. He'd thought having a large house would show people he
was worthy. In hindsight, he was putting his middle finger up
at the social workers who said he was nothing. He didn't need
therapy to tell him that then.

Although Karen, his therapist, was lovely. She would see him
every week on his own and then once a week with Kole as they
worked through the things that had happened. She also saw
Kole once a week, too, after he'd transferred from his previous
therapist to her. Beck wanted him and Kole to have a good

relationship, and if therapy was the best choice, then he'd do it every day for hours at a time if that was what was needed.

He'd always believed that what Drake had done to him hadn't affected him, except for the bottoming thing, but he had. He could admit that at that point in his life. After going through everything that had happened, he knew he had a lot of hang-ups that needed addressing, and he was grateful for every minute Kole gave him. He doubted he would ever feel like he deserved Kole's love, but he would work every day for it and would never make him regret it. He wanted to be worthy of it.

And speaking of worthy... He looked over his shoulder to the man who had pushed right up against his back while they slept, his hot breath teasing his back. Beck couldn't help himself. Ever so carefully, he rolled himself over to face Kole, nuzzling him onto his back with barely a murmur from the guy. In the early morning hours as it was, with the heating having only just turned on and therefore the air being chilly, the pebbling of his skin as he removed the cover was mesmerising. While he traced his fingers over the exposed skin, watching more goosebumps follow his path, he thought about what Kole had given him. He couldn't list every single thing or every single way that Kole had improved his life, but when it came down to sex, he'd done more than Beck could ever have wished for. Giving up control had always been Beck's fantasy, but the idea of trying it had scared him so much, he had never, ever contemplated even attempting to let someone do it. But as with everything since he'd met Kole, the man had blown that out the window.

Beck leaned over slightly and blew across Kole's nipples, watching Kole shiver as the nubs hardened to little points. As much as Beck did like having someone else take control, there was still something in him that enjoyed watching somebody find pleasure in what he did to them.

He skimmed his fingers further down Kole's stomach and around his groin, down his thighs to his knees and then back up again. He ran his finger up the underside of his cock, the perfectly sized shaft hardening little by little. Beck leaned down and flicked his tongue across the hardened nub at the same time as he rubbed his thumb across the head of his cock.

Kole moaned and squirmed. Beck glanced up, witnessing Kole's rise from his dreamland into the reality of the pleasure that Beck was creating. Kole swallowed, licked his lips and croaked, "Did I say you could touch that?"

Now it was Beck's turn to shiver, and he shakily exhaled. "No, Sir," he murmured.

"Well," Kole said, his voice hardening, "as you seem to be breaking all kinds of rules, how about you make me harder with your mouth." It wasn't a question.

Beck nodded once and scrambled down the bed, pushing Kole's legs to either side and laying himself between them, hissing slightly as his dick rubbed against the covers. All it would take was a few thrusts, and he was sure he'd go over the edge straight away. He wasn't stupid enough to get right to it. He paused in position, staring up at Kole, waiting. Kole stared back at him for a good minute, although it felt like an entire year. Finally, he nodded, giving him permission to start, and start he did.

He wrapped his hand around the base and fed Kole's cock into his mouth, moaning as the taste hit his tongue. He got the entire length as wet as he could and stroked as well as sucked and licked and nipped and flicked using every ounce of his knowledge.

"Fuck, that's so good." Kole groaned, canting his hips to make him go deeper. Beck relaxed his throat, and as Kole's hands palmed either side of his head, he removed his hands, braced himself on the bed and glanced up at Kole once more, giving permission with his eyes for Kole to use him.

Even so, Kole raised his eyebrows and waited for Beck to give him another confirmation that he wanted that. Beck nodded to the best of his ability.

Kole grinned. "That's what I like to see. Rise onto your knees, get them beneath you, and then put your hands behind your back—carefully—keeping your face where I can reach it."

Beck was quick to manoeuvre himself exactly how Kole wanted him and, though there was a slight ache in his back from the position, it made it all the more intriguing. Kole checked in once more with him, then slowly pushed his shaft further into Beck's mouth. When the head reached the back of his throat, he relaxed as much as he could and then swallowed around it. Kole hissed and pulled free before sliding deep again. They repeated the dance several times, Kole increasing his speed minutely each time. It didn't take long for Beck's jaw to start aching, but damned if he would stop. He kept going faster and faster, and Beck witnessed the rosy flush making its way through his body through Kole's body. Beck had never heard him curse as much as he had done in those last few minutes, and it sent a well of pride flowing through him.

"Stop," Kole ordered, and Beck froze. Kole pulled himself free, and he almost moaned at the loss. "I don't want to come yet," Kole said. "I want to be inside you when that happens." He moved to the side and patted the bed beside him. "Elbows and knees, facing the headboard."

"Yes, Sir," Beck said, wincing a little at the ache in his lower back, but the new position was better. When Beck was settled, Kole slapped his ass, the sound loud in the room, and after the slight sting, a warmth spread from the impact spot.

"Time for me to get you ready," Kole said, reaching into the bedside table to grab some lube and then kneeling behind him. "How are you feeling?"

"Needy," Beck replied, moving back slightly as if to make his point,

"Okay, well, let's get to it then," Kole said. "It's going to be cold."

The click of the tube and then the squirt of the gel had Beck's senses on high alert, and when the cold liquid touched his hole, he instantly tightened and tensed, but the moment Kole started massaging, he relaxed, letting the first finger slide in. Kole swirled it around, pushing it in and out, making Beck wish he could do something to make him go quicker. Kole must've understood though because he added the second finger, stretching him, the burn not that intense but intense enough to feel. All the while, Kole was murmuring pretty much nonsense, to be honest, but it was that kind of nonsense that helped Beck focus on what was happening, and he truly needed that. Despite giving control to Kole, he still needed something to reassure him he could stop things if needed.

When Kole pressed three fingers into him, he exhaled heavily, his head dropping between his arms, his elbows shaking with the need to bend and lower himself to the bed. The top of his head hit the headboard, and he rested forwards using it as a springboard to move himself backwards onto Kole's fingers.

"Oh, you like that, do you?" Kole murmured. "Let's get you completely ready for me."

With only that as a warning, Kole slid four fingers inside him, stretching him beyond what he ever thought he would be able to take. "That's it. You're gorgeous like this. I can't wait any longer."

Kole pulled his fingers free, and Beck sighed in both relief and mutiny. He wanted him back right away... yesterday, even.

"Hold on."

Kole's cock pressed against Beck's hole, and as usual, it initially shied away, but with the constant pressure, Kole finally thrust inside, sliding in and out in small increments until he was fully seated. He rested his hands on the bed, his stomach warming

Beck's back. Kole's lips pressed to his shoulder blades, and Beck found he would do anything to be able to kiss him right then.

"Are you ready for me?" Kole said.

"Absolutely," Beck muttered.

Kole withdrew slowly and then slid deep slightly, repeating the action a few times until Beck got used to it, and then, on the next withdrawal, he slammed his hips forward, hitting that most prized possession inside him and ensuring that he saw stars. He did it again and again until he was begging.

"Please, Kole. Please, Sir, please. I want to come with you, but I don't think I'm going to last," Beck admitted.

"I understand. This time, and only this time, you can come whenever you need to."

Kole increased his pace until all Beck could hear was the slap of skin, all he could smell was the sweat in the air and all he could taste was Kole on his tongue. He closed his eyes to enjoy the sensations, and his one good hand squeezed the slats of the bed, grounding him and halting his movement too far forward.

"That's it, Beck. You can do it," Kole panted. "I want you to come for me as soon as possible. You feel too fucking good, and I'm going to come. I need you to come. That's an order," Kole said, firming his voice.

And like that was all Beck needed, his body seized, wracked with contraction after contraction as he released onto the bed beneath him. All he could hear was white noise and cursing from behind him, and Kole's fingers tightened their grip on his hips as he held himself deep. A wave of heat flooded him, and it sent another shiver through him.

"Holy fuck," Kole said. "I can't remember the last time I came that hard. Are you still with me, Beck?" he asked as he pulled out.

"Uh-huh," was all Beck could manage. Kole manoeuvred him to the side, away from the wet patch. Beck lay there on his side, eyes closed, panting, body occasionally twitching with the aftereffects. "Holy crap," he breathed as Kole came back with a flannel. He flexed his injured hand but ignored the ache.

Under normal circumstances, Beck would have complained about Kole cleaning him, but for several reasons, he didn't. The main one was that he trusted Kole with everything inside of him, and he knew he would never harm him. So he let him do whatever he wanted to him without a second thought.

"That's it. All done," Kole murmured, sinking beside him to kiss his cheek. "You're perfect for me, Beck. You know that, don't you?" Kole whispered as he manhandled Beck while changing the sheets.

Beck wasn't quite there yet. He still wasn't certain he deserved Kole, but he refused to push him away when Kole didn't seem to want to leave.

"Well, that was certainly a wake-up call." Kole laughed as he lay beside Beck, pulling him into his arms and throwing the cover back over them. "I was just planning on bacon and eggs for breakfast, but we ended up with a lot more."

Beck chuckled. "We definitely did."

They dropped into silence, but as usual, it was never strained. There was always a point to it, and finally, Beck said, "I think I want to go to work today. I've cancelled far too many appointments lately, even several of the ones that I usually travel for. I want to get back to it. I miss it."

"Sounds like a plan. Let's have a shower, have some breakfast, and see if Joey or Dallas have destroyed the place."

"Nah, Ani wouldn't let them," Beck said.

"Ah, but when the cats are away, the mice will play."

"Why? Where's Ani gone?"

"Nowhere, I don't think. Just saying whenever Ani isn't there, they always do something to prank her or prank one of you.

Beck glanced at him. "That'll include you now, so keep your eyes open."

"Wonderful," Kole deadpanned.

They took their time getting ready—and having bacon and eggs—and Beck drove them to Life in Ink. The warm feeling spreading out from his stomach was welcome, and he grinned as he parked the bike in the car park behind the shop. After stowing everything, he grabbed Kole's hand and dragged him towards the door, Kole's laughter following.

The bell over the door sounded as they entered, and Ani glanced up from the desk, her smile, ready and eager to help a new customer, growing wider when she saw him.

"Beck!" She rounded the counter and threw her arms around his neck.

He let go of Kole and held her, dropping his face to her shoulder and allowing her to hold on to him as long as she wanted. The events hadn't just been tiresome for him; they must've worn on his friends—no, family—as much as they had him, and wasn't he an asshole for only just thinking about it?

"How are you doing?" Ani asked, cupping his cheek and staring into his eyes as if seeing into his soul.

For the first time in a long time, he didn't put on a mask. "I've been better, but I'm getting there." Ani's eyes widened, and he chuckled. "I'm learning."

She hugged him again and then stepped away. "You always did have a lot to learn," she teased with a wink, though he could see the wetness in her eyes.

Beck laughed and linked hands with Kole again, stepping closer to the counter when Ani moved behind it again. "Do I have anything on the agenda?"

"Not officially because I redistributed those clients who didn't want to wait for you." She gave an apologetic wince. "Sorry about that. But if you are planning to ink, you're welcome to have at least two that had originally booked with you."

"Who?"

"Maxim and Hilary." She tried to withhold her grin.

Beck rolled his eyes. "I don't know what it is about those two that you find so funny."

Ani leaned her elbow on the desk and rested her chin in her hand. "It could be that they always come in at the same time, usually see the same person, end up with similar tattoos and have yet barely spoken to each other. They're obviously into each other. I think they're just too shy to make the first move."

"They might have tattoos all over their bodies if someone doesn't first," Kole said. "Not that I've seen them."

"You're not playing matchmaker, Ani," Beck warned.

Ani pouted. "Why not?"

Beck sighed. She would do whatever she wanted, anyway. "Just be careful. But, yes, I'll take them. What time?"

"Eleven and twelve-thirty."

Beck nodded and faced Kole. "You want to watch?"

Kole smiled. "Always."

He turned back to Ani, her gaze bouncing between them, and sighed. "Stop," he muttered.

"So cute," she whispered, not quiet enough for Kole not to hear if the chuckle he let out was any indication.

He dragged Kole towards the stairs. "I'll let you know when I'm all set up. Not sure what state I left it in, so might take a bit to get sorted," he called over his shoulder.

"Sure thing!" Ani said.

When they closed the door to Beck's studio behind them, he sighed and laughed. "I missed that," he admitted.

Kole leaned against his front, sliding his arms up and around Beck's neck. "It won't take them long to get back to normal. The events of the past few weeks have been a shock for them all, but they're still your friends, Beck. They'll be eager to get back to the relationship you had before, just as much as you are."

Beck buried his face in Kole's neck, inhaling deeply, and just relaxed for a moment. Then he pulled back and cupped Kole's jaw. "I love you so damn much."

Kole beamed up at him. "And I love you." He kissed him, far too chaste and proper for Beck's liking, but Kole laughed and pulled away. "Now get to work. I want to see my man in his element."

Beck's cheeks heated because, although Kole had seen him work before, it had a different atmosphere to it. Then he had an idea. "While I'm working today, I want you to design me something."

"What?"

"Anything. I want your design on my body," he murmured.

Kole looked him up and down and bit his lip. "All right. Anywhere in particular?"

Beck smirked. "Your choice. You know what space I have left."

Kole licked his lips and nodded slowly. "Okay. I'll see what I can come up with."

He moved towards the desk in the corner of the room, and Beck stepped up behind him, halting his movements, leaning in to whisper in his ear, "And you'll be the one inking me."

22

KOLE

The shiver that ran through Kole was at odds with the heat that also flowed from his head to his toes. As much as he was in control in the bedroom, he would never forget how dominant Beck could be, pretend or not. When it came to inking, Beck was the professional, and he knew it.

He pulled away and settled himself onto the chair in front of the table, although he placed it along the side so he could watch everything that happened—as long as the client agreed. Pulling out his drawing pad and pencils, he settled into place and watched Beck potter around, tidying, cleaning and sterilising everything that needed it.

Kole was drawn to the man, and his hand began moving on the page, sketching the strength of Beck's body, the muscle definition, the chiselled jaw hidden by his beard, the softness in surprising places. It all merged to become the person Kole knew as Beck Cavanagh.

"I'm done," Beck said, leaning against the counter and crossing his arms. "You seemed far away."

Kole glanced down at his drawing and smirked. "Someone distracted me." He turned it to face him. "It's not the best."

Beck's eyebrows rose, and he moved closer, taking the pad. "I knew you could draw patterns, but I didn't know you could draw people, too. This is bloody amazing, Kole."

"It's not my favourite because I get, for want of a better word, anal about the minor details. If they're not right, it annoys me until I've figured it out or I give up. Patterns don't take as much brainpower."

"I'd disagree. Patterns have a lot of nuances that you need to think about. It's no less valid than something you find difficult." Beck flicked the pad towards him, making his drawing visible. "This is fantastic, Kole. You're fantastic."

Kole ducked his head but smiled. "Thanks. How's your hand?"

Beck leaned down and kissed him, chaste though it was, and said, "It's okay. Aches a little but I mainly use it to wipe at the skin, so I should be good to go. I have to let Ani know I'm ready because I'm sure Maxim is already here."

Kole stared at the drawing while Beck sorted his appointment, scrutinising the details, and found he quite liked it. He flipped to another page and smoothed it out, his mind wandering. What design could he draw for Beck? Should it be something similar to what he already had, or something completely different? While he considered it, he doodled, letting his pencil skim across the page until voices broke into his concentration.

Beck entered the room, talking. "—have someone in to watch, if that's okay? This is—"

"Kole. Nice to meet you," a guy said, striding over and holding out his hand. He was lean but tall, with a shock of black hair that made his bright blue eyes shine.

Kole shook his hand with a frown. "How did you—"

"Know?" He winced. "Sorry. I've seen the news following the case. It's hard not to know who you both are now."

"You must be Maxim?" Kole guessed.

The guy grinned and nodded. "Yes! You must've been talking about me, Beck."

Beck chuckled. "Only to say who my client was. Confidentiality and all that." He bustled to the counter. "You know what to do, Maxim."

Maxim removed his coat and shirt, placing them over the back of a nearby chair. His body was covered with ink, with only a few random spaces; one, Kole saw, was right over his heart. "I see Hilary is back again, too."

Beck met Kole's gaze above Maxim's head and smirked. "Yeah, you always seem to have appointments at similar times."

"She's lovely. I talk to her a lot when we're here. She's as addicted to tattoos as I am. We have a lot in common, it seems."

Beck worked his jaw, narrowed his eyes and nodded. "Would you like her to come in and watch as well? We certainly don't mind." Maxim's eyes widened, and his mouth opened and closed a couple of times. "Never mind. It was just an idea."

"No! No, that..." He inhaled. "That would be nice, actually. If you're sure?"

"Absolutely," Beck said.

"I'll go ask her," Kole said, rising and heading for the door, not giving Maxim that chance to say no again. He'd listen if the guy changed his mind, but he could see how much he wanted her there. But so much for Ani being the matchmaker; Beck apparently was, too.

Jogging down the stairs, he smiled to himself before entering the front of the shop. He stepped up to Ani and whispered, "Is this Hilary?" Ani frowned but nodded, opening her mouth, but Kole didn't give her the chance. "Hilary?" The brunette looked up from her phone. "Maxim would like to invite you to watch. I'm watching while Beck works, too. Would you like to join us?"

Hilary blinked at him a couple of times before physically shaking herself. "Are you sure that's okay?"

Kole nodded. "Beck offered and Maxim agreed. If you'd like to, they're more than happy to have you there." He was careful with his words, not wanting to scare her off and also not wanting to promise more than he could.

"Sure, thanks." She collected her things and stood.

Kole glanced at Ani, winked and led Hilary up the stairs. He held the door for her, and she entered slowly, as if worried about the reception of her being there.

"Hi, Hilary," Maxim said with a smile.

"Hey." She glanced at Beck, wringing her hands around the handles of her bag. "Are you sure this is okay?"

Maxim smiled. "Absolutely. We both love tattoos, so this is a great way to see someone else getting one, don't you think?"

Hilary smiled back and nodded. "Yeah." Kole brought over a chair for her, and she settled into it. "What are you having done?"

Maxim thrust his hand into his pocket and pulled out a piece of paper. "This. At least, I hope," he added, flicking his gaze to Beck. His hands shook as he held it out.

"Oh, I love that," Hilary breathed.

Kole stepped closer, as did Beck. The design was elegant in its simplicity, a slight contrast to what he already wore on his skin, but he could see how it would potentially work with the current designs.

"I can do that. Where do you want it, Maxim?" Beck asked as he stepped over to his working table, fiddling with some ink bottles.

"I was thinking it might fit in the space on the back of my neck. What do you think?"

Beck nodded. "That'd work. It might have to be a little smaller, but if you lie down, I'll check the available area."

Maxim sent a smile to Hilary and climbed onto the table, face down. Kole settled into his chair and rested his drawing pad on his knee, watching all the others as they interacted. Beck discussed the placement and created a copy of the drawing, slightly smaller, but still as detailed, and then took a photo so Maxim could confirm he was happy.

"Looks good to me. What do you think, Hilary?"

Kole couldn't see Hilary's expression, but her voice trembled as she spoke. "It looks amazing."

Kole swapped a smile with Beck and divided his attention between his drawing and the couple—and he was sure they would be a couple soon—in Beck's care. He smiled whenever Beck made them laugh, watching him weave his spell over them, though Kole knew he didn't know he did it. His personality, despite his trials and tribulations, drew people to him. They wanted to be near him, to know him, to take just a little of what made Beck as strong as he didn't believe himself to be and help themselves to be strong, too.

The clock said it had been an hour and a half when Beck finally rose and stretched after covering the tattoo with cream. He had shaken his hand out a few times during the process but hadn't complained.

"All done. You know the drill, so I won't bore you with the details."

Maxim exhaled as he stood. "That's going to sting for a bit." He huffed a laugh.

"Yeah, you chose an area close to a bone. You know how that goes," Beck said.

Maxim turned his back to Hilary. "How does it look?"

"It looks great. It suits you."

Maxim beamed. "Thanks." He pulled on his top and glanced at her as he smoothed it down. "I better leave you to it." He grabbed his coat. "Thanks, Beck."

"You're welcome. See you soon, no doubt."

Maxim nodded, looked at Hilary once more with a smile and headed for the door.

Hilary bit her lip, eyes darting across the floor, until she finally stood and said, "Wait!" Maxim paused, gaze solely on the woman wringing her hands. "Will you stay?"

"Are you sure? I don't want to make you uncomfortable."

Hilary's smile returned, her shoulders lowering again. "You don't." She turned to Beck. "It's just finishing off, anyway."

Beck nodded. "If you're okay with that, then by all means."

Hilary swallowed but smiled, putting her bag on the floor by the table, and pulled her top off, revealing her bra. She had a slight flush to her cheeks, but she settled onto the table on her front, exposing her back.

"Oh, wow," Maxim breathed, stepping closer.

Kole felt the same. The ink on her back was…beyond words. Patterns, images and words, all mingled to make a massive, full back spread. It was incredible.

Beck smirked at them and then got to work. Kole continued with his drawing, in between watching Maxim. If the man hadn't been fascinated before, he certainly was at that point.

By the time Beck stepped back, Kole's design was done. He closed the book, unable to look at the design any longer because it was raw. Unadulterated emotion and love, and it hurt. The band around his chest tightened with every breath, and he could barely swallow. He had never experienced such a thing before. None of his drawings had ever made him feel as bare as he was then. He wasn't sure he could show Beck even.

"All done," Beck said. "You know the routine. Don't do anything daft with it."

Hilary chuckled as she rose, slipping her top back on. "Thank you, Beck. I really appreciate it. And though this one is finished, there is a lot more skin for me to choose."

Beck laughed. "I know you, Hilary. It won't be long before you come back. Or you either, Maxim."

Beck's words seemed to shake Maxim from his stupor. "Absolutely. As much as I hate this, I also love it."

"I'll see you both soon, then."

Maxim opened the door and gestured for Hilary to go first, which she did with a flush and a smile. When the door closed, Kole could feel Beck's gaze on him, but he couldn't look at him. He would cry if he did; that's how close to the edge he was.

When a hand cupped his cheek, he jumped. He hadn't heard him move.

"What's wrong, Kole?"

He breathed through his nose, trying to stem the emotional torrent overwhelming him. "I just…" He swallowed. "I wanted to…show you how amazing you are." Glancing up at him was a mistake because tears escaped his eyes.

"Let me see," Beck whispered, crouching in front of him.

He handed him the book with shaky hands, the pencil he'd used bookmarking the page, and then closed his eyes. The creak of the spine was loud, and he could hear the brush of Beck's fingers over the paper. Then silence reigned until it was too much for him to take, and he opened his eyes.

Beck had his hand over his mouth, silent tears dripping over the back, as he stared at the page. Seeing those wet drips always made Kole want to join him, but he stayed quiet until Beck lifted his tear-stained face.

"You really see me like this?" Kole nodded. "It's amazing. No, that's too small a word. It's breathtaking. I want it."

Kole licked his lips and nodded. "Okay." There were so many words in that one word he didn't have the energy to say, so he capped it off with the phrase that meant so much to them both. "I love you."

"I love you." Beck surged up and caught Kole in a fierce kiss, and he took every lick, every bite, every nip until he had to pull away to breathe. "I love you so fucking much."

Beck stared into his eyes, nothing but sincerity showing, and although they'd shared the words so many times, it settled something inside Kole to know how much Beck meant it.

"How's your hand?"

Beck rolled his eyes. "Aching but good."

"Shall we get some food?" Kole asked, trying to break the tension.

Beck shook his head forcefully. "I want this now." He pointed at the design.

Kole spread his hands. "I don't know how to tattoo."

Standing, Beck grinned. "But I know lots of people who do and can teach you as you go along."

"No. I don't want the first thing I do to be this design. I'll mess it up."

"No, you won't."

"Yes, I would." Kole stood firm. "I'm not doing it until I feel more confident."

Beck visibly sulked. "But I wanted to be the first person you tattoo."

Kole grinned. "You still can be, but it needs to be something small in a place where no one will see if I mess up."

Beck laughed. "Really? A place no one will see? I'm sure that can be arranged."

Feeling his cheeks heating, Kole backhanded him. "I'll end up castrating you if I do it there, and I like it too much to damage it."

"It? It!" Beck stood, hands on hips. "What about me?"

Kole jumped up, wrapping his arms around Beck's neck. "And you." He stole a kiss.

A knock sounded before the door opened. "Beck, your next—Oops, sorry!" Finn said, backing out of the room with his hands over his eyes.

Beck laughed again, and Kole decided he would make that happen as much as possible. It was a beautiful sound. "It's all right, Finn. Come on in."

Finn popped his head back in before stepping inside again. "Ani asked me to let you know that your next client is here."

ELOUISE EAST

Beck frowned. "I don't have another client, do I?"

"She said you'll want to take this one." Finn scrunched his forehead. "And that you might need...support, which is why I'm here."

Kole's stomach churned. Who the fuck was it?

"Who the fuck is it?" Beck echoed his thoughts.

"Seven women who each want something small on their hands."

Kole's heart started a rapid tattoo, an inkling of who it was filtering through his brain. But seeing the confusion on Beck's face, he hadn't made the potential link.

"Why would I need support for that?"

"Because of who they are," Kole guessed.

Beck glanced at him. "Who?"

"I'm only guessing, but I bet it's the seven women who stood up against Drake."

Finn nodded slowly. "It is."

Beck let out a long breath, rubbing his hands over his lower face. "Do you think I can do it without breaking down?" he asked Kole.

"I think they won't care if you do."

Beck stared into space for a few seconds. "Okay. Let them in."

Finn paused for a moment and then nodded and disappeared.

"Are you okay?" Kole asked.

"I think so. This is hard, but it'll be nice to do this for them."

A knock sounded again, and Finn entered, followed by Becca and the others. Becca stepped straight over to Beck and hugged him.

"Thank you for agreeing." She pulled back. "We wanted something to unite us when we go back to our normal day."

"It's a great idea. Do you know what you want?"

226

She wiggled her head, glancing at the others. "Not really. Just something small we can have on our hand that when we see it, we remember."

"How about a ribbon?" Kole said, suddenly remembering something his mother once said to him. "No matter how tangled it gets, it is still one entire piece." Silence in the room, and he fidgeted. "And it's something different to the usual semicolon, but you don't have to."

Becca smiled. "I love that idea." She turned to the women. "What do you think?"

"I like the idea, but how would it look?" a woman said.

Beck glanced at him. "Want to design something?"

Kole blinked. "Um, I could." He grabbed his book. "Give me a minute."

Settling into the chair, he flipped to a blank page. He tried a few designs, but quickly dismissed them, although he'd still show them in case they worked better for the area being tattooed, but then hit on an idea. As his pencil scratched across the paper, his excitement grew. When he finished, he studied it for a second and then stood, heading over to where they were all chatting. Just his initial standing got their attention.

"These are some ideas."

Becca took the book and everyone crowded around it, discussing which they preferred. When Becca pointed at the last design, Kole smiled. Beck took it and chuckled.

"So simple, yet so poignant. Perfect." He winked at Kole, then turned to the women. "Are you all sure?" They nodded. "Okay, who's first?"

"Me," Becca said.

Kole had expected Finn to offer to help, but he seemed to know that this was Beck's role, and Kole couldn't have agreed more. As Beck tattooed Becca, Kole watched. The ink took the form of an infinity symbol made of ribbon, which extended into a couple of loops before the loose end flew free. They had chosen a teal colour because it was widely known as a symbol of healing, courage and strength.

Kole's phone rang, distracting him. He frowned at the private number, tempted to ignore it, but he excuse himself into the corridor.

"Hello?"

"Mr Peterson. It's Officer Kirby. I thought you'd like to know that we've arrested Andrew for arson. His prints were on the petrol can. While here, he attempted suicide, so now he's on a psychiatric ward and being looked after. You shouldn't need to worry about him now."

"Thank you, Officer." Kole exhaled as he hung up. As he entered the room again, Beck raised his eyebrows. Kole put his thumbs up. He'd explain later.

When Beck finished with Becca, Kole felt a sense of pride. Not because his design was now inked onto skin, but because Beck was seemingly taking some power back from being able to do it for them. When he finished all seven women, Becca stepped closer.

"What about you, Beck? Would you like to join us?"

Beck's throat bobbed several times before he nodded. "Finn?" he croaked.

Finn took Beck's place and, as Beck met Kole's gaze, tattooed the man with the symbol of a survivor. Something he didn't need, but so truly deserved.

23

BECK

Nine months later

"Welcome to our eighth Bonser event!" Joey said to the Life in Ink crew before the doors opened on the first morning.

It was, once again, the third weekend in January. Beck could feel the phantom cramping in his hands before he'd even started, a reminder that it was going to be a long day, and he wasn't as young as he once was. His left hand had healed beautifully with only minor residual aching on occasion. Their space had five reclinable chairs and trolleys that had been filled with their tools, and a table stood in front where Ethan and Ani would speak with the potential clients.

"How many do you think we'll get done this year? Will we beat last year's?" Dallas asked. The same question he asked *every* year.

"It's got to be more," Finn said. "We have Kole now."

Beck glanced over at his boyfriend, seeing the flush heat his cheeks when they all looked at him. He'd been training for the past nine months to tattoo, and he was damn good, though he refused to tattoo anything big at the event. He said he wasn't ready. The plan was for him to do the smaller tattoos, but Beck was sure he could slip in a bigger one now and then. Kole was also going to do some designing, so it would truly make a difference to their number count.

As Joey's spiel ran on, Beck reflected on how so much could change within a year. That time last year, he had no inclination of a relationship with anyone, let alone Ethan's best friend. But at that point, he could barely remember what his life had been like before Kole had entered it. And he much preferred it that way.

"Let's do this!" Dallas shouted, throwing his muscular arms in the air and sending out an almost visible wave of energy.

By the end of the day, they were all flagging, even with a surprise visit from Donovan and his family. Two adorable kids that Wally had been nannying before they got together. Beck's hands weren't thanking him, cramping with every movement; Finn's finger had a brace on it—he thought he'd sprained it; Dallas had resorted to sitting down, which he rarely did; and Joey appeared barely awake. They were getting old.

As for Kole, he was a bloody machine. With not being used to inking so much, Kole's hands had given up on him far earlier than the rest of them, but he had continued to draw design after design. There was no way they hadn't smashed the record from the previous year, even on the first day of that year.

"Ani, what did we do?" Beck asked.

"I don't even have the energy to tease you," she said from her perch at the table, head resting against one hand and eyes closed. "Sixty."

Beck's jaw dropped. "You're fucking kidding me, right?"

"Nope. I don't even think I'm going to be able to move tomorrow, and I've been just talking to people all day." She groaned as she stretched her legs out.

"Holy shit," Dallas said, and even he seemed less than enthused by the number. "Boss? I think we're going to have to trade our bodies in for younger versions."

Joey snorted. "You're the fittest of us all, so imagine how *we* feel."

"I really don't want to," Dallas complained. "I'm even considering not going out tonight."

Finn huffed a laugh. "The only thing I'm doing tonight is sleeping."

"True that," Joey agreed. "Come on. Let's get the stations cleaned. Our tomorrow selves will be grateful for it."

They all groaned and moaned but did as they were told, and when one of them faltered, the others helped to finish. Silence reigned as they stumbled back to the hotel, each going their separate ways with barely a wave to the others, and when the door closed behind him and Kole, he stripped off his coat and fell headfirst onto the bed.

"Do you want something to eat?" Kole asked, his voice as tired as everyone else's was.

"Nooo," Beck moaned. "Get into bed, Kole. We can eat at whatever time we wake up."

"Yes, boss."

Beck wrapped himself around Kole, both fully clothed, and fell asleep while inhaling the scent of his lover.

At close of business the following day, once they were all packed up and ready to leave, Beck pulled Kole to one side.

"Don't tell anyone, but you and I have another night in the hotel." He winked. "I thought we could celebrate a year of chaos and a year of us."

Kole beamed. "We didn't exactly start our relationship a year ago."

"Close enough. I remember inking clients last year and my eyes kept straying to you. You were far too beautiful for your own good."

"Sweet talker." Kole kissed him. "It'll be nice not to have to drive back tonight. You know I'm not a fan of riding the bike in the dark. We can be anonymous in a random hotel for a night."

"Yeah. You and me, room service and a bed. What more could we want?" He placed his finger over Kole's mouth. "And don't say sleep."

"I still can't believe we nearly missed the start of the event."

Beck shook his head. "I should've set my alarm. If it hadn't been for Ani..."

A heavy hand landed on his shoulder, making him jump. Something that, a year ago, would've made him freak out. But after working with his counsellor for so long, he was learning new techniques.

"I'm staying another night here. I'm going out tonight and making up for what I missed last night," Dallas said with a grin.

Beck and Kole looked at each other and shared a smile. He knew it was too good to be true to be completely alone, but never mind. Dallas would be out and about most of the night, and if he found someone, it was unlikely he would bring him back to the hotel. He liked to be as anonymous as possible. Though how he believed that would work, Beck had no idea. They were all famous in certain circles, and more of the public knew them than any of them realised. Beck maybe more so than the others due to his newfound newspaper-worthy past and the fact one of his clients was a prince.

"Don't have too much fun," Kole said.

"There is no such thing." Dallas grinned. He twirled with surprising grace, considering his six foot six inches of pure muscle, and headed back over to the crew.

"Hey, Dallas!" Beck called and waited for him to turn. "Wishing you all the luck in your endeavours. Not that you need them."

Dallas lifted his thumbs in the air and continued on his way.

"I wish he would find someone," Kole said. "He's so lonely."

"How do you know?"

Kole glanced at him. "Can you not see it in his eyes?"

Beck glanced back at Dallas's retreat and realised it was something he'd never acknowledged. He'd figured out that Dallas liked his privacy when it came to his private life and had believed he was looking for something, but it had never occurred to him to look past Dallas's jokes and size.

"Hey, it's all right. He'll find someone. It just needs to be the right someone at the right time," Kole said, bringing his attention back to him.

"Have I ever told you that I love you?" Beck teased.

Kole scrunched his nose. "Now that you mention it...no, I don't think so."

Beck grinned as he took the kiss he so wanted. He couldn't wait to have Kole in bed and let him do whatever he wanted with him. It was so freeing.

They finally made it back to the hotel, brushing off anything concrete about when they would arrive home, and slipped into the room, locking the door behind them. Beck dropped onto the bed and stared at the ceiling.

"I still cannot believe we inked over one hundred clients this weekend. That is mad," he said, stretching his arms behind his head.

"Definitely smashed last year." Kole laughed, stripping off his coat and kicking off his shoes. He strode to the bed and pulled Beck's shoes off, throwing them behind him. Crawling on hands and knees, he stalked up Beck's body, eyes feasting on him until he was level with him. "I'm glad to have an entire night to do whatever I want with you, and you'll take it all, won't you?"

Beck's mouth dried up. "Yes, boss."

"As much as I like my position, get up and strip for me. I want your naked body against mine in ten seconds."

He scrambled to his feet, his fingers fumbling with everything he touched, but eventually, he was naked, though he was sure it was longer than ten seconds. He jumped back into position on the bed, sliding his body beneath Kole, who hadn't moved an inch while Beck had been working.

"Good. Now touch me."

Beck happily ran his hands over Kole's body, his fingertips finding every ridge in his even-more-defined-body-than-ever. His boyfriend had found a love of the gym and spent time there several times a week. His body was showing the results of his commitment, and Beck loved it.

When he reached Kole's cock, he paused and met his gaze. Kole's mouth quirked at the corners, but he nodded. Beck wrapped his hand around the shaft, scraping his teeth along his bottom lip as the heat sank into his palm. He was hot and stiff, and Beck wanted him inside him straight away, but he wouldn't get his wish yet. He knew Kole well enough to know that.

Kole's eyelids fluttered, but they never closed completely. "That's it. You know how I like it. But you also know when to stop."

At that, Beck stopped because the words were a warning. Not that Kole was about to come, but that he didn't want to go too fast. Unfortunately, Beck didn't think he was going to last long, even with them only having just started. And Kole understood that, too, by his expression when he looked down at Beck's groin.

"Hmm, someone's raring to go." Kole hummed and tutted, staring at Beck as he held his cock in his hand. "Okay. Just this once."

Beck frowned. Just this once, what? "Um, boss?" Kole raised his eyebrows. "What do you mean, please?"

Kole smirked...and took Beck's cock into the back of his throat and sucked him so hard and fast, Beck's orgasm was wrenched from him in seconds. His head spun, all the blood rushing to his dick while Kole's mouth cleaned him.

"Holy fuck," Beck breathed.

"Yum," Kole said. "But don't expect that every time."

"Uh-huh."

All of Beck's brain power had gone. He had no hope of revival, but he wanted to reciprocate.

"Sleep, Beck. We have all night."

"Nope. I need this." He blinked several times, trying to wake himself, and between eye rubs, he managed to surprise Kole and flip him. "My turn. This'll be quick."

"Good."

He leaned down, engulfing Kole's cock in his mouth and groaning at the salty, bitter taste. A taste he was addicted to. Using every skill he knew, he sucked, licked, nibbled, swallowed, stroked and sucked some more until Kole trembled beneath him. He wanted it so badly. Needed it. He doubled his efforts, and Kole's fingers tightened against his shoulders.

"Fuck, yes. Jeez, Beck. I'm gonna come."

Beck kept going, and with a groan, Kole released into his throat. He drank down every drip and cleaned him with his tongue before lifting his head. Kole had a sheen of sweat on his face.

"Fuck, that was good."

"We're not finished."

Kole raised his eyebrows. "Who said?"

"You did."

Kole rolled his eyes and shook his head, slamming his head back against the bed. "I've created a monster."

Beck grinned. "A monster for your cock."

"Oh, god. That was bad. If you keep going, I'll find something to occupy your mouth."

"Is that a promise?" Beck waggled his eyebrows.

Kole shook his head again. "Maybe I should get the tattoo inked on you now. That'll shut you up."

Beck lifted to his elbows. "Really? Doesn't your hand hurt?"

"A little, but I should be good. If you still want it, that is?"

"Of course, I do!"

Beck scrambled off the bed and grabbed his bags. It had been far too long since Kole had drawn the design that pulled emotions from them both. He'd been pushing it back and pushing it back because Kole hadn't felt like he had the skills to make it look good, and Beck didn't want to keep asking for it. So, he'd left it until Kole brought it up again. He wasn't saying no.

"Here."

They set up the kit, and Beck laid on the bed on his back. He'd insisted he wanted it on his front so he could see it every day. Kole went through the motions of preparing Beck's skin, his hands visibly shaking, but Beck wasn't worried. Kole would steady his hands before he started because he'd seen it before.

"Ready?"

"Always," Beck replied.

The buzz of the machine, the silence in the room, the careful but heavy breathing of his tattooist all made for an experience Beck wanted to remember forever. The bite of the needle didn't phase him. In fact, it made him emotional because it was Kole doing it. Instead of watching the design evolve, he watched his boyfriend. The slight furrow of his brow. The pursed lips. He was the best thing that had ever happened to Beck.

It took a while, but when it was done, Kole exhaled. "I think that's it."

Beck stood, stretching before heading for the bathroom mirror. He could've looked down and seen it, but he wanted to see the full effect. While he stood in front of the mirror studying the design, his emotions filled him again. It was a design that encompassed what Kole had always loved drawing, alongside a few quirks that seemed to resonate with Beck. Swirls that turned into letters, that turned into a heart. It was epic, and he couldn't wait to show everyone.

"Thank you," he said to Kole when he slid his arms around his chest and kissed his shoulder.

"You're always welcome. Sorry it took me so long to gather the courage."

"It doesn't matter. It's there now."

Beck trailed his fingertips around the edges. It would remind him of their love every day.

"Officer Bryant, what can I do for you?" Beck said when he opened the door to their home a week later.

It hadn't taken them long to decide that they wanted to rebuild Beck's home, so after a long time of dealing with builders, architects and every other person who could possibly be involved in a house, they had an almost replica of the original house with a few small alterations to make it better. He couldn't have done it without Kole – probably wouldn't have done it without him. Now, they shared a wonderful home and couldn't be happier.

The officer was wrapped up warm with rosy cheeks, probably from being in his car with the heater on. That observation didn't detract from the surprise of his visit.

"Mr Cavanagh. Sorry to show up unannounced, but I thought an in-person visit would be the best option, considering the news."

Beck's blood ran cold. He'd only ever experienced that feeling once before, and that was when he'd been in Drake's clutches. What had happened to warrant the officer turning up?

"Come on in," he said, instead of what he wanted to. "Would you like a drink?"

"No, I'm good, thank you."

Kole entered the room. "Who is...? Officer Bryant. This is a surprise."

"I have news."

Kole stepped to Beck's side, threading his arm around his waist and tethering him to the ground.

"What news?"

"I'm here to let you know that Drake Price is dead," Officer Bryant said.

Beck stared at him, his breathing increasing. "What? How?"

"His inmates didn't take too kindly to his proclivities. He was stabbed in the yard and didn't make it through the surgery."

Beck turned away, disentangling himself from Kole, and paced across the room. "Why does that asshole always get away so easily?" He sighed. "He should've suffered so much more."

"As much as I...*should* explain this with a straight face and no emotion, I won't." Bryant smirked. "Between you and me, the fucker got what he deserved. A stabbing was the least of what officially happened."

Beck stared at him, and there was a glint in the officer's eyes that made him realise something bad—excluding dying—had happened to Drake, and it settled his agitation. "I'm glad. He deserved everything he got."

"I heartily agree. Unofficially." Bryant nodded, becoming the serious officer again, and headed to the door. "If you need anything further, you have my number. But, and I mean this in the best possible way, I hope we won't need to cross paths again. Oh, and Haynes and Conrad send their regards."

"Same goes for you. Thank you," Kole said.

Beck was frozen to the spot. Drake was dead. Gone. No longer in this world. "Officer Bryant!" Bryant turned back. "Do the others know?"

"I'm telling them next." He nodded and left, Kole closing the door behind him.

Kole settled beside him. "I don't know what to think if I'm honest," Beck said.

"You don't need to think anything. Just let it settle in its own time. The main thing is that he won't be bothering anyone ever again."

"Yeah." Beck shook his head. "That's going to take time to sink in."

"Do you want to see or speak to Karen?"

Beck considered the question. "Not at the moment, I don't think. I think I can wait until our next appointment, but if it starts bothering me, I'll change it."

"Okay, so what would you like for dinner?" Kole asked, pressing a kiss to his cheek.

"Surprise me."

And that was only one reason he loved the man. Kole smiled and pivoted, heading for the kitchen.

"Kole?"

He stopped and looked over his shoulder. "Yeah?"

Staring into his boyfriend's eyes, he asked, "Will you marry me?"

A smile crept across Kole's face. "Of course." He blew him a kiss and disappeared into the kitchen.

Beck stared at the empty doorway and grinned. Pulling out his phone, he opened the group chat.

BECK: *I'm getting married!*

Now he would let Kole know what the space on the back of his neck was for: Kole's name.

Thank you so much for reading! I hope this book has taken you away from real life and given you a world you can escape to. That's all I hope for my books, is that it will provide you with somewhere you want to disappear into. Read on for a teaser of Dallas, book 3.

I'd love for you to check out my other books. You can find all my social media links below. You can also buy all my books on my website.

And for a taste of the free short story you get if you sign up to my newsletter...

FREE!

Jason doesn't have the strength to fight his stepfather for a happy life, so, to stop the man from turning his fists and words to his younger siblings, he takes the brunt of his anger himself. He vows to get those children away from him as soon as possible. Then, when there is one bruise too many for his best friend's eyes, they come up with a plan for a fake boyfriend for Jason—someone who's really a bodyguard.

Darius doesn't get asked to the royal family's domain often, but he doesn't say no when he is. Being asked to be a fake boyfriend is far from usual, but he's happy to do it if it means he gets to spend time—and protect—the man he can't stop staring at. When things don't quite go the way Jason hopes, Darius offers another option. One that might backfire. But with Darius at his side, Jason finds more strength than he ever thought possible.

And maybe, he might've found the one person who could give him his happily ever after.

This is an MM bodyguard romance that spans both the Club Royal and Guarding Royalty series.

Get this book FREE by signing up to my newsletter.

DALLAS

S ix foot six of solid muscle etched with ink, Dallas is one of the veins of Life in Ink. His laughter is often the loudest in the room, his ability to crack jokes at the drop of a hat. To his friends, he's a fiercely loyal giant, always ready with a playful shove or a word of support. But beneath the surface, a yearning lingers. His restless energy searches for a connection that remains just out of reach. Despite being surrounded by his chosen family, his mind remains in the past, with a man who doesn't want him.

Letting Dallas go is the worst thing Lachlan ever did. When his family had told him he couldn't be gay and needed to stop talking with his best friend, he'd listened, and then Dallas disappeared, and Lachlan had been left with a gaping hole. The hole still hasn't been filled, despite trying his hardest. But then his ex-best friend had popped up in the news and he'd been riveted.

A planned trip to Perth to see a client ends with an unexpected reconciliation. Why is Lachlan in Perth, and why can't Dallas say no - but then again, he never could. It was why he had to leave in the first place.

The gentle giant finally finds the connection he secretly craves – with the man he's always loved. It's time to look to the future instead of the past, but can they?

Dallas is a story about a tattoo artist with a broken heart and his childhood best friend who wishes he could go back and fix the past.

Sign up to my newsletter to receive chapters fortnightly.

Books by Elouise East

Life in Ink
Joey
Beck
Dallas
Finn

Guarding Royalty
Protecting his Past
Protecting his Heart
Protecting his Secrets
Protecting his Life

Club Royal
Royal Firsts
Rogue Royal
Secretive Royal
Grieving Royal
Disowned Royal
Trained Royal
Awakened Royal
Commanding Royal

Illuminate Matchmaking
Ignite

Blaze
Kindle
Scorch

Boys, Daddies, Snuggles & More
Need Him
Trust Him

Daddy
Love Me, Daddy
Soothe Me, Daddy
Spoil Me, Daddy
The Complete Daddy Series

Love in Flames
Fight Fire with Fire
Up in Smoke
Smoke Signals
Smoke & Mirrors
Love in Flames Collection

Crush
Love Conquers
Instant Desire
Primary Seduction
Deep Down
A Crush for Christmas
Life Support
Covert Strength
Love Scene
Lawful Attraction
Crush Collection Volume 1
Crush Collection Volume 2

BECK

Crush Collection Volume 3

Just A Little Crush
First Kiss
He's Behind You
A Special Love

Standalone
Treehouse Whispers
Star-Crossed
Protecting the Thief
Sizzling Chauffeur
A Home for Barney
Mattie

Elouise R East (taboo)
Dark & Divergent
Forbidden Temptation
Too Many Secrets: A Life of Secrets
Too Many Secrets: The Lake House
Secrets in his Eyes

Collide
When Fantasies Collide
When Dreams Collide
When Pleasures Collide
When Cravings Collide
When Hungers Collide

Dark
Defying Sanity
Stronger Together

About Elouise East

E louise East writes sweet and steamy connections in gay romance. She also touches on taboo stories under the name Elouise R East. She writes books that are emotionally realistic, even if liberties are taken with other aspects of the stories. She doesn't know any other way to write. It comes from deep inside.

Books that tell the stories where friendship and family are the focal point - be it blood family or chosen - are very important to her. That's why she includes a variety of personalities, talents, ages, situations and abilities.

Her characters come to life on the page for her as well as her readers, their stories unfolding in front of her as she writes. Just like real life, the lives of her characters change with every choice, every interaction and every conversation. And she wouldn't have it any other way. She wants her characters to be real, to be relatable, to be free to have whatever views they tell her they have. And trust her, most of the time, she does not have *any* say in the matter!

Stalk her here… ;-)

Website : https://elouiseeast.com
Newsletter : https://elouiseeast.com/newsletter
All links : https://elouiseeast.com/links

www.ingramcontent.com/pod-product-compliance
Lightning Source LLC
Chambersburg PA
CBHW060540190726
48283CB00003B/806